Go Nitro
Rise of the Blades

Jeremy Dooley

ISBN:
ISBN-978-1097972791

DEDICATION

For Kat Dooley
Derek Dooley
Deepjyoti Deb
Krishna Soni &
Nick Candelino

The original Nitros

CHAPTER 1: A MEETING

Professor Phillip Redman stood in a small metal room, with his hands folded behind his back. He stared through a sheet of glass into the next chamber. His eyes were locked on what was within. Redman was a man en-route to becoming the most famous, and infamous scientist in history. He was a man with a million possible sins plaguing his mind. A man who was lost in an endless maze of thoughts.

One of the most important meetings in existence was about to take place, and on the other side of the glass was the subject. His creation. A science project. Not his first, but by far his most important.

Prof. Phillip Redman was in his mid-sixties with streaks of gray coating the sides of his otherwise brown hair. His face pushed inwards under his defined cheekbones, two long wrinkles ran across his forehead, and round glasses balanced delicately on the end of his nose. A long white lab-coat hid most of his body. The crisp new fabric was, as of yet, unblemished. His old coats were tucked away, hiding the stains and scars of past experiments and failures. Some called Redman 'old,' but most referred to him as experienced. Redman was known for his inventions designed for the betterment of mankind. Years of his life had been dedicated to pushing humanity further and further into the future. Though, no invention... no creation... had ever been as drastic as this one, and Redman was still unsure whether or not he had made the right decision.

Sitting on the other side of the glass was a young man at a single table, with his hands open in front of him. His name was Nicholas J Bruno. Eighteen years old. His hair was a disheveled mess of brown, and his skin was rough with unkempt facial hair. He was staring down at his palms with a level of concentration that most boys his age would find impossible. But this boy was anything but ordinary.

After another second or two, Nick pushed himself up from the table and began to pace. He ran hands through his hair and every now and again would mutter a few words to himself.

Redman knew he and Nick needed to have a chat, but how could Redman handle this delicate situation?

Nick's pacing footsteps reverberated off the walls as he walked. The door to his room slid open.

"Nicholas!" Redman's voice called out. The breaking silence made the word seem louder, almost causing Nick to jump. He started to turn, sighing while he did.

"Listen, Professor. We haven't had a chance to really talk yet, and I..." Nick opened his eyes and threw his arm up into the air, catching a clipboard only inches from his forehead. Several pages flew out of their locked position after the sudden stop and fluttered into Nick's face before lightly falling to the ground. As the pages cleared from in front of him, Redman came into view.

He was standing in the doorway, his arm still out from throwing the clipboard at his target. He smirked, reached down, and straightened his jacket. "Nice reflexes," he complimented, smoothing a wrinkle from his sleeve.

"What the hell was that?" Nick lowered his arm and waved the clipboard to the side. Redman turned to a small bin next to the doorway and pulled out another clipboard. Nick threw out his arms in exasperation, "Great... you've got another one. Are you planning to throw that one as well?" Nick couldn't be sure, but he thought he saw the slightest gleam of amusement in Redman's eyes.

"Increased reaction speed and reflexes. Check," Redman chimed off, scrolling his finger down the sheet of paper.

"You know keeping all these papers is a waste of

resources, right?" Nick asked. "There's such a thing as tablets."

"Less secure," Redman replied. "Tablets can be hacked and taken. Papers… not so much." Redman looked back down at his clipboard and continued reading. "Increased strength?" He glanced up. Nick waited a beat before pointing at his chest.

"Are you talking about me right now?"

"Am I?" Redman lifted his pen and motioned toward the clipboard Nick was holding. Nick sighed and grabbed the clipboard with two hands before effortlessly snapping it in half.

"Yeah, Redman, it's a clipboard. Doesn't take much to…"

"Snapping steel with minimal effort," Redman noted, without even acknowledging Nick. "Increased strength. Check."

Nick slowly looked down at the two halves of the clipboard, seeing the tear was made across bent and shredded metal, and not the thin wood he was originally expecting. He shook his head a couple of times, dropping the pieces to the ground. He barely even tried, and yet here he was holding a broken piece of metal. The halves clanged off the metal floor. Nick started to chuckle a little bit. "You're kidding me, right?"

Redman made another mark on his paper before turning to a switch next to the door. "No," he replied.

"People tell me I don't have a great sense of humor."

"You threw a clipboard at my head."

Redman flipped the switch with authority. The wall behind Nick began to hum and growl like some kind of monster. He turned around as the wall split down the middle and begin to retract, revealing another small room hidden behind it. This one was filled with human-like targets. Sacks of dirt covered in discarded pieces of Kevlar armor to mold them into the proper shape. Symbols that Nick didn't recognize were scratched into the chest pieces. Almost like the letter 'B' but comprised of two sharply etched triangles.

Some of the targets were moving, while others were stationary and holding guns pointed in Nick's direction. Nick glanced back and forth at a few of the targets before grinning. He turned to Redman, pointing a thumb over his shoulder at the mannequins.

"You're serious?" he asked. "A firing range?"

Redman shrugged and stepped forward. "Basically." Redman raised an eyebrow. "You could use practice." Nick looked down at his hand. He rotated it, closely examining his knuckles and every line on his palm.

"You're not talking about…"

"It wasn't a dream, Nicholas," Redman interrupted while getting closer.

Nick couldn't help but take a step back as Redman approached. Redman was an enigma to Nick. He had been ever since the day he arrived on Nick's doorstep. Nick had gone back to his home to collect his things and instead found Redman there waiting for him. Once the promise of justice for his family was made, Nick found it hard to turn away from Redman.

Now, it seemed like Redman knew things Nick had never even thought about and was always at least two steps ahead. Nick's only dilemma was deciding whether or not that was a good thing.

"I know your memory isn't in perfect condition, but the procedure must be in there somewhere," Redman said gently.

"Of course it is," Nick snapped back. Redman paused, seeing the stress building in Nick's face. It was as if every memory for Nick seemed harmless on the surface, but pulling it only revealed a tangled web of gnarled roots underneath.

He only ever saw flashes of his past, fragmented images, and broken recollections. Nick closed his eyes and shook his head.

When his eyes opened again, he was lying on a metal table, with both his arms strapped down tightly to his sides. The room was dark, only illuminated by the flashing lights on the many consoles around him. The tension was so high that Nick could actually hear his heartbeat. Nick pulled against one of the restraints, but it had no give.

"Is this really necessary?" he asked Redman. Redman patted Nick on the shoulder and looked off into the shadows. Nick could see another figure nod back to the scientist.

"Trust me, it's for your own safety, as well as everyone else in here."

"You strapped me down," Nick stated, turning back to Redman as he snapped back into reality. "Put this giant... *thing* over my arm."

Nick was back on the table. A large machine slid along a track on the ceiling above him. The sound of the metal actuators and servos driving it forward instantly drowned out Redman's words. The machine perfectly positioned itself over the center of Nick's arm. Nick could barely form thoughts through his fear and anxiousness. It felt like his entire body was tensed and incapable of relaxing again.

As the machine started winding up and buzzing to life, a large needle slid down and lined itself up just below his elbow. The needle was several inches long and led up to a large glass tube above it. Nick could see a red liquid within the tube, bubbling and churning like it was magma. "Redman!" Nick yelled. The needle retracted a tiny bit, preparing to spring forward. "Redman, wait! I don't know about..." The needle fired down into Nick's arm, burying deep into his skin. A blistering pain shot through Nick's veins and began boiling his blood. The edges of Nick's vision blurred and suddenly all he could see was red.

Back in reality, Nick glanced down at his arm, watching his veins glow a faint red underneath his skin like they were on fire. He slowly clenched his hand into a fist and closed his eyes.

"Next thing I knew, I was here," Nick said. "After laying on a table, asleep, for two years. Two years of my life are gone because of this, and the only thing I have to go on is your word."

"I'm sorry, Nick," Redman began, looking away. "I couldn't completely anticipate the pain this procedure would put you through." Redman nodded to himself. He looked up again, but not at Nick. His gaze simply went off into the distance. "But, I could anticipate the results."

Nick opened his eyes.

"I told you I wanted to help you make things right, and that's exactly what I've done. Given you the ability and the opportunity to do extraordinary things. Now, I can't *make* you do anything," Redman shrugged, "and, honestly, I don't want to."

"Then what *do* you want, Redman?"

Redman relaxed his stance. He faced the targets and darted his eyes from one mannequin to the next. "I want you to do what's right. I want you to make a difference for yourself and for everyone else in this city. You and the others on your team will be exactly what this city needs."

Nick was silent, staring at the professor, who seemed to be refusing to look back. Nick turned slightly and examined the targets downrange. He closed his hand into a fist, causing his veins to begin glowing again.

"Okay, Redman," Nick quietly agreed.

Redman looked back as Nick turned to square up on the range. "Just do me one favor?" Nick said.

Redman raised an eyebrow.

Nick peeked back over his shoulder, meeting eyes with the professor. "Stand back." Nick closed his other hand into a fist as well, right before his entire body began tensing up. He slowly turned his head back while taking in a deep breath. Once his long inhale ended, he lifted his hands while slowly spreading out his fingers. He pointed them in the general area of the targets and then began to exhale. As he did, he felt a warm sensation travel from his spine and slither its way through his veins. It snaked past his shoulders, through his arms, and collected in his hands. The pressure that built up in his palms made it feel like two heavy weights were suddenly crushing down on his knuckles. His exhale gained a voice. He couldn't keep in a faint yell as the pressure released, and fire began to leak out from under his nails. The fire crawled around his fingers. It gathered in his palm, increasing in brightness the longer it stayed there.

Nick assumed this was the closest he would ever feel to

a God. An immense power was now under his control. Something as ferocious as fire had to do whatever he said. It felt good.

With one final push, he forced his hands forward. The fire leaped from his skin and exploded outward in a fiery cone. The light from the fire reflected off the metallic walls, bathing the room in a blinding cascade of red and orange. As Nick turned, the fire followed, torching every target in its path and setting them ablaze.

Redman stepped back, covering his face with his clipboard to guard against the intense heat.

Nick closed his fingers into the fire, collapsing it into a thinner, even more intense inferno. He pulled his hands back toward his chest. The fire was now a thin beam of blinding yellow. Nick threw his arms out to the sides, making the fire evaporate into a few lasting flames and sparks. Small wisps of fire danced in the air around Nick as embers fell to the floor and faded to black.

Redman slowly lowered his clipboard to the sight of Nick standing with his hands by his sides.

Nick was breathing heavily, never taking his eyes away from the targets. Sweat was dripping down his face, and evaporating into steam before getting a chance to drop to the floor. The charred remains of the mannequins were still crumbled apart. The fire Nick created has been so intense that the metal weaponry they held was still glowing a faint orange.

"Nick..." Redman began. He paused for a moment, before realizing there were hardly any words to really say.

Nick slowed his breathing and wiped some sweat from his forehead. He had surprised himself with the ferocity of those flames. As he looked over the destruction in front of him, it became clear that this was a responsibility he'd have for the rest of his life. A responsibility to keep this fire in his control and never accidentally create a scene like this. He tried to find the right words to say to Redman. After a few moments, he settled on some.

"That..." he started between heaves of oxygen, "was pretty damn awesome."

CHAPTER 2: A REUNION

Another mannequin was loaded onto a spring, waiting for its moment. It had its back to the floor, with a weapon firmly in its hands. In an instant, the spring released, flinging the mannequin up and into the battle. Less than a second later, its head was engulfed in flames, sending its helmet flying off and falling with a smoke trail to the ground like a comet. The helmet clanged off the metal floor. It twisted and spun in one position and then wobbled to a stop. Nick closed his hand into a fist and shook it in the air a little, nodding while he did. Traces of smoke and embers floated away from his fingertips. Another mannequin sprung up. Nick threw his hand forward, causing a perfectly round fireball to hit the mannequin directly in the center of its chest. A third sprung up but was immediately disarmed. Nick relaxed his stance as a timer on the wall read out his current record.

Nick glanced at it for a moment before shaking his head while turning away from the course. It had become a routine at this point to him. Nothing new. Just the same target practice over and over again. He constantly felt like he had gotten good enough, but Redman never gave the official seal of approval.

Nick grabbed a small towel from the back of a chair, wiping some residual sweat from his forehead. The room had received some upgrades in the past week, including an improved firing range, a rest area, and Nick's personal favorite, a brand new 60" television.

Not only had Nick been asleep during Project Nitro for two years, but now another two weeks had passed since that meeting with Redman. Those two weeks were almost entirely spent within these walls, training and practicing. Therefore, Redman had insisted that the television's only purpose was so Nick could keep up on current affairs, which Nick had done... slightly.

Nick knew Grant Stel, the former senator from Maine, was now the nation's president. He knew technology pioneered in Lattice Light City was now being implemented in massive cities across the nation, like Los Angeles and New York. However, this quest for know-ledge didn't stop Nick from playing a cartoon or two every so often. It was a good way to escape the weirdness going on around him. It brought him back to a time when his family was still around. When Nick, his parents, and his brother would sit together and watch these cartoons in peace. A much, much different time.

Dropping the towel back onto the chair, Nick grabbed the remote just as the door to his room slid open.

"Finished training already, Nicholas?" Redman asked, walking into the chamber.

Nick shrugged, placing the remote back down. "Been trying to beat my time from two days ago," Nick commented. He stretched out his arms and sighed. "Must be past my prime."

The door slid open again, and Linda Carmicle walked in. She was a lab worker with red hair tied back in a bun and extremely thin glasses shielding her eyes. Nick had grown fond of her over the past two weeks, as she was always around to talk if Nick needed it. It was a comfort that Nick didn't take for granted. In her hands was a tray of food. She approached the table and carefully placed the tray next to the chair. She slid it into place, making sure it was straight enough for her preference.

"Hope you like your steak medium rare, Nicholas," she commented with a smile. The smell of the food hit Nick. His stomach rumbled in anticipation. A bit of light red liquid was pooling next to the steak, and the carrots alongside it were beautifully orange.

"Wow, thanks, Linda," Nick stated with a confused, upward inflection to his words. "I could've just gone to the cafeteria myself, you know?"

"Ordinarily, yes," she replied, "but not today, Nick. You have a busy day ahead of you."

Nick raised an eyebrow as she turned and made her way to the door. "Umm, okay," Nick said quietly. Before Linda could leave completely, Nick raised his hand and called out to her. "And, hey! Tell Shea that whenever he wants that rematch, I'm ready! I've been practicing that game all..." Nick stopped and turned his sight to Redman.

Redman folded his arms and patiently waited for Nick to finish.

"...all last night after I was finished with my training, of course." Nick lifted a finger and shook it in her direction. "Why would you even suggest anything otherwise?"

Linda smirked and quietly left the room.

Redman shook his head. He sat down at the table across from the tray of food. "Nick, you really need to focus on handling your abilities," he stated. "I can't let you just run free with your new powers without first being absolutely sure you know how to control them. They're dangerous, to say the least."

"Did you see my best time, Redman?!" Nick asked, motioning toward the firing range. He grabbed a carrot off the tray and crunched into it, continuing to talk while he chewed. "And accuracy. Oh, man. Don't get me started."

Redman adjusted his glasses slightly and began to open his mouth to reply.

"I mean, how long are you planning to keep me in this

lab before you finally let me go home again? I have things I need to see and figure out for myself. People I need to talk to.

Redman laid his clipboard down on the table in front of him. He lightly tapped his finger against its surface. "Nick," he began, carefully, "you don't have a home there anymore. You know very well the Nitro enhancement process took two years to complete. Your old house has probably been sold since then. There was no one to live in it."

Nick placed his hands on the table on either side of his food tray. He knew Redman was right, but nothing inside of him was prepared to accept that. Nick kept hoping everything he remembered about his family was just a nightmare. He was hoping he'd wake up and his family would be back, waiting at home for him.

Nick shook away the thoughts. He knew it was time to move on, however difficult that may be. He nodded to Redman and leaned in a little closer to his food.

"You're probably right, Redman, but there have to be clues in that house," Nick added. "I'm not gonna go through life not knowing who took my family from me." Redman glanced away, letting Nick finish. "And what about my cousin Dante, and my uncle John?" he asked. "They went from seeing me almost every week to not a single time in two years. Don't you think they might be worried, or want to talk to me? Find out I'm still alive?"

"Dante Bruno?" Redman asked, looking back up again.

Nick took another bite of his steak and spoke through careful chews.

"Yeah," he said with a full mouth. "We were pretty close growing up." Nick put down his fork, never removing his stare from Redman's eyes. "Why do you ask?"

"Enlisted into Project Nitro at the age of fifteen," Redman continued. He broke eye contact with Nick. Instead, he looked down to one of his papers, reading it carefully. "The first one to awaken and so far the most proficient at controlling his enhancements."

Nick was silent. His mouth was slightly open, and he couldn't bring himself to close it. "Redman…" he spoke, in almost a whisper, "what are you…?"

"I didn't want your mind clouded during your initial training," Redman interrupted, tucking the paper away, "but yes, you're not the only Bruno to be brought into Project Nitro."

Redman reached his hand into his coat, fishing something out of a pocket within. He pulled out an electronic tablet and placed it on the table, sliding it toward Nick. Nick gazed down to the screen as a video began to play. He instantly recognized the boy it was featuring. He was taller than Nick remembered. Brown hair pushed forward into a spiked mess. A pointed chin, a bright white smile and a focused determination in his eyes. It was Nick's cousin, Dante. Dante was talking to someone off-camera, laughing and pointing to a few other people in the room. His chin was lifted up in pride. Nick watched in amazement as Dante turned away from the camera and threw his hand forward. A wave of crystal emitted from underneath Dante's feet. It sliced its way across the ground, firing shimmering spikes up into the air as it went. It was like a creature in the way it moved. In what seemed like a millisecond, Dante lowered his hand again, and the floor before him was covered in a thick sheet of ice. It glittered brightly in the light of the chamber. Dante turned back around and held out his hands to the people standing off-camera like he had just put on a show. Nick slowly shook his head and took a deep breath.

"There's…" he tried to speak, but the words barely came out, "there's no way." Nick looked up to see Redman nodding, with a small smile. "Dante? But… why would… I just…" Nick focused his eyes on the tablet. He had been afraid of how to approach his cousin once again. How to show up years later after disappearing with superpowers and try to make everything seem okay. Now, Nick was on the other side of this interaction. His cousin was there in front of him, and just as powerful as Nick. Not only that but after worrying about whether or not Nick would even *see* his cousin again, he instead learned he'd be working with his cousin constantly.

"The five of you will do great things," Redman said. "Especially with you as the one leading the group."

Nick's head snapped up. "What?" he asked. "Leader?"

"Yes," Redman replied. "The Nitros will need a leader, and you're it."

"Why me? What makes you think I could pull that off?"

"Captain of several different teams in school," Redman chimed off. "A high GPA and willingness to learn. Avid chess and video game player, demonstrating a high level of problem-solving abilities. Most importantly, an extremely likable personality among your peers. That'll help you lead your team and accomplish your overall purpose."

"Purpose?" Nick asked. "Isn't my purpose to find who killed my family?"

"Again, Nicholas, you think this is all about you, and what you've lost, but it isn't." Redman adjusted his glasses and shuffled through a few papers in front of him. He pulled out a series of large photographs from within his coat. Without taking any time to look them over first, he handed them to Nick. They were security camera photos of men wearing body armor. In their hands were a variety of high-powered assault rifles. Grenades were strapped to their sides, and masks hid their identity from view. They all had the same symbol scratched into the chest of their combat vests. Some of the photos depicted the men throwing innocent people to the floor, or worse, stepping over the bodies of the ones who hadn't listened.

"What exactly am I looking at, Redman?"

"They call themselves the 'Blades,'" Redman began

before Nick could fully finish his question. Nick picked up one of the photos to study it closer.

"Yeah," he said slowly, digging through his thoughts. "I've heard of them. They were wanted by the police in Lattice Light City before I even started the procedure." Nick put down the photo, returning his eyes to Redman.

"I'm guessing they didn't stop?"

Redman shook his head. "Worse than that, I'm afraid. The Blades came across stolen pieces of a past experiment. A substance called Otrolium. After finding it, they built up their supplies and ranks. They've become more of a military force than a gang. It wasn't something the media advertised in years prior, but their actions have grown so bold that they've become impossible to ignore. They're organized, and ruthless. An army, hellbent on finding the rest of the Otrolium."

Nick moved the photos until the final one came into view. He lifted it off of the table and began to absorb the horrible scene. Five bodies were lying in an alleyway. Their skin was shriveled up and hugging bone, like a skeleton with fabric barely stretched over the top. The limbs from several of them had somehow crumbled into nothing but dust and were scattered across the pavement. On the wall of the alley, words were scribbled over the brick using a substance blacker than charcoal.

"What you built, we will destroy," Nick read softly. He tried to drink in the image in front of him, but his brain was refusing to let him accept it. "How could someone do this?" His left hand closed into a fist. "Why would someone do this?"

"The leader of the Blades is a merciless, dangerous man, Nick," he stated, closing his eyes like he was trying to accept the reality. "That's why you're here. You and the other Nitros."

Nick looked back up.

"Are you serious?" Nick asked. "I knew I'd be fighting bad guys. I knew I'd be helping people in Lattice Light, but you *never* mentioned the Blades before." Nick glanced to the side, at the target range. His brain instantly starting replacing the mannequins with the soldiers he had just seen. The fake weaponry seemed much more sinister. Their armor seemed much more sturdy. Their eyes seemed much angrier. The symbol etched into their armor made "You really think I can take him down without knowing anything about him?"

"Yes," Redman quickly replied, opening his eyes. "You have to. There's no easy way to tell you this, Nick, but... the Blades are responsible."

Nick snapped his eyes back to Redman.

"Nicholas, these men are responsible for the death of your family."

Nick's world shattered. All these years he had heard stories of the Blades. Their name would come up on news programs in the background while Nick joyfully spoke with his parents. He knew the gang responsible for his family's death before it even happened. Nick's veins began to glow. He could feel the pressure building up in his hand.

"Your father's job at the Faraday Research Center is what made him a target," Redman explained.

"The Center?" Nick asked. "The one that exploded?" Nick knew too well about that eruption. His father had been a security guard at that complex and sounded the alarm after he saw a thief had broken into the building. The ensuing gunfight resulted in the entire center going up in smoke. Nick's father escaped, along with half of the workers inside, but 400 souls never made it out of the building. The explosion was so intense that there was nothing left of the victim's bodies to recover.

"Yes," Redman replied. "The Faraday Research Center exploded because a large quantity of Otrolium had been stored there. That's what caused the eruption. A man named Scott Cells broke in to scout out the complex for its location for a later heist. After your father caught him and sounded the alarm, a bullet hit a tank of Otrolium, and the rest is history. When the Blades found out what your father had done, they came after him and the rest of your family for the loss of the Otrolium and Scott Cells."

Nick looked down again and grabbed the photo, rereading the words written on the wall. The bodies in the photograph were people he had never met, but the more he stared, the more they started to resemble the ones he loved most. The ones he would never see again.

Redman watched as smoke started to wisp into the air, and some small flames leaped from the edges of the photograph, curling them into black nothingness. A tear came to the corner of Nick's eye. A familiar tear that traced the same path down his face it had taken a thousand times before.

Nick closed his eyes. The photograph was now completely engulfed in flames. The heat in the room was rising. Nick winced in pain as the tear on his cheek sizzled away into steam. He could feel himself starting to lose control. He was fighting what was happening in his own mind. Redman reached out toward the fire but stopped when a voice cried out in the chamber.

"Nick!" it shouted. Nick's eyes shot open. He dropped the photograph to the table, letting it crumble into nothing but ash. He snapped his head up and looked toward the door. A young man energetically stepped in. He had a massive smile painted on his face as he looked at Nick. Nick's mouth was wide open; he couldn't help himself. He pushed away from the table, causing it to bump into Redman and almost knock the man from his chair. Nick stood up and took a step toward the young man.

"Dante?" he asked. Dante's smile grew even larger, which Nick didn't even think was possible. Dante took off across the room at breakneck speed. He hugged Nick so fiercely he had to take a step back, almost toppling to the ground. Dante's feet kicking with excitement in the air as Nick held him up. Dante threw one of his fists into the sky in celebration.

"Holy crap!" Dante yelled. "It's actually you!"

Nick dropped Dante back to the ground, but it was impossible to get Dante to stay away from him. He was like an excited dog without a leash. Dante put his hands on Nick's shoulders, drinking in the realness of the situation.

"Wow," Dante said again, beginning to calm down, "they told me you were here, and I just kind of thought they were messing with me."

"I told you," Redman chimed in while lifting his hands in the air, "none of my staff are going to 'mess with you,' Dante," he said while making air quotes.

"Dante," Nick began, "how are you here?" Maybe there was a better way to ask Dante about the events preceding this, but finding those words wasn't easy for Nick. He imagined seeing Dante years down the line, when the two barely knew each other anymore. Yet here they were, standing together and embracing like no time had passed at all. "Why are you here?" Nick continued without letting Dante respond. "What about your Dad?"

Dante sighed and shook his head a little. Nick expected an immediate response. When none came, he knew that it wasn't good news.

"My Dad put up a great fight, Nick," Dante replied sadly.

Nick took himself back to his days before Project Nitro. The times he would sit with Dante next to his father's bed. The three would talk and play, but Dante's father could never be far from the machinery that kept him alive. He had been very sick for many years. The family had known, unfortunately, it was just a matter of time. Nick immediately made the assumption that that time had come.

"I'm sorry, Dante," Nick said, quietly and sincerely.

Dante smiled again. The excitement of the situation hadn't completely faded from him. It seemed his happiness outweighed the memories.

"Thanks, man, but he was in a lot of pain toward the end. Glad he's not hurting anymore. And hey! Shortly after all that, Phil here came up to me and invited me into the project. Help you make things right for yourself."

"Professor or Redman will work fine, Mr. Bruno."

Dante threw his hands out to the side. "Oh, c'mon. Why can't we be on a first name basis, Doc?"

"I'm also not a doctor."

"So, they did the procedure on you as well?" Nick asked. Dante's eyes sprung to life again.

"Oh, man I totally forgot! Check this out!" Dante lifted his arm into the space between Nick and himself and spread his fingers apart. He slammed his hand into a fist, causing ice to erupt from the creases and crawl across his forearm. Some pieces of ice shot out a few inches and took the form of dangerous-looking spikes. Dante rotated his arm around, showing Nick every side of the ice-gauntlet he now wore. "Pretty cool, right?" He leaned in closer. "Get it? Because it's ice."

Nick laughed and stared in amazement.

"Dude…" Dante lifted his other hand and put up one finger. "Also this." He pushed his gauntlet outwards, causing a blade made completely of ice to spring out several feet. It shimmered in the light as Dante began to swing it around. "Ice sword!" he yelled. "I can't wait to do some damage with this thing!" He continued to swing it, making swooshing noises while he did.

Nick was laughing at the display as his cousin began fighting off several invisible enemies. Nick couldn't express how relieved he was that Dante had retained his carefree and playful nature. When Nick's family was lost, Dante's attitude was one of the only things that kept Nick together. It was a comfort that Nick was scared he'd lose by joining project Nitro.

Dante spun completely around, bringing the sword in for a massive attack. He barely managed to stop it in time before it hit Redman. He was standing only a few feet from Dante.

Redman didn't even flinch as the sword stopped mere inches from his face. He simply stared, in an almost disappointed manner. "Are we finished here?" he asked.

Dante's ice sword melted back into his hand. He leaned in a little closer to the professor.

"You are terrifying," Nick said quietly.

Redman turned toward the door and motioned over his shoulder. "Come, come now," he called out to the two. "Time we went to meet the others."

Dante stood up straight again and turned to Nick. "Oh, dude," he started, "you're going to love these guys."

"You've met them?" Nick asked.

"Oh, yeah, we've been hanging out for a while." Dante started to head for the door but turned around to face Nick while he walked backward. "We were just waiting on you, man. Something about your enhancers took longer than ours. Redman didn't want us hanging out until he was sure your powers were safe. Guess you got the green checkmark." Dante picked up the pace to catch up with Redman.

Nick's smile slowly faded away, as the two disappeared outside the door. He sighed and looked back down at the embers and ash left over from the photograph. He closed his eyes for a moment.

"I'm gonna make this right," he spoke with purpose. His only hope was that his family could actually hear him. Nick looked back toward the door, and ran to the exit.

CHAPTER 3: A TEAM

"Look alive people!" Dante yelled as he trotted into the room. Redman followed close behind, shaking his head while he did. Nick followed in after him, cautious, but intrigued. The room he entered was similar to his own. Metal walls and floors, a solitary table in the center, and what seemed to be a form of firing range off to the side.

"Did we just go in a circle or..." Nick began. Dante quickly turned around and put his hands out to the side.

"No, no!" he yelled back. "Don't be fooled. This place may look exactly like your room, but in reality..." He walked to one of the chairs around the table and dropped down into his seat, "...It *is* exactly like your room." Dante leaned back and popped his feet up onto the table. "But this is my place. At least for now."

Nick was nodding through his cousin's speech but was sufficiently distracted by something else. Three other people sat in the room around the two Brunos. All of them had their eyes locked on Nick, and none said a word. There was tension in the air. Nick wasn't very interested in being the one to break it. It was like he was the new kid in school and was already being judged by the current students. Nick never had many issues speaking in front of crowds or meeting new people, but this situation was a bit different. Nick wasn't worried about who these people were, he was more worried about what they could do.

"Everyone," Redman started, "this is the final member of Project Nitro. Nicholas J Bruno."

The first to acknowledge Nick was a young man standing near the target range. He quickly turned on his heels and jogged over to the table. He had dark tan skin, sleek black hair, and a well-kept goatee. He was, by far, the largest person in the room, standing almost six and a half feet tall. His shoulders seemed like they were wider than a car, which almost matched the speed at which he charged toward Nick. He was wearing a big smile on his broad face as he ran up. Before he had even finished his approach, his hand was out and waiting.

"Hello, Nick!" he yelled through a thick Spanish accent. "It's so great to finally meet you."

Nick slowly reached out and accepted the handshake.

"Thanks. Nice to meet you too… uh…"

"Diego Cortez," he replied as he continued to shake hands with a force that made Nick think he might lose his arm at any moment. "The Professor has told us so much about you."

"Not really," another voice added. This one was from a girl sitting at the table, tapping her fingers across the metal. Her shoulder-length brown hair was tucked behind her ears, except for a few strands hanging down in front of her left eye. Her green eyes were locked on Nick in a focused stare, without so much as a blink. Nick couldn't tell if she was genuinely interested, or just trying to intimidate him. Either way, it made him uneasy.

"What are you talking about?" Diego asked. "This is him! Nick Bruno!" Nick cocked his head slightly.

"Yeah, I get it," she stated as she slowly stood up. She approached the two and put her hands on her hips, looking Nick up and down. "Sure, we've heard his name a bunch, and we know his enhancement was more concentrated than ours, but what do we actually know about the guy?" She whistled for a moment like she was calling a dog. Nick looked up and met her eyes. "So what's your deal, huh?"

"Megan, that's not nice!" Diego yelled. "Give him a break. He's only been awake for a few days." Nick shrugged and motioned toward the others.

"Well, how long have you guys been up?" Dante stood up from his chair.

"About a month there, chief," he replied, stretching out his arms. "Apparently the DNA enhancers they used on you took a little longer to cook. Redman's been drilling that into our brains almost every day."

"Actually," Redman interjected.

"Oh for God's sake," Dante muttered, rolling his eyes at Redman.

"We have a binding agent that we use to properly adhere the enhancements to your DNA. Nick's formula called for a higher dosage of this chemical, meaning it took more time for his system to adjust."

"But he still works, right?" Megan asked, pointing a thumb at Nick. "Like, his powers and everything? If he's supposed to be our 'incredible leader' he should be pretty great, right?"

Nick instantly put his hand up, stopping Redman before he could respond. He took a second to roll out his shoulders. He tilted his head to both sides hearing a satisfying pop and then confidently stepped forward.

"Don't worry Redman, I got this one." He tucked his hand behind his back, leaning like a professional pitcher lining up to the plate. He focused for a second. His eyes scanned the mannequins in the firing range, selecting the perfect target. Nick wound up and hurled a fireball out of his palm. It careened across the room, leaving a thick smoke trail as it went. It cracked against the helmet of a mannequin, knocking it off and sending it crashing to the floor. It skittered several yards before coming to a smoldering stop. Nick grunted in satisfaction, stood up straight, and blew the smoke away from his fingers. He turned his eyes back to Megan. With a few cocky raises of his eyebrows, he spoke.

"Pretty cool, right?" said Nick, smirking at Dante.

"Hey!" Dante complained, snagging Nick's attention. "That's what I say after I use my powers!" He sat back in his chair and folded his arms. Somewhat to himself, he said sulkily, "It makes much more sense."

Megan looked back and forth between the two Brunos before sighing. She locked eyes with Nick. Without even turning to look, she threw out her left hand toward the firing range. A small purple orb began to materialize in front of her palm. It was so bright that Nick couldn't look directly at it. Megan was unfazed and kept glaring at Nick. It was like she was daring him to watch. The orb seemed to be spinning, as bright light and shades of purple swirled and darted around within its walls. After a few moments, the orb launched from Megan's hand and rocketed toward the range.

Nick tried to keep his eyes on the orb, to judge its accuracy. His hand was up in an attempt to shield his eyes from the blinding light. However, all he could see was the orb disappear into the sea of targets. The light faded into nothingness, and for a short time, the room was completely still. No one moved as they waited for something to happen.

Nick began to lower his hand just as the immense light returned, even more brilliantly than before. It was immediately followed by a loud explosion, which shook everything and everyone in the room. Nick stepped back as shards and broken pieces of the targets erupted from the range and clattered across the floor. Purple smoke billowed out and clouded everyone's vision, leaving the aftermath a complete mystery. Large chunks of metal spun through the air. Some missed crashing into Nick by mere inches. As the smoke dissipated, the devastated landscape came into view. The range was completely obliterated. Nick's mouth slowly dropped open as he observed the destruction.

Megan lowered her hand and took a step toward the shocked Nitro.

"That's more what I would call 'pretty cool,'" she stated. She turned her head to look at Dante, who leaned back and put up both of his hands in surrender.

"Hey," he began, "it's all yours."

Megan nodded.

"That," Nick said between deep breaths, "was…"

"Completely irresponsible!" Redman roared.

Nick could see a flicker of guilt wash over Megan's face. She was like a puppy who knew she had done something wrong.

"Your powers are far too dangerous to use in your little version of flexing your muscles. I thought we covered this already!"

Nick stepped in front of Megan and put his hand out toward Redman. "Hold up, Doc," he butted in.

"Professor!" Redman corrected, angrily.

"It was my fault," Nick continued. He looked back at Megan and then to Dante. "I'm sorry, I was trying to impress them, but I guess I'm still getting used to the idea of not being the only one."

Megan sighed. "Yeah, I, uh," she said, stepping up to Nick as well, "that was stupid of me."

Dante began nodding. "Yes, Megan, yes it was," he said childishly.

"Thank you, Dante," she snapped. She turned back to Redman. "I swear I won't get out of control again."

"Aaaaaannnddd…" Diego egged her on as he stood next to Dante. Dante closed his eyes and started to giggle to himself. Diego put a hand on Dante's shoulder, laughing quietly as well. Megan darted her eyes to the two. There was only a brief moment before they instantly stopped laughing and instead stared innocently up at the ceiling.

"And," she began, taking the hint from Diego, "I'm sorry." Nick smiled a little and turned to Megan. He put out his hand.

"Let's try that again, shall we?" he asked in as kind a voice as he could. Megan glanced down at his hand. "Nick Bruno. It's a pleasure to meet you."

Megan smirked and took his hand, shaking a few times.

"Megan Sods. And the pleasure is all mine." Nick was still a bit unsure of Megan. She seemed very headstrong with flashes of kindness. Nick assumed only time would tell which of those characteristics took the helm more often.

The moment of silence and understanding between the two was suddenly broken by loud, obnoxious noises as Dante clapped. Each impact was slow and loud as he could possibly make it.

"Bravo!" he yelled. "Oh, that was just spectacular."

Dante lowered his hands and sighed. As he did, he turned to look at the last person in the room. He was sitting at the table with his hands folded in front of him. Nick had noticed him, but the boy had made zero attempts at an introduction.

He had very pale skin, and blonde hair that was either a tangled mess up top or was dropping down in front of his face. He had very sharp features and a low brow that kept his eyes temporarily out of view. One of the most noticeable traits was the long scar that ran down over his left eye and cheek.

"What about you, huh?" Dante called out. The boy glanced up, meeting Dante's eyes. His right eye was a brilliant shade of blue, while his left eye was much paler. "Why don't you tell Nick your story there, morning glory."

The boy turned to Nick and strummed his fingers a few times.

"Steven Reynolds," he said quietly, in his slightly raspy voice. He looked straight ahead again as Diego moved behind his chair.

"Awww, c'mon, Steve," Diego began, "don't be so glum."

"Please stop talking to me," he said in a monotone manner.

Diego reached down and put his hands on Steven's shoulders. He gently began rocking him from side-to-side.

"We just want to be your friends, man," he reasoned.

Steven continued to stare off into the distance, not moving a single muscle. He spoke very clearly, as if his words were directed to everyone in the room. "I'm not here to make friends," he announced. "We have a job. *I* have a job. Nothing more, nothing less." Nick glanced over at Redman who was slowly shaking his head.

"Not a typical childhood," Redman remarked to Nick. "You can't blame Steven for that."

Diego leaned down next to Steven and rested an elbow on his shoulder.

"No, but I can blame him for being a sourpuss." Diego got his face closer to Steven's and puckered his lips. "Aren't you a little sore-spot? Yes, you are."

Steven turned his head slightly so he could look at Diego.

"I hate you... very much."

"Eh, leave him alone, Diego," Nick said. "Let's talk more about the big question with you. What kind of powers did you get from the enhancers?"

Diego perked up. "Oh, right," he stated, twiddling his

fingers in the air. He motioned Nick to follow him as he ran toward the back of the room.

Nick slowly followed, past the other four. Dante stood up and joined Nick. As they approached another area of the room, Nick noticed that the floor began to change. It went from consistent tiles to a few missing here and there, to no floor at all. Eventually, the three were walking on top of nothing but soil and some patchy grass.

"This is," Nick started, turning toward Dante, "a bit odd."

Dante smirked, but motioned his head toward Diego, essentially telling Nick to pay attention.

Nick turned back as Diego stepped out into the center of the uncovered area. He widened his stance once he reached his mark and dropped his arms down to his sides. Nick couldn't see Diego's face from the angle, but it didn't matter. He could feel the concentration emanating from where Diego was standing.

Diego put his palms flat toward the ground, and then slowly lifted them up to the level of his shoulders. As he did, the ground below him began to shake and shift.

Nick could see fault lines quickly trace through the dirt and draw careful paths around Diego. Two sections of earth started to fight their way apart from the rest. The two patches quickly grew into two columns as they rose out of the ground under Diego's palms. They were comprised of a twisted marbling of dirt and rock.

Diego turned his head to look over his shoulder at Nick and smiled. "Check it out!" he yelled back to the Brunos. "Earth powers! I can move rock and dirt around and form it however I want."

Nick stepped forward. It was amazing to see something like rock acting on its own. To Nick, rock was like the epitome of inanimate, and yet here it was moving around like an animal.

Diego snapped back to position, and then took two massive steps forward, punching out his fists while he did.

The two columns split from their base and took off forward like bullets. They slammed into the metal wall in front of him and shattered into shards and pebbles. When the dust settled, two massive dents in the metal faded into view. Diego stayed locked in his position for a moment, taking a few deep breaths, before relaxing and stepping back. He turned back to the Brunos and put out his hands. "Not bad, right?"

"Yeah," Dante remarked. "Pretty impressive. I think Redman might have a conversation with you later about that wall, but still, not bad."

Diego raised an eyebrow before glancing back to the two colossal dents in the thick metal wall.

"Oops," he quietly muttered.

"Nothing to worry about, Mr. Cortez," Redman announced from back at the table. "I'm beginning to get used to actions like that one."

As the three walked back from dirt to metal floor, Nick's eyes set on Steven. He was still sitting at the table, not even turning to watch Diego's demonstration. As Nick got closer, he motioned his hands out to his sides.

"Sooooo," he egged on.

Steven glanced up at Nick, still unfazed.

Nick didn't say another word, but did move his hands like he was hoping for more.

Steven sighed and slowly reached his hand across the table. He grabbed a glass of water and dragged it back to his body. He turned his eyes back up to Nick one last time before waving his other hand in a circular motion over the table.

Nick felt a strange uneasiness fall over him as Steven's hand grew in pace. The surface of the table below Steven's hand began to change, and move as if the metal was beginning to boil. Then, from the center of the movement, a blackness began to grow. It was the darkest shade of black Nick had ever seen. A circle with no definite edges. Instead, it seemed to just fade off into nothingness. As Steven continued the motion, the dark circle grew larger, until it was roughly two feet in diameter.

Steven stopped moving and sat back in his chair, motioning his hand out toward the darkness.

"Ta-da," he said, deeply and without any hint of excitement or enthusiasm.

Nick stared at the marvel and leaned in to get a closer

look. However, no matter how close he got, the circle never gained any more form or detail.

"Wow," Nick said, examining it further. He then tilted his head and looked back to Steven. "Umm, what it is?"

Steven sighed and lifted his hand again, this time moving it in a circle next to him. Another black circle formed in the air beside his head. This one was just floating without contact to any surface. Steven then slid the glass of water across the table. Once it came in contact with the blackness, it tilted to one side and fell in, disappearing into the shadows. Almost instantly the glass shot from the other circle next to Steven and fell perfectly into his hand. Steven nodded, lifted the glass, and took a sip.

Nick had never seen anything like this before. It was like something out of a video game or a sci-fi movie. The other thing coming over Nick was a feeling of hope. Taking down the Blades seemed almost impossible, but after seeing the incredible powers of his teammates, victory seemed definite.

"Portals?" Nick asked. "That's pretty awesome."

"It's a bit more complicated than that," Redman began.

Nick stood up again as the two portals faded away. They slowly shrunk until there was no trace of them remaining.

"You see, scientists spent years researching the universe, and what holds it together. Trying to solve what was in that area between stars and planets. Scientists collectively began calling this area, 'the Void.' As we researched it further, we discovered that the Void is completely made up of a substance called 'dark matter.' This dark matter is present throughout the galaxy, including here."

"Because of that, I can use resonant dark matter in the area to connect myself to the Void," Steven added. "Those portals are more like gateways. I can enter the Void from here, and exit anywhere else in our universe."

"No way," Nick said in almost a whisper. "So, people can go in?"

"Well, yes," Redman replied. "One." He lifted his hand and pointed toward Steven. "The Nitro enhancements we used on Steven adapted his body to survive within the Void. No one else can, and even Steven would succumb to the forces in there if given enough time."

"Hear that, Reynolds?" Dante asked. "No going in there for quality time away from us."

"Any time away from you will be 'quality time,'" he muttered back.

"That's enough," Redman interrupted. "I understand that you've hardly had a chance to meet one another, but the five of you are a team. You were inducted into Project Nitro to work together. I don't expect you to love one another, but I do expect you to respect one another. You all hold incredible power in your hands, but if you don't act as a team, you won't stand a chance against the Blades."

Nick and Dante glanced at each other, and then back to

Redman.

"You cannot take on this responsibility lightly. All of you know what it's like to lose someone close to you. To have them taken away." Redman carefully darted his stare to the eyes of everyone in the room. "The Blades took them away from you, and they aren't going to stop there. If you can't end this, here and now, no one can."

Nick nodded, mostly to himself, and then turned to look at the others.

Megan and Dante were staring right back at Redman, while Diego and Steven were looking away. Both seemed to be digging new holes for memories they'd prefer to remain buried.

These men and women standing next to him couldn't just be strangers anymore. This was his team. The photos of the bodies left behind by the Blades were still fresh in his memory, and again the bodies reminded him too much of his own family. He knew he was either going to stop the Blades with these new partners or end up dead alongside them.

"I'm willing to do this, Redman," Nick spoke out, still looking at the others. Nick didn't move for a moment, choosing his next action carefully. He lowered his head. "I've lost too much because of the Blades. We all have."

"Here here!" Dante shouted. "I know not everyone here is lucky enough to have a family member on the team, but I'd be surprised if we didn't feel that way soon enough."

Suddenly Dante and Nick were pulled forcefully together as Diego threw his arms over both of their shoulders. "Sure, I could see that happening!" Diego added.

Megan started to chuckle and folded her arms. She shrugged and stepped toward the others. "What the hell? Can't be that bad working with you guys, right?"

"Yeah, I don't bite," Dante replied. He leaned closer to Megan and spoke quieter. "Much." He growled like a cat, causing Megan to unfold her arms and place her hands on her hips.

"That. What you just did there. That needs to not happen anymore, got it?"

"Message received," Dante quickly responded.

"What about you, Steven?" Diego asked.

Steven stared at the other four but still didn't stand up from the table. He sighed and faced forward again, before slowly raising one of his fists into the air.

"Yay, woo, go teamwork," he said dryly.

"I'll take it," Redman snapped. He grabbed his papers off the table and nodded to his Nitros. "Well, then. Follow me. Time to get you suited up and ready for action." Redman turned away and began walking out, motioning the others to follow. "I think the city is ready to meet you."

CHAPTER 4: A MISSION

Nick and the others followed closely behind Redman as they snaked their way through hallways they hadn't even known existed. Redman was like a trained mouse in a maze, knowing exactly where to turn and when to do it. Clearly he was the man in charge, as almost every person passing by nodded to him or made a significant effort to look busy. As the Nitros passed by lab workers, the workers would immediately stop, stare at the five, and whisper to one another. As the Nitros passed another startled group, Dante leaned closer to Nick and spoke very softly.

"I get that some of these people are seeing us for the first time, but this doesn't exactly look like excitement to me," said Dante.

Nick leaned in as well, not looking at Dante, but getting closer so he could lower his voice.

"What do you mean?" he asked.

Dante motioned toward another group as they all avoided eye-contact and quietly murmured to one another.

"It almost looks like they're afraid of us."

Megan stepped up between the two Brunos and made her way past them. As she did, she turned her head over her shoulder.

"Wouldn't you be?" she asked. She continued past them, leaving Nick to just shrug to Dante.

As the group continued around another bend, Redman came to a stop in front of a large metal door. He lifted his hand to a red panel next to the frame and laid his palm flat across it. The device scanned each of his fingers. Small, glowing circles traced around his fingertips, one at a time. A quiet beeping filled the air while it did. A few seconds later, the door churned to life and began to slowly slide out of the way. Nick examined the panel as the group entered the new room.

"So, Redman," he started, examining the intricate machinery around him.

Redman glanced back but continued on his path forward.

"How do you... you know... afford all this stuff?" Nick asked.

Redman smirked. "Do you, Nitros, know why we call our city, Lattice Light?" he asked, instead of giving an immediate response.

"Sure," Diego began, "it's the street grid. The city used

to be called… uh…"

"New Exeter," Megan finished. "This was the first city in the U.S. to adopt the street grid as a standard. No more manual-control vehicles allowed. They renamed the city because of the blue lights coming out of the sides of the street. Looks like a lattice pattern from above."

Redman nodded as he approached the center of the large room they had entered. "The mechanics underneath the asphalt don't just direct the vehicles, Megan," he added, "it powers them. The longer the cars spend on the road, the more energy they gain from it. All that energy is fed in through solar panels along the buildings and hydro-electricity generated from the currents in the ocean. While it will take years for this technology to become a standard across the entire nation, Lattice Light is a shining example that it can be done."

"Looks like you know a lot about it," Nick pointed out.

Redman shrugged and leaned over a large desk in front of him. "I assume I should. I'm the man who invented it, after all. That and many other things to better help the advancement of mankind." He put out his hands. "Hence, the funding for projects like this."

Nick raised an eyebrow. He turned from the professor so he could better learn the details of the room around him. It was enormous. Several tables and chairs were strewn across the floor, while Redman's desk sat in the center, and up a few feet from ground level. It was like he was seated on a pedestal. A massive computer screen essentially covered an entire wall, with several control panels underneath it that Nick could never hope to understand. Displayed across the screen was a wireframe map of Lattice Light City. Nick couldn't help but move closer, as his curiosity grew. He looked over the city, at each building and alleyway. He had been in the city many times before, but the streets and towers now had a very different meaning to him.

Somewhere in the shadows, the person responsible for the death of his family was hiding. Nick leaned forward to get a better look and rested his hands on one of the panels below the screen. He squinted at the wireframe map. His brain desperately tried to take a mental snapshot of every single inch.

However, before he could make any progress, a voice cried out. "Watch it!" it shouted.

Nick snapped away from the control board and turned to face the woman standing next to him. She was holding several binders, each stuffed to the brim with papers. Her red top perfectly matched her fiery red hair, which was curled up in a bun. She had pale, freckled skin and large glasses that seemed to magnify her eyes.

"That is very sensitive equipment. One wrong move and we shut down an entire section of the street grid. Unless you want to be the one explaining to the mayor why downtown Lattice Light is at a standstill, I'd suggest moving away."

Nick folded his hands behind his back and took a few more steps back. "Oh, ummm, sorry," he muttered. "I... I didn't realize..."

"Ahh, Kristen!" Redman interjected. He turned to the others and motioned toward her. "Nitros, this is Kristen McConnell. She's the head tech in this lab. Days spent keeping the grid up and running, as well as everything in this building. Trust me, that's no easy task."

"No, it isn't," she added, "but it's important." She firmly nodded. A small smiled formed as she faced Nick once again. "Still, pleased to meet you. I've heard so much about you." She took hold of the binder topping her stack. "I mean how could I not? The Nitros. You guys have been the biggest news around this place in years." She handed the binder to Nick and continued to move toward the other Nitros, handing them each a binder as she went.

Nick looked over the cover, squinting at the title etched into it. Kristen was still talking in the background, but her words seemed to fade out as Nick's attention fell elsewhere.

"Subject Nuclear?" he asked. He turned to look up at Redman, shaking the binder a bit while he did. "That doesn't sound good."

Redman chuckled and adjusted his glasses. "Believe me, it is," he replied. He stepped down from his desk and walked toward Nick. "Like it or not, Nicholas, that's you."

He pointed his finger at Nick's chest as he made the remark. "At least, what went into making you."

Nick looked down at the binder again. He opened the front cover, revealing the first page contained an image of him, with all of his information scribbled next to it. His name, home, height, weight, hobbies, blood type. Everything was there. Another flip of the page showed newspaper clippings and internet articles about the attack on his family. A third turn revealed information about Dante, as well as a list of people Nick had been in contact with before the procedure. As he turned more pages, the information became harder and harder to understand, until it eventually became gibberish that would make Einstein scratch his head. Formulas and equations next to lists and lists of chemicals.

"I'm Subject Nuclear?"

"Well, technically, yes."

"I told him the name was stupid," Kristen noted as she took her seat in front of the computer.

"Each project had a codename associated with it while it was in production," Redman continued, without acknowledging Kristen. "We here at the lab grew attached to them over the years of work."

"Subject Blast?" Dante asked from across the room. Redman nodded again while pointing down to the binder.

"You see, each one of your enhancers has a little bit of Otrolium laced in," Redman explained. "It's what we used to bind the chemicals to your DNA."

"Hold up," Steven interrupted, "didn't you say that stuff was dangerous?"

"Yeah, like, super radioactive dangerous?" Dante added, flailing his hands around. "Isn't that why you shut down that project to behind with?"

"Yes, but the Otrolium isn't dangerous in the amounts we used," Redman assured. "Regardless, we decided to base your codenames off of its explosive nature."

"But why do we even need codenames?" Nick asked. "We're not exactly hiding our identities from people."

"No," said Kristen, "but Redman thinks having names like that will raise the spirits of people in the city. Like superheroes or something."

"Exactly," Redman agreed. "With things being as bad as they are right now, the citizens of Lattice Light need figures they can look up to. Not just another human. They need something more. Something they truly believe can fight against the Blades when no one else could."

Nick sighed. He closed the binder with a loud thud. The name Nuclear was embedded cleanly into its cover. The light from the room was shimmering off of it and casting a bright glow on Nick's face.

"If that's what you think is best, then fine, Redman," Nick said, calmly. "Feel free to call me Nuclear, then. It'll take some getting used to, but I'm sure I can learn to like it."

Dante nodded and slapped his binder closed, making an echo in the room. "Subject Blast, reporting for duty!" he chimed off while deepening his voice. He closed his other hand into a fist and punched the air in front of him a few times. "Yes! That sounds so awesome."

"And I guess that makes me, Reactor?" Megan added, pointing to the cover of her binder. "Not bad. Could have been worse."

"Like 'Atomic?'" Diego asked. "Cause, you know, that's what mine says. Don't you think that's a bit violent?"

"The names are based on explosives, chief," Dante noted, "of course they're going to sound violent."

Steven stepped up to stand next to Diego, holding his binder down by his side. "Mine says 'Subject Explosion,'" he muttered. He lifted his hands out to his sides a bit before letting them drop back down. "You just ran out of names, didn't you?"

"Haha, yes!" Dante laughed excitedly. "Blast, Nuclear, Reactor, Atomic, and Explosion!" He rattled off the names, pointing powerfully at each member as he called them. "A real life team of superheroes! This is so badass." He turned to Nick and leaned in, talking a little quieter. "This is like a freaking comic book, dude! This kind of stuff only happens in the movies!"

"If you think fancy names make this a comic book," Megan started, from further away, "you haven't seen anything, yet."

Dante and Nick turned to look at her, seeing she was now standing against another wall in the room, examining six glass tubes. Inside of them were six uniforms, displayed proudly on the bodies of mannequins. The material making up most of the suits seemed stretchy, yet at the same time, thick and strong. Like a type of carbon fiber disguised as fabric. The combat boots were heavily padded on the bottom and sported several buckles along the sides. The top and bottom sections of the uniform connected at the waist underneath a thick belt. A large buckle was the centerpiece of the belt, which had the letter 'N' engraved across it. The suits were all identical, except for one key feature. The boots, belt, sleeves, and designs along the chest and inner parts of the legs were a different color on each suit.

"You have got to be kidding me," Steven groaned as he stepped closer to them. "We have to wear matching uniforms?"

"Ah, yes," Redman chimed in happily, like he had forgotten all about them. "These suits aren't just for looks, everyone. They are specifically designed to handle your unique abilities. For example, Nick's suit can withstand extremely high temperatures, while Steven's is designed to blend with the darkness of the Void, making him nearly invisible when in the shadows."

Nick stepped toward the red uniform and reached out, lightly touching the glove. He could feel a certain, but very faint, roughness in the fabric.

"Permeated," Redman noted. "Small, almost undetectable pores in the gloves, so any fire you create from your hand doesn't remain trapped underneath the suit."

Nick wanted to smile and was somehow finding it difficult. The suits were pretty impressive to him, but something was throwing him off about them. It only took him a few more seconds to realize exactly what it was.

"Hey, Redman," he began. The professor glanced over, ready to answer whatever questions Nick had brewing. "I'm guessing this red suit is mine?" Redman nodded.

"Seemed appropriate for fire," Redman responded.

"Silver for Dante?"

"Blast!" Nick's cousin corrected, almost before Nick had finished speaking.

"Shut up," he snapped back at him. "Purple for Megan. Green for Diego. And black for Steven, right?" Redman continued to nod throughout.

"That's correct. Excellent guesswork, Nicholas. I tried to base the color scheme on your powers as best I could. I'm not really much of a designer, but the team I put in charge seems to have done a satisfactory job. My main concern was with their functionality."

"Yeah, yeah," Nick said quickly, trying to finish his thought. "That's fine, Professor, but what's with the sixth one? You know, the blue one?"

The others followed Nick's stare and also found themselves looking at a sixth uniform. While the other five suits were lit up and nicely displayed, this one was left dark and almost seemed to just blend into the background like it was trying to be forgotten.

"Yes," Redman said quietly, almost like he was admitting something. "There was once going to be a sixth Nitro. It was in the original plans, but unfortunately never ended up happening." He motioned toward Kristen, who still had one binder in her hands.

Nick turned to her, and she immediately handed it to him. Nick ran his hand over the cover, tracing his finger across the embedded name. "Project Uranium," he whispered to himself. As his finger ran across it, a thin layer of dust stuck to his skin.

"Too unstable," Redman answered before Nick could even ask the question. "That particular enhancement was one of my earliest designs when Project Nitro was being developed. It didn't hold up to my standards."

"Clearly it went pretty far," Megan pointed out. "I mean, you made the suit. You still have the file."

"Because there's still hope for it," he replied, "but not now. There are more important things on the agenda than perfecting something we don't need. For example, your first mission assignment."

Taking the hint, Kristen began typing away on the computer. Within seconds the massive screen was filled with information. Words, formulas, and images were detailing a device spinning in the center. The machine looked like a metallic box with two empty, circular slots in the center. Several large pipes extended off the box and connected to a large glass tube next to it.

Nick read through the measurements and was shocked to discover the machine stood over eight feet tall.

"Wow," Diego muttered, stepped forward to stand next to Nick. "What the heck is that thing?"

"This," Redman began, "is the Otrolium Matter Converter. This machine is how we manufacture the substance. Items go in the tube, and the energy from the atoms and electrons within the item is harvested. The item is destroyed, but Otrolium is the product. The Converter is the only way to make more of the Otrolium, meaning the Blades have been after it ever since they learned it existed."

"Not to step out of line here, Professor," Megan said, holding out one of her hands, "but why not just destroy it? The Blades can't steal it if it's gone."

"Because I've received specific orders to avoid that at all costs," Redman replied. "You need to understand that Otrolium is the closest thing humanity has to an alternate fuel source. Fossil fuels are diminishing, and not even the street grid's technology is enough to replace it completely. Destroying the Converter now would be like stepping fifty years into the past. Uncountable amounts of progress and innovation gone in an instant."

"Okay, okay," Dante interrupted, "we get it. Destroying the machine. Bad. So what's your plan?"

"The government has granted me access to one of the most secure facilities in the nation. Your job will be to safely escort the Converter there."

"What?" Kristen asked, turning from the computer. "You mean it's not already in one?"

Redman shook his head but didn't look at Kristen. "We've had it hidden in this lab since the project began."

"It's here?!" she exclaimed again.

"Yes, which is why the Nitros will be making sure there are no issues with the drop-off. It should be simple, as long as the Blades don't catch wind. Even with a police escort, the journey will take around ten hours. Get the Converter to the base, lock it up, and check that worry off our list. They should be readying the Converter for transport as we speak."

Almost as soon as Redman's mouth closed, a red light on the ceiling began to flash, and rotate around the room. Accompanying it was a blaring siren. The information on screen quickly vanished one line at a time and was replaced by a map of Lattice Light City. The map zoomed into a specific block and flashed a red dot over a building near the water.

"That escort might have to wait, Redman," Kristen reported, in almost a panic. It one swift motion she spun back to her keyboard. "We have police reports coming in from a warehouse on the docks." After a few more lightning fast keystrokes, words and stats began to appear next to the building on the map. "Warehouse… 77. Armed soldiers with Blade markings were seen forcing their way inside."

Redman squinted his eyes. He walked away from his desk, getting a closer look at the screen. "Warehouse 77?" he reiterated. He didn't speak for a few seconds while his brain processed the information.

Nick could see Redman trying to reach a conclusion, but something seemed to be stopping him. "That facility has already been cleared out. There shouldn't be any Otrolium there anymore. Why would the Blades be attacking it?"

"Maybe you missed some?" Dante suggested.

"Unlikely," Kristen responded. "We're very thorough in our sweeps after Otrolium has been located."

"Then it must be some rogue soldiers," Redman reasoned. "Maybe just looking for somewhere to lay low."

"Going to have to disagree, Professor," Kristen snapped. She slowly turned away from the computer, setting her eyes right on Redman's. "Patrick Zealo is leading the group."

Redman's eyes widened. "Stunner?" A silence fell over the Professor. His eyes drifted to the side as he wrestled with the possibilities. He knew the crimes Patrick Zealo was guilty of committing under the persona of Stunner. Everything from assault to suspected murder. Redman now had to make a big call. Were the Nitros ready to take on a challenge like him?

In a moment of acceptance, Redman turned and ran to the uniforms. He furiously typed into a keypad in front of them, causing the glass coverings to move away. The mannequins within the suits began to shrink down, allowing the uniforms to collapse down to the bottom of the tubes.

"Redman, what the hell is going on?" Nick demanded with his arms out to the sides.

"Patrick Zealo is a high ranking member of the Blades," Redman responded. "We don't think he has direct contact with the Blade Leader, but he probably knows someone who does." Redman pushed away from the tubes taking Nick's suit with him.

"What's with that name?" Diego asked. "Stunner?"

"He constructed a portable device that he wears on his back. It funnels the energy of Otrolium into tangible beams of light. The device is so destructive that LLPD has been given strict orders not to engage him. Luckily," Redman began, throwing the uniform to Nick, "you aren't part of the LLPD."

Nick looked down at his suit, running his thumb on the thick, but flexible material. The red color was bright and new. He could almost see his reflection in the shine of the fabric.

"So what's the mission?" he asked, slowly looking back up. Redman glanced at each of the Nitros, before taking a deep breath and folding his arms.

"The Converter will have to wait. Get to the warehouse. Stop the Blades from getting whatever it is they're after. Disarm Stunner, and get him to tell us where we can find the Blade Leader."

Nick turned to look at Dante, who was now retrieving his suit from the tube. The other Nitros began filing in to do the same.

"How are we getting there?" Dante asked. "Got a car or something?"

"Yes, actually," Redman responded while examining a few more items on the screen. "I've been working on a custom vehicle that I can control from here using the grid. Should be able to transport you anywhere in the city within minutes."

"Sweet!" Dante yelled. He lifted his hand and moved it across the air in front of him like he was highlighting a headline in the news. "The Nitromobile!"

"It isn't finished yet!" Redman snapped, cutting him off. "It needs more work, and it absolutely will not be titled 'The Nitromobile.'

Diego has been practicing an ability that can move you across the asphalt at a rapid pace. He'll be able to get you there."

Nick looked toward Diego, who gave him a quick nod.

"They don't know you're here," Redman added. "The Blades have no idea what they're up against, now."

Nick returned his gaze to Redman as the professor took one last breath, calming his nerves. "I think it's time we showed them."

CHAPTER 5: A BLINDING LIGHT

The wind felt almost unnatural to Nick as it snaked its way through his hair. It had been years since he was last outside. Even though most of it was spent unconscious, his body still somehow knew it had been deprived. Even the moonlight felt like it would be enough to burn his skin. Nick was standing tightly against Dante, Steven, and Megan.

Diego was in front of them with one leg lunged out further than the other. His hands were angled downward, and his eyes were locked ahead in concentration. The asphalt was pulling away from the road underneath the Nitros, pushing them forward onto the next moving slab, and then calmly settling back into its original spot. Slab after slab moved them toward their destination, and closer to their first mission as a team. The neon blue lights coating the edges of the streets gave momentary clarity to the world around them, before plunging into darkness again. People on the sidewalks froze mid-step and stared as the five uniformed bio-humans tore down the street. All the bystanders could see was the road ripping up to transport them away, and Dante happily waving off the back.

"How long have you been practicing this?" Megan called out to Diego. He maintained his focus but tilted his head slightly to acknowledge her.

"Redman gave me the basics only a day or two after I woke up," Diego replied. "Let me take a few laps around the outside of the lab."

"And you got it first try?" Nick questioned.

Diego didn't respond right away. "Well, no, but I don't think you want those details right now."

Nick stiffened his lower lip and nodded. "You're probably right."

Nick didn't want to question Diego too much. He knew Redman wanted him to fill some sort of leadership position, but Nick was exactly brimming with confidence. He had no idea how these new people would react to him suddenly trying to bark orders, especially Megan and Steven. Nick figured his best move on this mission would be to watch and learn how each member preferred to operate.

As the Nitros got closer to their target, the stillness of the night was broken by the distant appearance of blue and red lights, alternating back and forth. The pace of Diego's moving road slowed as they reached the series of police vehicles. They broke apart but stayed in close formation. They cautiously dove into the sea of police. The officers around the cars took their eyes away from the warehouse, finding themselves staring at the five figures that just arrived instead. The police chief had a small smile on his face as he looked up and down each of the Nitros with his arms folded tight.

"You know," the police chief began, "I had never been more certain I was on the receiving end of a prank phone call." He walked toward Nick, closely examining his uniform. "And, yet, here you are. The biohumans they called us about."

The chief had a slender head with defined temples and thin, emotionless lips. His tan skin had a certain shine to it, and his fine black hair was cut short. Nick nodded to him and then glanced to his side. The large number '77' painted across the warehouse was barely visible through the night air.

"You can call me Nuclear, and we're here to help," Nick said with a purpose, not turning back to face the chief. Nick was trying to stay serious, but on the inside his brain was on fire. He barely ever interacted with police officers before, and now he felt like he was supposed to speak to them like a coworker. He figured the best he could do was act like the cops he used to watch on TV. No nonsense and straight to business.

Not taking offense, the chief tipped his hat and put his hands on his hips.

"You can call me Deb," he introduced. "I'm not gonna try and pretend I understand everything that's going on with you guys, or what exactly you are, but if you really think you can help us with this Blade situation…" Deb turned his attention back to the warehouse, before releasing a small sigh. "Let's just say we can use all the help we can get right now."

"So what's happening in there?" Steven interrupted, clearly getting tired of the formalities.

"Patrick Zealo and around ten Blade soldiers were seen entering the building," Deb reported. "We wired into the city's surveillance system once we got the call. They're held up inside at the moment, but we're not exactly sure why. Only thing we can guarantee is that they know we're here."

"Is there Otrolium inside?" Nick asked. Deb squinted and turned his head slightly.

"Is there *what* inside?" he questioned. Nick didn't answer. He didn't know how much the police force knew about the Otrolium. As much as he wanted to explain the whole situation, he didn't want to overstep whatever Redman had decided was better left unsaid.

Nick instead motioned at the other Nitros, before taking a few steps forward. The other four Nitros hung back for a second, watching Nick march toward the warehouse. This was Nick's first moment to prove he was worthy of his powers. If he could take down Stunner it would send a clear message to the rest of the Blades.

"Nuclear," Dante started, quickly running in front of his cousin. He put his hand on Nick's chest. Nick stopped and raised an eyebrow. "I think it's pretty safe to assume the Blades are well armed in there. We need a plan going into this."

"Blast has a point," Megan added. "Going in blind could be suicide." Steven didn't directly address the others as he stepped up.

"I might have an idea," Steven began. "If you're looking for suggestions, Nuclear."

Nick nodded. "I think we'll take what we can get at this point."

Steven turned to Dante and pointed to the small device sitting over his ear. Each Nitro had a matching one to stay in communication if they were separated. "Redman gave us these things for a reason," Steven said. "Let me get inside and report back to you guys with whatever I see."

"You're going in?" Diego asked. "You know they're not exactly going to let you barge in through the front door."

Steven slowly lifted his right hand and began to move it in a circle next to him. The night became even darker around him as the Void began to leak into existence and create a portal beside him. Steven stared at it, slowing his breathing while he did. "I don't plan on using the front door," Steven replied. He cautiously reached his hand toward the darkness. It was as if he was breaking the surface of a pond when his fingers finally made contact. Ripples through nothing but shadow as the Void slowly engulfed his arm up to the elbow. Steven turned his head back to the others, while still reaching into the portal. He had a look of concern on his face that sported a dangerous mix of optimism.

"I can use the Void to get inside and scout it out without them knowing," Steven explained. "I'm sure they're watching all the entrances. This is going to be our best bet."

"Are you sure about this?" Dante questioned. Steven took one last deep breath and squared himself up with the portal.

"No," he quickly responded, "but we have to try everything eventually." Steven closed his eyes and exhaled as he took two steps forward and disappeared into the darkness. As he opened his eyes again, he could see a tangled mixture of black and purple cascading around him. Distant stars twinkled in and out of existence. He was in another world, and yet the one he knew was still right in front of him. Outlines and shapes of buildings, the police standing at attention, and the vague but purposeful movements of whoever was inside the warehouse. He could see it all. Everything in his universe had their own representation in the Void made up of nothing but shadows and darkness. Their movements were slow, to the point where they seemed to be locked in stillness.

Steven began to approach the warehouse, stepping across the darkness, like he was walking across an ocean, causing ripples with his footsteps. As he got closer, the figures standing within became clearer. It didn't seem like they were set up with any purpose, but more like they were patiently waiting for something. Steven reached the edge of the warehouse and reached out to touch it, but instead of solid contact, his hand faded straight through the building's outline. Steven instinctively pulled his hand back, as his brain refused to comprehend what was happening. He closed his fingers into a fist and exhaled again. He began to move forward, in defiance of his own mind. He walked through the wall and stepped carefully into the building.

As he got closer the outlines of the men inside solidified into Blade soldiers, their details began to fill out. Steven could make out their armor and weaponry, each adorned with scratches and markings. A haggard letter B was crisply defined on their chests.

Steven knew how to handle himself in a fight, as he'd been doing it his entire life. However, the situation was a bit different when he was preparing to fight an army. Each time he saw another weaponized soldier, a bit of his confidence would evaporate and leave him questioning.

Steven glanced to the side at the darkest corner of the room, and with a few quick looks back at the soldiers, ran toward it. Steven knelt down into the shadows. He lifted both his hands slowly and purposefully. His concentration was coupled with the darkness and space around him melting away. Color began to seep back into his vision and the shadows folded away into concrete and metal. The world around him returned to normal as he lowered one of his hands. The other one lifted to his ear and activated his communicator.

"Guys," he started quietly, "you there?"

"Steve-!" Nick started. He turned his head over his shoulder to look at the officers behind him, listening closely. Using codenames was still a difficult thing for Nick to remember, but he was sure it would set in eventually. "Uhh... I mean... *Explosion*. Did you make it inside?"

"Deb was right," Steven said, ignoring the question. "There's ten of them in here. All of them have pretty significant weapons and armor." Steven darted his eyes around the room. "No sign of Stunner, yet, or at least anyone who would fit his description."

"Any Otrolium in there?" Diego asked.

"None. At least not any I can see. If there was, chances are they've moved it for extraction." Steven looked to his left, assessing the scene in front of him. "I think I have an idea. Reactor?"

"I'm here, Explosion," Megan quickly replied.

"See the wall in front of you, the one with the main loading entrance on it?" Megan looked up and nodded to herself.

"Yeah. Hard to miss."

"Do you think you could hit the top left corner with one of your bombs? We've got six soldiers up above on a catwalk, and it looks like it's anchored to a crossbeam in that corner." Megan smirked, stepping away from the other three Nitros.

"You got it."

"That leaves four other Blades on ground level," Steven continued. "If you guys break in at the same time Reactor's attack hits, we might be able to take down the rest before they know what's happening."

"Oh, trust me, dude," Dante interrupted, "they won't know what's happening. I don't think we're exactly something you plan for."

"On Reactor's mark, then," Nick instructed. "We need to go in fast and loud. We have surprise on our side, and that's probably better than all our powers combined. Sound good? Everyone ready?"

"Roger," Megan said.

"In position," Steven added.

"I'm ready," Diego reported.

"Can do," Dante finished. Diego, Dante, and Nick moved toward the front entrance. They hugged the outer wall of the warehouse closely.

Megan's hand sprung open, revealing a small, but extremely bright, orb. The purple light from it sparkled across the puddles on the pavement. Megan took a few extra moments getting her aim, before stepping forward and hurling the orb at the warehouse. It danced through the air. The orb got smaller and smaller in the distance, and almost completely disappeared from view. It blinked out of eyesight right at the corner of the warehouse, and for a moment, there was a deafening silence. A shockwave tore out through the sky, shaking every police cruiser parked outside. The blinding eruption ripped metal away from the rafters and sent bolts and screws firing from their positions.

The Blades inside ducked for cover. One looked up and pointed toward the ceiling when he saw the crossbeam overhead buckle at one end and shear away from its anchor. The entire catwalk began to buckle and collapse as the six Blades frantically tried to escape. They plummeted to the floor and smashed into the concrete. Metal bars and wooden planks dropped down on top of them, burying a few of the blades underneath. Dust and debris exploded outward around the entire room.

In almost the same instant, the front gate of the warehouse burst from its hinges and rocketed into the building. Nick leaped out of the dust and pitched a fireball. It slammed into the chest of a Blade soldier, causing him to drop his weapon and clutch at his smoldering armor. He swatted away embers like insects. After a few more panicked seconds, he dropped to his knee.

Another Blade, after watching his fellow soldier fight against the anguish, tightly gripped his gun and took aim in the direction of the front entrance. However, the harder he pulled on his rifle, the less it seemed to move. He turned his head and looked down, only to see his gun completely encased in ice. The ice crawled up his arm and started to circle his shoulder. "What the hell is this?!" he shouted. His knees began to shake as the ice pulled him toward the floor. More of it continued to swirl around his limbs. Soon, he was completely encased, with just his head poking out of the top and shaking vigorously.

A third Blade ran to his colleague but tripped and crashed chest-first into the floor. His gun slid from his arms. It skittered away, leaving a trail of sparks as it went. The Blade furiously crawled toward it. As he reached for his weapon, the concrete underneath it sprung to life, coating over the gun and absorbing it back down into the ground. The Blade stared in horror and shuffled backward. "This isn't real!" he yelled. "This isn't real!" Soon, the spot on the floor that just swallowed his only defense was adorned with two green boots as Diego approached him.

"I can understand why you'd think that," he chuckled, "but yeah... we're real." Diego lifted his right foot and stomped it down onto the concrete. Instantly a small pillar shot out of the ground and bashed the Blade soldier's chin. He flipped backward and collapsed onto his back, unconscious before he even hit the ground. "That makes nine!" Diego called out. "I thought Explosion said there were..." A small click echoed through the room as the barrel of a gun pressed firmly into the back of Diego's head.

"Ten," the Blade muttered through his helmet. "I don't know who or what you freaks are, but I have a feeling a bullet can still hurt you." He began pressing on the trigger. As the trigger reached halfway, the Blade snapped his head to the side just as a black portal formed out of the nothingness next to him. He tried to turn his weapon, but before he could finish Steven careened out of the darkness and smashed his fist into the Blade's helmet. The soldier flew across the room and cracked through a large piece of shelving, crumbling it and dropping all of its contents to the ground underneath it. Steven stood up straight as the portal behind him collapsed back to reality. He turned his eyes to Diego and nodded.

"You good?" he asked. Diego laughed a little as relief poured out of him.

"Wow!" he exclaimed. "That was a bit closer than I would have liked. Nice save, Explosion." Steven didn't exactly know how to respond to the comment. He felt like he was just doing his job by saving Diego, but now it seemed like Diego was looking at it as a friendly favor. A small smile fought its way onto Steven's face but immediately disappeared when Dante stepped forward with his hands folded together and pressed up against his cheek.

"What a hero!" he remarked, in a high pitched, feminine way. "Do you do autographs?"

"Enough!" Nick called out. "The Blades are down, but where the hell is whatever they were trying to take? There's no Otrolium or anything here. Why attack this warehouse?"

The silence in the room was suddenly cut by the rhythmic sound of clapping. Each clap echoed across the walls and sounded like it was completely surrounding the Nitros. They turned their attention to a figure walking toward them from the rubble and debris of the catwalk. He was wearing ratty, loose-fitting jeans and a brown t-shirt. Two bandoleers filled with different gadgets crossed his chest, and deep blue goggles hid his eyes from view. His hair was a shaggy, dirty brown that hung down in front of his brow. He had a wide face sporting a terrible grin, and he continued to applaud. What made him stand out against the shadows of the warehouse was the backpack peeking out over his shoulders. It glowed brightly with two tanks filled with Otrolium. Two black wires snaked out of the tanks and fed into the man's gauntlets that emitted a dim yellow light.

"Stunner," Nick growled. Stunner was just as intimidating as Nick feared, but after managing to take down ten armed soldiers, Nick was ready to take on anyone. This was Nick's chance to prove himself to

Redman and the rest of his team. Stunner wasn't going to stand in his way.

Stunner started to laugh as his clapping slowed and eventually stopped. He lifted his hand and motioned toward the Nitros.

"Well, just look at this!" he announced. "The five of you. Fresh off Redman's production line and straight into the fight. Can't act like that doesn't deserve a little bit of praise. Takes a lot of guts to dive into the ocean when you don't even know how to swim, yet." Nick's eyes widened, and he turned to Dante, who also was staring, horrified, at Stunner.

"What did you just say?" Nick asked, unsure of exactly what he had just heard. Stunner lowered his arm and shook his head a little in mock surprise.

"Please," he began. "You kids can't seriously imagine you're some kind of secret, right? That we wouldn't know about you? About Project Nitro?"

"You were expecting us to come here?" Diego asked.

"Expecting you?" Stunner quickly snapped, "hell, we were *counting* on you showing up, son."

Nick lowered his brow. He couldn't tell if Stunner was just toying with them, or if the Nitros had actually stumbled into a trap. If they had, how did Stunner and the Blades already know about the Nitros? The confidence that was just filling Nick's mind had already disappeared.

Megan stood up straight and put out her arms. She

motioned toward all the fallen Blades sprawled across the floor. "Looks like your little plan didn't work!" she mocked.

Stunner tilted his head to the side, letting the crack of his neck ring out around them. His crooked smile returned, one inch at a time. He slowly reached down to his gauntlet and twisted a few dials into place. A humming sound emitted from his backpack. The green light grew in intensity alongside the sound.

"Well, nobody here is claiming this thing is over, now are they?" Stunner took a large step toward the Nitros but suddenly stopped. He looked down at his arms as ice crawled up toward his elbows. He slowly turned his gaze back to the Nitros, centering them on Dante. "Oh, that's real cute," he groaned. The ice around his hand suddenly began to glow a bright yellow. Cracks traced around the ice, and each fissure was brighter than the last.

Stunner ripped his arms up as shards of ice shattered into the air around him. Two massive beams of light fired out of his gauntlets and tore into the concrete. Fractured pieces of the rock fired into the air around him. "You kids might be able to drop a couple of soldiers easy enough, but let's see how you step up to something with a little more… bite." Stunner lunged forward and punched both fists out in front of him. His gauntlets burst into life, shooting in a line-drive toward Steven. Diego jumped to the side and spread out his limbs.

"Watch out!" Diego yelled. The light smashed into his chest, forcing him backward into Steven and throwing both of them to the floor. Steven rolled back to his knees. He looked between Stunner and Diego, who now had smoke rising off his body toward the ceiling. Diego dropped the back of his head onto the concrete. His teeth were pressed together in pain.

"Get Atomic out of here!" Nick yelled back to Steven. He didn't want to give up on the help Steven and Diego would provide, but now his only concern was losing a teammate on the first mission. The more Nick thought about it, the more he wanted to pull his entire team out of there before anyone got seriously hurt. What would Redman say? Would Nick be a total failure at that point? He couldn't risk it.

"We can handle this guy!" Nick said. Nick, Megan, and Dante squared up against Stunner as he loaded up another shot.

"You've got a lot to prove here tonight, Nitros," Stunner said. "Well… so do I." Stunner pointed his gauntlets straight down. They fired into the floor a second before Stunner started raised his arms. The beams rocketed across the ground, kicking up chunks of concrete and dust in their path toward the Nitros. Nick leapt out of the way and rolled to a stop. Megan opened her hand and prepared a bomb for an attack.

"Reactor, no!" Nick yelled, reaching out in her

direction.

"It won't kill him," she assured, "but it will definitely take him out."

"The backpack!" Nick called out again. Megan turned to look at Nick. She opened her mouth to respond but was first tackled to the ground by Dante. Another beam ripped past them with a deafening static-like noise. Nick created a fireball in his hand and whipped his arm around, launching it at Stunner.

Stunner threw his forearms into the air, letting the fireball slam into his gauntlets. The fire and smoke curled around the metal. "There's Otrolium in his backpack!" Nick finished. "If those tanks break this whole warehouse is gonna go up."

Megan turned her attention back to Stunner as he marched toward the three.

"Go for the gauntlets," Nick ordered.

Megan nodded and jumped to her feet, charging at Stunner. She threw a massive punch, which Stunner ducked underneath. Megan could hear the whine of his gauntlet as he prepared to couple the next shot with a punch. As he brought his fist around, ice sprang off the ground and stopped the motion before he could finish. The beam fired off wildly into the distance and smashed against one of the walls. Megan quickly raised her knee and slammed it into Stunner's chest, knocking him backward. Nick followed up with two more fireballs, but Stunner managed to expertly blast both of them out of the air. He smiled and took another step back.

"You kids are pretty damn sloppy," he commented. "It's like you've never been in a real fight before." Megan ran up with another punch, but Stunner quickly crossed his gauntlets in front of him, absorbing the punch into the metal. He threw his leg forward, kicking Megan in the stomach and knocking her far enough back to line up his next shot. His gauntlets were just inches from Megan as they roared to life.

Dante lifted his arm, causing two pillars of ice to crack into the bottom of the gauntlets and knock the beams off course once again. Stunner growled and swatted Megan out of the way with a back-hand. She fell to the floor, taking a moment before trying to push herself back up.

"That's it!" Stunner shouted. He fired his gauntlets at Dante, who made a defensive wall of ice in front of him. The beam was too much, and shattered the ice directly into Dante, pushing him backward and making him close his eyes. As he reopened them, he was greeted with Stunner jumping through the shards of frozen water. Stunner's fist collided with Dante's temple, slamming the silver Nitro to the ground.

"Dante!" Nick cried out as he threw another fireball. This one pinged off of Stunner's shoulder, making him twitch in pain and snap his attention to Nick. Smoke rose from his shoulder, and a blackened hole with bright red edges was now a feature of his shirt. Stunner reached up to his bandoleer and grabbed a spherical device off of it. He threw it at Nick, who instinctively created a cone of fire in front of him to destroy it. As soon as the fire made contact, Nick was drowned in thick white smoke. Nick covered his mouth with one hand and closed his eyes. He coughed, flailing his other arm around, trying to dissipate the fog. However, before it could clear, two beams of yellow light careened through the smoke and ripped Nick off his feet. He smashed into the ground, gripping his chest in pain. Stunner stepped out of the smoke and walked toward Nick. He stood menacingly over him, gauntlets charging up.

"It's a real shame, you Nitros," he began. "We've been hearing about you for months...years even... and this is what we get?" He knelt down next to Nick. He puffed out his cheeks and sighed. "I had to read hundreds and hundreds of pages about you. Seemed like each one took more time to explain how you were Redman's silver bullet. I'm not gonna lie to you. You got some of the Blade members feeling pretty nervous. They started sweating about the possibility of five biohumans running around our city. Imagine their faces after tonight? The laughs we'll have when I tell all of them that the 'mighty Nitros' were nothing but five weak, scared, helpless kids." Stunner snarled at Nick. "Pathetic."

"Hey Stunner!" a voice called out. Stunner turned his

head just as a chunk of concrete hammered into his chest. Stunner stumbled back. The wind was instantly knocked out of him. He tried to regain his balance and take a deep breath but was just greeted by another boulder slamming into his shoulder.

Diego limped forward, still clutching his chest. "What's wrong? Couldn't finish me off?"

Stunner ground his teeth while getting back to his feet. Diego held his hands out to the sides, presenting himself. "We're way stronger than you, Zealo," Diego mocked. "You think your shiny gloves are gonna be able to stop us? You aren't like us. You're just a regular, everyday guy, who has some fancy tech. We're a lot more than that. A lot more than you." Stunner's brow began to twitch as he took another step forward. His gauntlets began humming as Otrolium fed into them.

"I'm going to turn you five into dust," he hissed. He reached down to his gauntlet and readjusted the dials. The humming from his backpack became even louder. The light grew more intense with each passing second. Diego was obviously still in pain but managed to muster up a smile.

"Then prove it, amigo. What are you waiting for?" Stunner growled and clenched his fists. He lunged forward, causing a blinding light to emit from the ends of his gauntlets. The beams rocketed toward Diego and disappeared only a few feet from him. The beams dove into a black nothingness. The ends of the beams faded into distant points as the Void swallowed them. Stunner stopped and raised his eyebrows.

"What the..."

"Good catch!" Diego cried. Steven gave a thumbs up with one hand, while the other maintained the portal between Stunner and Diego. "Now return to sender!"

Steven nodded. The portal suddenly collapsed down to a single point, and then quickly grew to its regular size again. Stunner had no time to react as his own light beams erupted out of it. The cut through the air in a straight path to Stunner. The beams fed directly back into the end of his gauntlets. The backs of them burst into a shower of yellow and blue sparks. Stunner fell to the ground and furiously shook his arms, trying to stop the inevitable. After a few more seconds, the gauntlets exploded into a shower of metal shards. Stunner yelled in pain and slammed his back against the concrete. He held his hands in the air. Blood dripped down from his palms and onto his chest.

Nick sat up again, seeing Megan and Dante doing the same. He slowly pushed himself to his feet, wincing at the pain in his chest. A wave of relief fell over him. Nick had been so concerned that he'd have to take control of his team and tell them every move to make, and yet here they were, solving the problems for themselves and handling the situation.

Stunner's cries grew fainter as the pain turned to

numbness. His anguished noises made it seem like he was trying to will his gauntlets back into working order. Any Otrolium in the tubes of his machinery quickly receded into the backpack. The bright glow faded away, and safety measures took over. Stunner's entire system shut down. He dropped his hands down the floor next to him and muttered quietly to himself in between gasps.

"It's over, Stunner," Nick announced, walking toward him. Stunner was still grinding his teeth together in pain but managed to chuckle a few times in between. Nick knelt down next to Stunner, looking over his injuries. Stunner's hands were a bloodied mess of metal splinters and bruises. The tubes feeding to his backpack were lying across the floor like two dead eels. "Now, what the hell are you these Blades doing here? What was the point of all this? Did the Blade Leader send you after us?"

Stunner shook his head and tried to move his hands, but all he got were shakes and twitching fingers.

"You kids must think pretty highly of me," he snickered. "I'm not high enough in rank to even see the guy, let alone get orders directly from him. Never have, and after this, never will."

"So what was the point?" Nick asked again.

"We need to get our hands on something," Stunner replied. "Plain and simple."

Nick sighed and turned to his right. Deb was approaching, along with several officers who began rounding up the Blade soldiers who littered the floor. The officers ripped them off the floor before cuffing them and carting them away to vehicles.

"Gotta say," Deb began, "I'm impressed. You Nitros actually managed to take down Stunner. And you responded to the call almost as fast as us. Good work and good timing. I'm still not completely sold on the idea of you five running around... but this definitely helped."

"Thanks, but whatever the Blades were here to steal is gone now," Megan remarked.

"What *were* you here to steal?" Nick interrogated. "What was here?"

"It's gone now," Stunner quickly replied. "If everything worked the way we wanted." Nick shrugged to Deb who scratched his head. "When we set out to steal something, you can be damn sure we're going to get it." Nick snapped his eyes back down to Stunner. Stunner was grinning to himself. He refused to open his eyes as Nick continued his interrogation.

"What the hell are you talking about, Stunner?"

"Wait a minute," Diego interrupted. "Deb." Deb turned to Diego. "Did you just say, we responded to the call as fast as you guys?" Deb paused for a second but then nodded.

"Well, yes," he replied. "We got a call about the Blades at the warehouse, got here, and you guys rolled in only a few minutes later. It was an extremely impressive response time."

"That's doesn't make any sense, dude," Dante noted. "We intercepted police reports back in the lab. That's how we knew this little party was going down."

"Exactly," Diego added, "we didn't get here until like… thirty minutes after that call." Deb looked back and forth between the Nitros and shrugged.

"I don't know what to tell you. We have the security camera footage. Stunner and his men weren't even here thirty minutes before you were."

Then, cutting through the silence, Stunner's maniacal laughter began to grow louder and louder. He would cough every now and again, but would then immediately fall back into that hideous cackle.

Nick started to look at every piece of this mission, and fix them together like a puzzle. There were too many things that didn't add up. Things that didn't quite fit. How could they have intercepted a police report, when the LLPD hadn't even been called yet? Why was there nothing in this warehouse for Stunner to steal? How did Stunner already know about the Nitros, when it was a top secret project? The questions kept scratching away at Nick's brain until a realization sprung up. Nick's eyes widened as he turned back to Stunner.

"There was never anything here to steal, was there?" he asked. Stunner continued to laugh but shook his head while he did, a glint in his eye.

"We're not out to steal any Otrolium today, punk," Stunner said through closed teeth. "In fact, we're looking to give some of it back to good old Phillip Redman." Nick lifted his hands to his head and gripped his hair.

"No... no, no, no!" He stood up and pushed his way past Deb.

"Nuclear!" Megan called after him, "what the hell is going on?"

"Stunner wasn't after anything here!" Nick snapped back as he turned to face her. "Nothing in here was important to them."

"So then why attack it?" Deb asked. Nick sighed, beginning to accept that suspicion was grimly becoming a reality.

"So we would show up," he stated. "So we would leave the lab. The Blades needed us away from the lab so they could steal what they were really after." The other Nitros were silent until Steven came to the same realization.

"The Converter," he whispered.

"We've been played like idiots!" Nick exclaimed. "Think about it. Who told us about Stunner being here?" The Nitros thought back to the moment the siren began going off in the lab. Everyone was frantically looking back and forth at each other.

"We have police reports coming in from a warehouse on the docks," Kristen chimed off.

"Why did the call just happen to come in immediately after Redman told us about the Converter?" Nick questioned.

"We've had it hidden in this lab since the project began," Redman stated.
"It's here?!" Kristen shouted.

"How did Stunner and the Blades already know about us, even though Redman assured us the project was a secret?" Nick asked the others.

"I've heard so much about you," Kristen spoke. "I mean how could I not? The Nitros."

"Kristen," Megan said quietly. "This whole time she … she's working with the Blades."

"They're after the Converter!" Diego added. Stunner was beginning to pass out, but the last of his chuckles were still escaping.

"I think it's worse than that," Nick began. "Stunner said they're giving some of the Otrolium back to Redman." Nick turned away from the group and looked out into the night sky. He knew that somewhere out there, the Blades were hard at work. Their plan was perfectly coming together.

"They're sending the Otrolium to Redman." An eerie silence fell over the Nitros, and Dante barely managed to get out his next words.

"Kristen is going to destroy the lab."

CHAPTER 6: A THREAT

"And you're sure about that?" Redman queried. Nick had his finger pressed tightly against the communicator in his ear. He spoke as clearly as possible but found it difficult through all the layers of panic.

"Without a doubt," he replied. "Kristen was the only one in a position to give us that premature police report. It got us out of there, just like she was hoping. She's trying to take the Converter, and worse, destroy the lab."

"Redman!" another voice shouted. Redman turned around as a lab worker ran into the room, desperately trying to catch his breath. He reached the professor and leaned forward, resting his hands on his knees. His chest was pumping in and out, and it seemed like his heart was going to burst at any moment. "Kristen was just spotted in… in the loading docks. She and two others are loading up a box-truck down there. We couldn't get the clearest view, but they appear to be Blade soldiers."

"Did anyone stop her?" Redman asked. The worker shook his head.

"None of the guards could get close," he reported. He motioned toward his own body like he was miming something. "She had on... some kind of suit. It covered most of her body, and it's somehow making her stronger. She was going to fry anyone who got near her." Redman thought for a moment and then widened his eyes, turning away from the worker right after.

"Project Hard-Drive," he whisper. He snapped back to attention and pointed at the worker. "Evacuate the building, now! We need everyone out and cleared to at least a three hundred foot radius." The worker nodded frantically. He turned away and ran from the room. As soon as he left, Redman put a finger to his ear. "Nuclear, you five have to stop Kristen. She's loading the Converter into a truck right now, and she's wearing experimental battle-tech from my lab."

"What kind of tech are we talking about here, Professor?" he asked.

"It's a suit codenamed Project Hard-Drive. That thing is going to make her stronger, and even more dangerous than Stunner was. The suit enhances her strength and agility, while also equipping her with wrist lasers, sensors, electrified traps, and..." Redman stopped. "Just... trust me. You need to be careful."

Nick glanced over at Dante, who was also closely listening to the conversation.

"I'm sorry, Redman," Nick began, "but Kristen can't be the biggest issue we have right now. That bomb is already on its way to the lab. If we don't stop it, you will lose everything and a bunch of workers there could die. We don't know how much time we have."

"Nuclear!" Diego exclaimed, running up to the red Nitro. "We could split up. Half of us go after the Converter, and the others stop the bomb."

"Not a chance," Nick immediately snapped back. "We're stronger as a team. You know that. If we separate now, we're just making ourselves weaker. Redman made me the team leader for a reason. We can't risk losing the lab."

"We don't have time for other options," Megan interrupted. "Leader or not, giving up on the Converter can't be your plan. Here me out. Diego can take me and Steven after the bomb."

"Steven and I," Dante corrected, with his finger in the air. Megan shot a warning glare at him, to which he shrugged and looked downward. "Not the time... got it."

"That just leaves the two of us to go after Kristen," Nick stated while nodding to Dante. "But how are we going to catch up to them without Diego moving the ground? Redman's vehicle still isn't ready." Dante stepped forward and put his hand on Nick's shoulder.

"I think I've got a plan for that one, cuz."

♦ ♦ ♦ ♦ ♦

The ground ripped away from underneath Diego, Megan, and Steven as they took off toward the lab. Megan stared at each passing street, hoping to see the bomb along the way. They had no idea what they were looking for but were under the assumption it would be easy to spot.

Redman was at the helm back in his lab, forcing all the cars on the road out of the Nitros' way. It was like a sea of traffic parting in front of them, without any intervention at all. A few moments later, a call came in on Megan's communicator.

"Go for it," she answered, with a finger against her ear. "Any signs of the transport?"

"We have readings from a truck heading for the lab just a mile ahead of you three," Redman stated.

"You sure it's the one we're after?"

"Not entirely, but it's certainly grabbing my attention. I can't control it using the grid. Someone has overridden its connection and appear to be driving it manually." Megan nodded and turned to Steven, who didn't look back. He simply kept his eyes forward.

"You catch all that?"

"Yes," Steven muttered.

"So you know there might be a driver in there," she told

him. "We need to get them out of the truck before we get rid of it."

"Why?" Steven asked. "Their goal is to blow up our base. Why should I care if the Blade responsible for it gets hurt?"

"Because we aren't killers, Steven," she snapped back. "It's one thing to accept he might get hurt, but it's another to just plain not try and save him." Steven didn't respond. He was already sick of Megan's insistence on saving the driver. As far as Steven was concerned, that was her job and not his. He grunted a little and moved some of his hair out of his vision.

"Target in sight!" Diego called out. They started coming up behind a large truck, tearing down the road and forcing cars out of its way. The truck was solid white with a thick red stripe down its side. It was moving so fast and low that even the slightest bump in the road would make the back scrape against the ground and shower the Nitros in sparks.

Diego lifted his arm, protecting himself from the spray. "I'll pull up alongside it." Diego lowered his arm again as they approached the truck's rear. "Steven, get the driver out of there. Try not to hurt them, okay, tough guy? Megan, check the back to see what we're up against here. If the bomb has a small enough radius, we might be able to find another place to detonate it."

The ground below the Nitros started to pull away even faster as they reached the truck. Megan jumped from the asphalt and onto the back rail, leaving Diego and Steven to get closer to the cab.

Megan gripped the handle to the back and ripped the door open. Her face was flooded with green light as soon as the covering was lifted. She shielded her eyes for a second, letting them adjust to the light.

"They've overridden the grid, alright!" Steven yelled from the front of the truck, "but there's no driver up here! This thing's on autopilot to the lab!"

"They must be piggy-backing off of the grid," Redman assessed, "but if I shut down that section of the grid, the truck will either come to a sudden stop or drive off the road and crash. Either one could cause the bomb to detonate."

"That might not be a big issue if the bomb is small enough," Diego replied, "especially since there's no one in the truck." Megan stepped into the back and gulped.

"The bomb might be… a little too big for that strategy," she said, grimly. In front of her were nearly thirty tanks of Otrolium, primed and ready to detonate as soon as the truck hit anything. The tanks were all wired into a large device, bolted to the interior of the truck. Megan absorbed the sight as best she could. Her confidence in handling this situation had plummeted. No training could have prepared her for the device set in front of her. She knew giving up wasn't an option, but right now it seemed like her only chance for survival.

However, her own stubbornness wasn't the main thing keeping her from fleeing. The tanks of the bomb were in a horseshoe formation around something in the center of the truck. "And as for no one being on the truck," Megan continued over her communicator. "That's not exactly the case, guys."

In the center of the tanks was a man, chained to a metal ring welded to the bottom of the truck. He had tape around his mouth and was furiously pulling against his restraints. He turned to look into Megan's eyes, showing no emotion other than pure desperation. "This might get tricky."

◆◆◆◆◆

"There's Kristen's transport!" Nick yelled. Nick and Dante slid across a thin pathway of ice that constantly formed in front of them. Nick was leaning one arm across the back of Dante's shoulders, while his other hand was aimed behind them. He was forcing a cone of fire into the air and propelling them forward at a blazing speed. They were fast approaching a box-truck racing its way down the street.

"I can't believe this is working!" Nick yelled to Dante over the wind.

"Of course it is," Dante replied. "We make a great team! Besides, this was my idea... so how could it *not* work?"

As the two approached the small truck, the back door

suddenly erupted off of its hinges.

"Heads up!" Dante yelled. The Nitros ducked under one of the doors as it went past. Nick glanced back in time to see the door slam into the pavement and begin to topple end over end away from them. Nick turned back around as a horrible sight took shape.

A massive figure stood in the open bay of the truck. It was Kristen, decked out in Redman's Hard-Drive armor. It was a menacing red, metal suit that covered almost every inch of her body. Tubing and wires snaked between the thick pieces of metal like some sort of futuristic skeleton. Small tanks of compressed air ran down her arms and legs, while large servos made up her joints.

"Just keep driving!" she barked over her shoulder to the other soldiers in the truck. "Get the Converter to the drop-off!" She lifted her hand and took careful aim, lining up a small tab on her wrist with Dante's head.

A buzzing noise began in her shoulder and traveled down the length of her arm until it reached a small device strapped to her wrist. A bright, red light emitted from within the device and focused itself into a red beam. A laser shot from the device, carving into the street. Without missing a beat, Dante put up his other hand. The pathway continued to form in front of the two, but now a giant wall of ice had sprung up in front of them as well. The laser deflected off the ice and into a building on the side of the road, crumbling a portion of the brick. More shots from the laser pinged off the ice as the Nitros got closer to the truck. Each impact would fracture the ice a bit more.

Kristen balled her hand into a fist and slammed it against the side of the truck in frustration, denting the metal.

"What do we do?" the soldier driving the truck asked, frantically.

"I'll deal with them!" Kristen hissed. "Do not stop under any circumstances!" Kristen lifted her arm and traced her finger across a series of buttons. She hit one of them, causing two pieces of metal to wrap around the sides of her face, connecting in front of her nose and mouth, while another piece slid from the back of her neck and over her head, sealing into place. Once everything was locked in, two red lights flashed on where her eyes should have been. She stood up straight and then took a massive step forward out of the back of the truck. Her foot hit the ground and embedded into the street. Her suit took the huge force without issue, and the truck continued at full speed, while Kristen remained in one spot, solid as a rock. She pulled her arm back in preparation. Two slabs of metal hooked out of their locked position on her forearm and connected in front of her fist. The metal plate they formed was connected to a compressed air cylinder, cocked and ready to amplify her strike.

As Dante and Nick approached, she threw her punch, annihilating the wall of ice Dante had created. Broken fragments of ice and droplets of water surrounded Kristen. The two Nitros lost their footing after the impact and went sprawling to the ground, rolling for twenty feet before skidding to a stop. Kristen lowered her arm and slowly turned to look at her new prey. Nick and Dante forced their way to their hands and knees, and then up to their feet.

Nick was faced with an even greater challenge, now. Stunner was a force in himself, but now Kristen was demonstrating that her suit was far more dangerous. Not only that, but Nick and Dante were on their own. Nick decided his best option was to try and end this without a fight.

"Kristen!" Nick yelled to her. "You're not going to get away with this! Give us the Converter and the suit, and it'll make things a lot easier for all of us."

Kristen snickered and put out her hands. "Sorry, Nitros," she said, condescendingly, "but there isn't any stopping this one. This plan's been in the works for years."

"What plan?" Dante questioned. "What does your leader want all this Otrolium for?" Kristen closed her hands into fists and took a step back, planting her foot firmly into the ground.

"You'll be fully aware when the time comes, *Blast*. Quite a codename." Nick and Dante could hear the servos powering up in her legs. "For me? I'll stick with Hard-Drive now." She pushed off her back leg and charged at the two Nitros, jumping into the air just before reaching them.

✦✦✦✦✦

"Just hold on, okay?!" Megan yelled to the man tied up in the back of the truck. "My name is Reactor. We're with a group called the Nitros. We're going to get you out of here!" The man was ripping his head back and forth, trying to free himself from the chains.

"Reactor," Diego yelled through the communicator. "You're running out of road real fast! The lab is only a few miles away! If I try and stop this truck myself, it could detonate from the sudden change in speed."

"Well, I can't blow it up," Megan added. "Not without taking down an entire block with it. Explosion, can you hear me?"

"Yeah," he quickly replied. "No luck up here. I can't get this thing rewired. What's the plan?"

"You're going to have to teleport the truck into the Void."

The driver's side door of the truck had been ripped off. Steven was leaning into the cab, fiddling with whatever he could find in an attempt to stop the vehicle. Upon hearing Steven's plan, he leaned back out of the cab. His hair whipped around his face as he stared at the back of the truck. He turned around and looked ahead at the lab, which was now coming into view.

"No can do," he said. "I've never made a portal that big before. Even if I did, I could probably only manage to teleport it a few feet. Nowhere safe enough for this thing to go off."

"Why not let the bomb detonate in the Void?" Diego asked.

"No one fully understands that place," Steven snapped. "It's entirely linked to our world in ways we don't completely comprehend, yet. You want to set off a bomb in it and see what happens? Be my guest."

Diego nodded and looked up toward the sky. He studied the stars for a bit, and then looked into the back of the truck. Megan was tensely waiting for a plan.

"Another question," Diego began. "If you made a vertical portal to catch the truck, could you make it come back out of a horizontal one?"

Steven was still staring at the lab. "I guess." He looked up as well, and then back at Diego, realizing exactly what Diego was envisioning. "What are you, an idiot?" Steven asked. "You want me to launch this thing upward? What the hell is going to happen when it comes back down?"

"It won't get that far," Diego stated, nodding to Megan while he did.

It took her a moment to form the entire plan in her head. Did Diego seriously think she could hit a moving target with one of her orbs? Let alone a bomb-loaded truck flying through the sky? It'd be an extremely difficult shot and if she missed... she didn't want to think about what would happen if she missed.

Megan looked down at the man in the truck again. This was her only chance to save him and all those at risk from this bomb. Megan gulped away her doubts. She quickly turned and ran to the captive. She grabbed the chain holding him to the truck with both hands and started pulling as hard as she could. The metal ring welded to the bottom of the truck cracked and buckled as it pulled away from the metal.

"Damn it," Steven grunted. He sighed and began moving his hand in a circle next to him. A portal appeared, traveling in the air alongside the moving truck. He grabbed the door of the truck with both hands, took a deep breath and then pushed himself away. He fell backward into the darkness and rolled out in front of the lab. The inertia of the truck was still with him as he smashed onto his back. Steven flipped himself onto his stomach and gripped his fingers into the dirt. He looked up and saw the truck barreling toward his position.

Guards and lab workers were rushing out of the building around him, and police were circling the streets. The loud noise of the evacuation was drowned out to complete silence as Steven sized up what he needed to do. He had no idea if he could bring himself to make a portal the right size or hold it open long enough. He had practiced with his portals leading up to this, but nothing of this magnitude. He could feel himself getting angry at Megan for risking everyone's lives for a single captive, but at the same time, couldn't completely blame her.

Steven pushed himself up and planted his feet firmly on the ground. He lifted both of his hands and tensed up his knuckles. His hands began to tremble. Beads of sweat appeared on his forehead. Darkness formed in front of him and on the ground next to him at the same time. It would bleed into existence for a few seconds and then flash back out as it tried to boil into reality. The portal grew once again, before rapidly expanding and then collapsing into nothingness once more.

Steven's hands snapped away from their position, and it felt like someone had kicked him in the chest. He dropped to one knee and groaned at the pain. He exhaled, and to his astonishment, a cloud of black fog erupted from his mouth. It danced away into the night sky. The Void was powerful, and even he was finding it difficult to control.

"We're running out of time!" Diego yelled. "Get the guy out of the truck and get that portal up."

"I can't do it!" Steven shouted back. "I already told you! It's too much! I've never made a damned portal this big before! You're resting your entire plan on something that can't happen!"

"You can do it, man!" Diego said. "I know you can do it! Keep trying!"

Steven closed his eyes. He could see swirling images dancing before him as the Void drifted in and out of his mind. Among those images was one of a familiar face. A boy with short blond hair and a jersey hanging loosely off his body.

"Derek," Steven whispered to himself. Steven could see his brother walking through the Void. His brother who had always believed in him and pushed him further. The one who never let Steven give up on his dreams of a better life or a higher education. Derek was everything to Steven right up until the day he died.

"You can do it, Steve!" Derek yelled. "I know you can do it!"

Steven's eyes shot open. He held his hand tightly to his stomach, trying to will the pain in his body away. He shook his head a little and slowly got back to his feet as the last of the evacuees left the lab. A hand grabbed his shoulder and twisted him around.

"Explosion!" one of the guards yelled as she ran out of the lab. "We have to get you out of here. Now!" Steven stared at her. She had a look of concern and fear in her eyes. It was a look Steven had unfortunately seen before and was now painted across everyone in the surrounding area. He could hear the truck approaching but didn't even bring himself to look at it. Steven then grabbed the guard's hand and threw it away from him.

"Get yourself and everyone else to a safe distance!" he

ordered. "Now!" The guard took two steps away, not moving her eyes from Steven's. She solemnly nodded and then turned to run back to everyone else.

Steven exhaled and looked back toward the truck. He lifted his arms and began moving them both in circles. His brain started to cloud, and he could feel himself wanting to black out. The portals were beginning to form, but straining to get to the right size. Blackness started to leak out of the sides of Steven's eyes like tears made of ink. His teeth were pressed tightly together, and his knees were beginning to give out. Steven's entire body began to convulse and would snap around every few seconds. Black smoke poured out of his nostrils. The whites of his eyes deepened until they were blacker than pitch.

"Almost there!" Megan strained as she continued to pull off the metal. The creaking intensified until finally, the metal snapped away, freeing the man from the chains. Megan grabbed him, and without even looking, jumped backward out of the truck.

Diego swooped in on his moving road and caught the two of them. He slowed to a stop, letting the truck careen forward away from them. It rocketed toward Steven at a tremendous speed. Steven pushed his arms forward a little further and shut his eyes, causing more darkness to bleed out from under his eyelids.

"Come on!" Steven yelled. The truck reached Steven and suddenly vanished into a massive black circle. Dirt off the ground continued past the portal and spun in tiny twisters around Steven's legs. The area around the lab went from a loud panic to absolute silence in an instant. Steven opened his eyes again and stared at the nothingness in front of him. The portal was gone, and all he could see was the crowd of people just beyond the grounds of the lab, staring in disbelief.

Steven chuckled for a second and then fell to his knees. Just before he dropped to his stomach, another massive black portal appeared on the ground next to him, and the truck came flying out. It took off in a line drive, straight up into the air. The truck bent and turned as it flew into the sky, getting higher and higher. The crowd of people began to scatter as bits of the truck tore away from the sheer force.

"Can you get a clear shot?" Diego asked. Megan was holding a purple orb behind her back and had one eye closed, taking careful aim at the flying truck. It was beginning to slow down as it reached the top of its jump.

"It's moving really fast," she admitted, "but that doesn't mean I'm not going to try." She jumped forward and whipped her arm around, pitching the orb upward into the sky.

♦♦♦♦♦

Nick threw his fist downward, but Kristen managed to

block the attack and knock him away. Nick skidded to a stop next to Dante and prepared to jump in again. The two stood shoulder-to-shoulder as Kristen paced back and forth, waiting for one of them to make a move. She was like a dog on a leash, hoping one of them would get close enough.

"She's strong," Nick quietly admitted to Dante. Dante nodded and wiped a little blood away from his lip, trying to catch his breath. Nick scanned every inch of her suit, desperately trying to figure out how to break it. With most of his team away catching a bomb, Nick was starting to doubt his chances. "She's just brushing off everything we've thrown at her. We need a way to get through her armor."

Kristen only had a few scratches on her, but for the most part, remained unharmed. She laughed a little and pointed down the street behind her in the direction of the lab.

"That bomb is going to reach your precious lab any second now," she mused, "and even Redman won't be able to track the Converter for much longer. The Blades won this battle. It's only a matter of time before we win the war as well."

"Why do this, Hard-Drive?" Nick demanded. "Innocent people are going to die! What could the Blades possibly offer you that makes any of this worth it?"

"How about even a single ounce of respect," she

snarled. Kristen's tone grew angrier as she spoke. "Everyone looks up to Redman like he's the greatest thing ever dropped on this damned planet. Well, he's not! That bastard has lied to me, the people of this city, and even you. The Blades are a group devoted to truth and fairness. Power to the people who deserve the power, and justice to the ones who really need it. Redman could never offer that. He always claims he's doing the best for this city when all he's really doing is torturing the people who live in it. Putting thousands out of work with his street grid, endangering lives when it malfunctions, and of course making Otrolium. The most dangerous substance this world has ever seen. The Blades are the ones running this city now."

"Well darn," Dante snapped, "I guess we'll just give up then. You cool with that, Nick?" he asked, slapped his cousin on the chest. He turned back to Kristen and put out his hand, pointing a finger at her. "Lady, you put up a great fight, and I just gotta say, bravo." Dante began to clap and shake his head at the same time. "Fantastic. Just fantastic. Wouldn't you agree?" He looked at Nick, widened his eyes for a second before returning to normal like he was trying to communicate something. Nick squinted at his cousin and then looked back at Kristen. He could a small patch of ice forming behind Kristen, and growing slightly larger with each clap. Nick gave a small nod before perking up his bottom lip and joining in with the clap.

"Just terrific," he added while nodding.

"Oh, brilliant performance," Dante continued. "You really had us fooled. You know, you could be a famous actress someday."

"Maybe in a sequel or something," Nick corrected, "I don't know if she's exactly first movie material, but you know what, we'll work on it. We'll work on it."

"What the hell are you two doing?" she questioned, angrily.

"Keeping you looking over here, of course," Dante replied. "Honestly, I'm applauding our performance more than yours."

"It was good, wasn't it?" Nick asked. Kristen snapped her head around in time to see a giant wall of ice behind her grow several spikes and lunge forward. She raised her arms and blocked several of the spikes, severing them in half, or blasting them apart with her wrist lasers. A few managed to sneak through her defenses and smash into her metal armor, denting it and ripping some of the panels on her shoulders away. She fired her lasers at the base of the ice wall, letting the beams connect and focus. The bottom of the structure shattered. The massive pillar of ice crumbled around Kristen.

She growled and twisted around to stare at Nick and Dante. Sparks were flying out of the exposed sections of her shoulders and arms where the armor had been torn away. The sparks would bounce off of the rest of her armor, leaving small, black scorch marks. Dante moved his hands around, making the ice around Kristen begin to lift off the ground and snake around her.

"This isn't going to stop me, Blast!" she yelled as she reached down and grabbed onto the ice. She began ripping away chunks of it and tossing it to the street. "A little frostbite isn't going to get through this armor. It was made for bullets and tank shells. You're going to have to do a lot better than frozen water!"

"Maybe," Dante admitted, "but how about when it isn't frozen anymore?" Nick pushed his hands forward and created a cone of fire, while slowly walking toward Kristen. The intense heat of the fire was enough to make Dante close his eyes and take a step back. The fire engulfed the ice and flash melted it. The water dropped onto Kristen, leaking into the exposed areas and splashing around the frayed wires. Kristen's glowing eyes began to blink and pulse as she stumbled her way out of the water. Her suit began to move in erratic ways without any control. Her fingers were snapping around, and her wrist-lasers were periodically charging up and powering down.

She managed to gain enough control to twist her head toward the Nitros but was met by Nick charging up a punch. It connected with the side of Kristen's head, knocking her to one knee. Before she could recover, another punch collided into her chin. She leaned backward and was kicked in the chest by Dante. She smashed to the ground on her back. Her suit sparked and sputtered as its most basic functions shut down. As the suit powered off, her face shield slid upward and to the sides, revealing Kristen's face while she struggled to move.

Nick took some deep breaths and shook his head while looking down at her. Kristen was just another insurmountable challenge that the Nitros managed to conquer. At this point, all Nick wanted to feel was confidence. However, with half his team trying to disarm a massive bomb, that was an impossibility. Nick lifted his finger to his ear and spoke urgently.

"Kristen is down," he reported, "what's happening with the bomb?" He waited for a response, but nothing came. "Guys?! The bomb, what's going on?! Is anyone there?!"

"You're too late," Kristen yelled. "Our leader has been planning for you guys for years, and now this bomb will wipe everything you and Redman have off the planet."

Nick looked in the direction of the lab, fearing the mushroom cloud that could appear over the skyline at any moment. After a few more seconds, there was a bright flash, almost blinding. Nick's heart sank as the sounds of screams and a loud explosion echoed through the allies. He shielded his eyes but tried to keep the massive eruption in his view. Once he got a closer look at it, a different story made itself known. The explosion was like a firework several thousand feet in the sky, and it covered the entire city in a bright green light.

Kristen just stared as the explosion faded away into nothing but dust and particles, and the night fell silent once again. Moments later, the communicator clicked to life.

"Bomb is taken care of," Megan replied. "We're going to need a little bit of a cleanup here, but there's no significant damage." Nick took a second, releasing the breath he had been holding for several minutes now. He was finally ready to feel total confidence in his team. The situation was handled and the Blades' first attempt at destroying there team was in pieces. If this didn't get the Blade Leader's attention, nothing would.

"Great to hear," he said, relaxed.

"Also, LLPD is bringing Stunner back to the lab for questioning before taking him away. You should get back here."

"No problem," Dante cut in. "We'll have some of the cops swing by to scrape Kristen off the pavement before she starts rusting."

"Assuming that means the fight went well?" she asked.

"Did you ever have any doubt, sweetheart?" There wasn't an immediate response. Dante simply stood still, waiting for a chuckle at the very least. Instead, Steven replied, even more monotone than usual.

"Just get your asses back here."

CHAPTER 7: AN INTERROGATION

"Thank you." The man from the van sat in a chair off to the side in the lab's main chamber. He was wrapped in a blanket, and Megan had just handed him a glass of water. He took a timid sip and coughed a few times after he managed to swallow. The man had very short black hair and light-tan colored skin. His eyelids were hanging lazily over his eyes like he was tired. He was dirty, and his entire body would shiver every few minutes.

"You're pushing your limits, Redman," Deb said. He stood close to Redman and kept his voice low to keep the other from overhearing. "Everyone here should be back at the station by now. Bringing them here is a massive breach in protocol, and you know that."

"We got Patrick and the other soldiers out of that warehouse without a single police casualty," Redman replied. "The least you can do is give the Nitros a chance to learn some answers for themselves as quickly as possible. This is our best opportunity to learn where we're going next."

"Shouldn't you be the one to ask the questions?" Deb asked. "Why are you letting these kids handle it?"

Redman sighed through his nose. "They need to handle this themselves. They are the heroes here... not me."

"So, why did the Blades have you tied up in that truck?" Nick asked the man. He didn't respond immediately. He looked at each of the Nitros. He was understandably cautious, but also had a hint of fear in his eyes.

"We saved your life, pal," Steven muttered. He stood off to the side, leaning against a wall with his arms folded. "Least you could do is answer a simple question instead of wasting our time." The man slid himself away from Steven, essentially refusing to look him in the eye.

"Don't worry about him," Diego stated, kneeling down next to the man. He rested his forearm on the back of the man's chair and pointed a thumb at Steven. "He likes to talk tough, but in reality, he's just a big softy." Steven scoffed at Diego and stepped away. "We're just here to help, I promise. We're the good guys," said Diego. The man gulped down another sip of water. He took a deep breath before speaking.

"Okay," he finally said, in a rasped voice. "I'm sorry, it's just... you guys are like... unreal. I feel like I should be dreaming right now." He pointed at Diego. "You were moving the ground, and you made some big portal thing," his finger went from Steven to Megan, "and you broke metal with just your hands. And you…"

"Dude," Dante interrupted, "please. The question. It's important."

"Oh, right," he said, calming down. "I'm sorry. I want to help you guys. I really do, but I don't know anything about who took me, or why. I'm not anyone important. You can look me up if you want. My name's Thomas Hessen. I was grabbed on my walk home from work about a week ago."

"The Blades had you captive for an entire week?" Megan questioned. "Why?"

"I don't know. They blindfolded me. Threw me in a truck." Thomas's eyes drifted to the side. "It felt like we were driving for days. Next thing I knew they threw me in some kind of cell. They told me they needed me to test something. I guess the plans changed when you showed up. Instead of whatever they were planning, they put me in that truck and sent me away."

"Do you know what it was they were planning to test?" Redman asked.

"No," he quickly replied, "but I think it has to do with that Otrolium stuff that was in the truck with me. I heard them talking about using people as… I don't know… lab rats, I guess. Honestly, I don't think I was the only test subject they had." Nick and Dante solemnly glanced at one another. "They believe the Otrolium does something to people. I think they're trying to make some sort of weapon with it. They would have conversations around me sometimes. Not often, though."

"A weapon using Otrolium, huh?" Dante said while holding his chin. He turned to Redman and shrugged. "Where do you think that goes on the scale from horrific to terrifying?"

"It most certainly is not good," Redman responded. He turned back and nodded to Thomas. "Thank you for your time, Thomas. An ambulance is waiting to take you to the hospital. We'll keep in touch in case we have any further questions."

"Wait, Professor," Thomas called out. Redman turned around to face him again. "Please, is there any way I can help you guys? I feel like I owe it to you and… I mean…" Thomas turned his head downward and mumbled something very quietly.

"And what?" Redman asked, leaning in.

"You guys are really cool, okay?" he admitted. "I know I don't have any superpowers or things like that, but I can help with other stuff, too. Like marketing, maybe? Help with your public appearance?" Redman shook his head. He looked at the other corner of the room.

"That's not necessary, Thomas," Redman replied while turning to walk away, "but thank you for your offer." Redman grabbed Nick by the shoulder, urging him to follow. "Nicholas, did you get Kristen to tell you anything about the Blades or their plans? Now that they have the Converter, we need to figure this out as soon as possible."

"Sorry, but no," Nick replied. "It's like she's brainwashed. She kept going on about the Blades being a 'new beginning.' She was also very adamant that you have been lying about something." Redman stopped. "You and your inventions were like some sort of obsession with her." Redman thought deeply. He shook his head and then started to walk again.

Nick didn't want to believe anything Kristen had told him, but Redman wasn't exactly making that easy. Redman was a man with many secrets, and always seemed to be letting on less than he actually knew.

"She's probably a former member of the R.A.N.T.," Redman stated, continuing to lead Nick across the room.

"I'm sorry, the what?"

"The Resistance Against New Technology," Redman begrudgingly replied. "See, when several pieces of my tech were released to the public, especially the street grid, there were many people against it. They believed it would end thousands of jobs and put lives at risk." Nick nodded.

"And, it didn't. Right?"

"Of course not," Redman snapped. "Sure, some roadwork jobs were no longer necessary, but no substantial harm."

"And no one ever got hurt because of the grid," Nick

continued to probe. Redman stopped walking. Nick quickly came to a halt behind him, waiting for his next move. There was a stillness between the two. The sigh that escaped Redman seemed like a key unlocking something Redman preferred to keep safe. He turned his head back to Nick. Not his whole body, simply his eye glancing back over at the Nitro.

"It was almost like the R.A.N.T. took it as a victory," he said quietly. "Shortly after the grid was installed as a standard, some cars began having issues with their tracking. It was simply because not every manufacturer knew what they were doing. They would lose sight of the grid momentarily and sometimes skid off the road. They were all cases of minor damage to the car and whatever it hit." Redman closed his eyes. "Except for one. There was one instance of a vehicle that didn't hit a building or a street sign. It hit a boy." Nick looked away from Redman. His mind was picturing the horrific scene, even though he didn't really want to.

"So what happened to him?" Nick asked. Redman's eyes didn't open. He stiffened his lip.

"It was a turning point for the grid," Redman said, instead of answering. "All manufacturers had to follow the exact same standard, and the problem was alleviated completely. I tried to help the boy's family following the accident, but they left the city shortly afterward. Either trying to get away from the grid or the spot where they lost their son. I fully understand both."

Nick nodded. He thought back to his conversations with Kristen. Then even further back, to Redman explaining the situation with the Blades. Nick could picture the photograph in his head. Shriveled bodies strewn across the ground and deep black letters etched into the brick wall.

"What you built, we will destroy," he said quietly. Redman finally opened his eyes again. He turned completely to face Nick. "That's the message the Blades wrote on the wall." Nick returned his eyes to Redman. "What if the Blades are all members of the R.A.N.T.?"

"I suppose it's possible," he responded, "but it still doesn't explain what they're up to." Redman motioned his head toward the corner of the room. Patrick Zealo sat there in handcuffs. His hands were wrapped up in blood-stained bandages and were hanging down in the center of his lap. His backpack had been removed, making him seem a lot smaller, and definitely less intimidating. "Kristen didn't seem to know anything we need, but maybe we can get some answers from *him*."

Nick nodded and approached Patrick.

Patrick continued to stare forward, despite hearing Nick approach. His head was bobbing ever so slightly, and his foot was rapidly bouncing up and down. It was like he was taking himself to another world.

"So, that whole plan of yours didn't work out, huh?"

Nick asked calmly. Patrick tilted his head up to look at Nick and smiled.

"Don't know if I'd say that, kid," he said in his snarky tone. Nick grabbed another chair from a few feet away and dragged it closer to him. He lined it up across from Patrick and sat down.

"Well, the plan was to attack us, right?" Nick held out his arms and motioned around to the other Nitros. "Here we are. We're all fine, but you," Nick pointed to Patrick's bandaged hands, "you aren't."

"The Blades have the Converter, smart-ass. Take that in for a second, and then tell me *all about* how much you won."

"How about you talk instead, and tell us what your leader wants that Converter for." Patrick sat back in his chair, casually leaning his forearms across the top of his legs.

"How many times do I have to drive this nail into your head, kid? I'm not a high enough rank. Folks on my level don't get that sort of info in a damned pamphlet."

"Then who is a high enough rank?!" Nick demanded, leaning forward. "Talk, Zealo! You must know something!" Patrick stared directly back into Nick's eyes, never blinking. He wasn't fazed by the outburst, and instead, a small grin crawled across his face.

"Sounds like someone's getting a bit desperate," he mocked. Patrick took his arms off his legs and placed them between his knees so he could lean forward, so his face was only inches away from Nick's. He spoke lower, in almost in a whisper. "See, you, your friends, Redman, and even the police think they have control over this city, but you don't. They put cameras up all over the streets. They doubled their police force. They put up posters and made ads on T.V. warning people about us, and yet here we are. You might have eyes all over this place, but the Blades came into power by remembering that every eye eventually has to blink."

"So you work in the shadows?" Nick interrogated. "Sounds pretty cowardly."

"There's a fine line between being cowardly and being smart. If you think we're actually cowards, I know a lot of graves you can dig up. Maybe the people buried in 'em can tell you how cowardly we are."

"Killing doesn't make you brave, Zealo." If was almost sickening to Nick. Face-to-face with something guilty of murder. Patrick was no better than the men who took Nick's family away from him. As far as Nick was concern, Patrick was just another step closer to ending this problem forever. Nick pushed himself out of his chair and started to turn away. "Clearly it didn't help you in the Blades, either. You're not even important enough to see the guy you take orders from." Nick took one step away before Patrick's voice called out to him.

"But I might know some people who are," he announced. Nick stopped and turned back around. He didn't say anything, but moved his hand in a circle, encouraging Patrick to continue. Patrick shrugged and leaned back once again. "I've been with the Blades for quite a while, but I didn't just happen to find 'em."

"Get on with it, Stunner," Nick urged impatiently.

"I have a brother and a sister. Matthew and Miranda. Both of them are in the Blades and higher ranking than me. I know for a fact they've both had direct contact with the Blade Leader. Find 'em, and maybe it'll get you what you're looking for." Nick thought for a second, staring intensely at Patrick.

"Why are you so quick to sell out your siblings?"

Patrick snickered and closed his eyes.

"Same reason Kristen told me only one of you was supposed to show up at the warehouse today." He opened his eyes again and shook his head slowly while snickering. "There isn't any honor among us. Some of us talk about being a new beginning, but in reality, all we want is power. Isn't that all anybody wants? If I'm going down, I refuse to sit back and let them flaunt their freedom over me. "

"Where I can find your siblings?"

"Sorry, kid, but that's where my usefulness to you is gonna end. Haven't seen them in years." Nick didn't say anything else to Patrick, and instead turned around and returned to the others. On the way there he nodded to Deb.

"He's all yours." Deb tipped his hat and lifted Patrick out of the seat. He handed Patrick off to two other officers who escorted the Blade out of the building. Redman was already typing away on his console, searching for any signs of Matthew or Miranda Zealo. Nick took his spot next to Diego.

"It's been a weird day," he stated, turning to look at Nick. Nick didn't look back.

"Yeah," Nick agreed, staring at the monitor, and waiting for any information to appear. He was hoping this was the exact information he needed to track down the Blade Leader, but he was losing confidence with each passing second.

"We've walked away on top from two challenges, man," Diego continued. "Seems like we're winning so far." Again, Nick remained silent. "So, why the long face?"

Nick sighed and walked toward the screen. He talked over his shoulder to Diego before entirely walking away.

"Because right now it doesn't feel like we are." Nick got to the monitor just as Redman's search was coming to a completion. Photographs began to appear of a frail-looking man. His ribs were well defined out of his sides, and his skin looked like it was on the verge of falling off. He had sharp facial features and a shiny, bald head. Dark black, tribal tattoos ran along almost every inch of his body and even crept up his neck and onto the bottom of his face. Most of the images that appeared were either mugshots or grabbed from security camera footage.

"That the guy we're looking for?" Dante asked.

"Indeed," Redman replied. "Matthew Zealo. Unfortunately, he's been off the grid for quite a while now, and we can't find any proof that Miranda ever existed at all." Nick stared at the photographs, carefully studying every detail.

"Well, I guess it's more than nothing," he said, trying to remain positive. "I mean, look at the guy. Someone has to have seen him." Nick turned and started to walk past a few of the Nitros. "We'll have to get his face out to police officers, and people in the city. Someone eventually might come forward and..." Nick stopped as he reached Megan.

She wasn't giving a single sign of acknowledgment to anything he was saying. She remained locked on Matthew's face, and her mouth was hanging open just a little. Her eyes darted back and forth all over the screen as she took in more and more.

"Megan?" Nick asked. Again, she said nothing. Nick walked closer to her and put his hand on her shoulder. As soon as he made contact, she jumped to attention, snapping her out of some kind of dream. "Megan, are you okay?" She didn't answer. She just looked at Nick, like her mind was refusing to understand what was happening.

"Yeah," she finally said, quietly. "Yeah, I'm... I'm fine. I just..." She looked back up at the screen. "I've seen him before." Nick looked back and forth between Megan and Matthew. He pointed at the photograph while addressing her.

"You've seen that guy before?!" he asked, flabbergasted. "Where?" Megan shook her head. Her expression never changed to one of sadness, and yet tears were starting to roll down her cheeks. They didn't look like they were stemming from pain. Either the tears were just the product of muscle memory, or Megan had already cried them too many times to be hurt by them anymore.

"The last time I saw my Dad," she replied. "Matthew he... he was there." Nick grabbed Megan's shoulders again. He turned her, so she was facing him. They stared at each other, and Nick leaned in closer. He couldn't get over the expression on her face. It's like she wasn't the same person Nick had met. She seemed so much more innocent now. So much more afraid.

"Megan, I need you to tell us everything you remember," he stated. "It might give us an idea of where to find this guy."

"No. No, I don't think it would." Nick let her go. She turned back to the screen as the memories transformed into words. "My Dad was a businessman. I'm talking, really wealthy businessman. He ran a company called Timesake Innovations back in Memphis. He worked a lot, but he tried, you know? He made as much time as he could for me. That was enough. You could at least tell he cared, even when he wasn't there." Megan looked off into the distance. She was picturing her father, standing in the room, nodding to her and smiling.

"He, invested with the wrong people, and eventually things got out of his control. His company began to fall apart. Scandals and criminal charges were popping up every week with someone else in there. It was only a matter of time before the whole thing went under." Megan laughed a little through the tears and shrugged. "I was actually kind of happy, you know? I thought that meant we'd get to spend more time together." Her smile faded. "But as soon as his company was gone, he kept telling me we had to leave. He just came in the house and told me over and over that we had to move. Start a new life somewhere else. I'd make new friends. Have a new school. Just a brand new life."

"But why?" Diego asked. "Why a sudden change like that?"

"I didn't know," Megan responded, "until I saw the police reports later. My Dad had a lot of enemies doing what he did. Apparently, the world of big business isn't a very nice one."

"So, one of his competitors was coming after him?" asked Nick.

"Worse than that. My Dad didn't care about himself. He cared about me. He was afraid one of them was going to come after me. So he bought some protection. When his company went under, he couldn't afford to pay that protection anymore," she paused, remembering.

"It started with him just being more cautious, but then notes for him starting showing up at the house, and eventually, our home started to get vandalized while we were asleep. The left messages on our doorstep threatening to come after us. That's when he started to yell about leaving and starting over somewhere else."

Megan shook her head and took a deep breath, trying to relive a piece of her life she wished she'd never experienced in the first place. "The last place we went was his company's old building. He had some possessions stashed away inside that he thought would help us get away.

The newspapers all claimed something else, but I know what happened that day. Someone was waiting inside for him. They chased him to the roof... and..." She stopped talking. Everyone was left to make the same horrible conclusion to the story. Megan returned her eyes to the screen. "The last thing I remember seeing, as I was running to his body, was someone leaving the building. No one else should have been inside that day."

Megan's lip twitched. Her lowered as she spoke. "I think my Dad was buying protection from the Blades," she pointed angrily up at the photograph, "and when he couldn't make the payments anymore, Matthew's the one who came after him." Another tear began to slide from her eye, but she quickly wiped it away. She didn't face Nick but spoke directly to him.

"We're going to find this guy." She met Nick's eyes. "*I'm* going to find this guy."

"I'm so sorry, Megan," Nick said quietly. Nick so far had only ever seen Megan as a headstrong person, but now she seemed so different. He realized more and more how similar she was to him. The tears he saw her crying were the same ones Nick cried after his family was gone. The drive she seemed to have toward Matthew was the same Nick had toward the Blade Leader. Nick was finally beginning to understand Megan. These feelings and realities were all things she was trying to hide, maybe to seem stronger than she was, or maybe to keep others out of her own problems. Either way, Megan had just become a whole lot easier to understand.

Megan shook her head. "We've all lost someone, Nick," she spoke. "We all have our reasons to hate the Blades." She glanced up at Matthew one last time. "This one is mine."

"Well," Dante butted in, "it sounds like the Blades use this freak as some sort of assassin. That might be something we can use."

"Assassin?" Thomas asked. The Nitros turned, seeing Thomas being escorted out of the room by two paramedics. He pushed away from them and approached Megan. "Wait… I actually think I can help with this."

"How?" Nick asked.

"When I was being held captive by the Blades, I

overheard a conversation between two people," Thomas began. "I couldn't see them very well, but they were talking a lot about some sort of job. Taking someone out and other euphemisms like that. It didn't take a rocket scientist to figure out they were out to get someone. The first guy kept saying that he'd get the job done, but the second guy was ordering him not to."

"Ordering?" Diego jumped in. He looked at Nick. "If that was Matthew that Thomas was hearing, he may have been getting orders from the Blade Leader."

"Matthew!" Thomas exclaimed. "Yeah, that was the first guy's name. I remember them calling him that."

Nick nodded, but then stopped and thought about the situation Thomas was describing.

"But why would the Blade Leader order Matthew *not* to kill someone?" he questioned. "That doesn't make any sense if Matthew is supposed to be some sort of assassin."

"I don't know," Thomas replied. "He was very adamant that the first guy lay low for a while. He was telling him to skip town until 'things blew over.'" Thomas made air-quotes around the final statement.

"Skip town?!" Megan asked in a panic. She pushed away from the computer, diving into the conversation. "Damn it! If the Blade Leader is onto us, he might be trying to get Matthew away before we can get to him." Megan snapped to Thomas and pointed a finger directly at his face. "When is Matthew leaving?!" Thomas shivered at her outburst and gulped.

"Ummm, well," he tried. "I… well… the conversation I heard happened a few days ago, and the guy said he would be getting out of town before the weekend."

"What?!" Dante cried. "But it's Friday, dude! It might as well already be the weekend in my book. If that was Matthew, he could already be long gone by now!"

"Wait, wait," Thomas interjected, throwing out his hands. "I can help! I'm telling you, I can help you guys. The man I was listening to said he would lay low until he could safely leave. He rattled off a few places. If he hasn't left yet, he might be hiding out in one of them."

"Where?!" Nick demanded. Again Thomas had a noticeable twinge of fear run through him. He was like a man without a spine, who wanted to curl up and hide anytime someone addressed him directly.

"Ummm, one is an abandoned apartment complex called, uh, Midnight Grove. Another was the discontinued train station at Cedar Square. I used to work next to it. The last one was a hotel set for demolition sometime soon. Grand Temple Inn. That's all I heard before they left. I don't know which one he went to, if any. I just remember thinking to stay away from those places if I ever got out." Redman was typing the information into his computer almost faster than Thomas could give it. The map of Lattice Light city popped up on the screen once again, and three blue markers appeared over the different locations.

"Crap," Steven muttered, "they're miles away from each other. Even with Atomic, getting there and sweeping all three locations in gonna take a while."

"We don't have time for that," Megan exclaimed. "Matthew is our only lead toward the Blade Leader, and as far as we know, he's leaving town. The more time we spend talking here, the more time he has to escape. We're going to have to split up." Suddenly, a fourth dot appeared on the map, accompanied by a loud beeping sound. This one was red and was blinking rapidly.

"What the hell is that?" Nick asked.

"Armed robbery," Redman stated. "Liquor store on 22nd."

"We can get there," Deb called out. "You guys seem like you have your hands full."

"Could be the Blades trying to distract us," Diego reasoned. "We should be the ones to handle it." Redman sighed and reached into his desk. He stood up and made his way away from the console.

"I still don't like the idea of you splitting up," he started, "but I understand the urgency of this situation." He threw a small box to Megan. It had a blue light on the front of it, but otherwise, looked completely plain. "That will activate your vehicle. You and Nuclear can get to the robbery in progress while the others sweep the locations on the other side of the city."

"You got the Nitromobile working?" Dante asked.

Redman turned around. He started to return to his desk.

"Well, I guess we'll find out, won't we? The boys and girls down in engineering have been working tooth and nail to get it running." Redman reached his desk, and then immediately snapped around, like his brain had just realized something. "It's not called the Nitromobile! It's called the Grid Enabled Multipurpose Instant Nitro Interchanger." Redman perked his head up and wore a broad smile. "We here call it the G.E.M.I.N.I." None of the Nitros said anything. The only sound to pierce the air was the slapping of Dante's palm against his forehead.

"How... long did it take you to come up with..." Diego tried.

"Enough," Nick interrupted. "Reactor and I will get to that robbery, stop it, and then head for the hotel. They're only a few blocks apart. The rest of you can sweep the train station and the apartment complex. Sound good?" Diego saluted to Nick and jogged toward the door. Steven slowly trudged behind him, letting his arms hang lazily at his sides.

"Just had to put me with them, huh?" he asked, passing Nick. Dante patted him on the shoulder as he moved past.

"C'mon, Sparkles, it'll be fun!" he said.

"Train's leaving," Diego called from across the room, "last one on is a rotten egg. Which is funny, because I think a rotten egg would be in a better mood about this whole thing than Steven right now."

"You two are insufferable!" Steven yelled as he got

closer to the exit. Megan twiddled the device around in her hand as she turned to Nick. Nick shrugged and also started toward the door.

"Who knows?" he began, "maybe Matthew is the one at this robbery. Could make our lives easy." Megan followed as the two left the main chamber.

"Nick, if this day has taught me anything so far," she started, "it's that nothing is easy."

CHAPTER 8: A STICK-UP

"So," Nick muttered to himself, "no radio, huh?"

He and Megan were sitting in the front of the Gemini as it tore down the road. It was a sleek vehicle, low to the ground and very aerodynamic. The glass was all bullet-proof, and the outside was armor plated, with deep, black carbon fiber in between the panels. The wheels had a protective shell covering which sported very similar blue lights to the sides of the road. Other vehicles on the street were being forced out of the way as the grid carried the Nitros to their destination.

The sun had just risen. The Nitros had been out, fighting and interrogating all night. It was starting to wear on Nick, but he knew a well-needed rest would come soon.

"Maybe I can get you some music in a future upgrade, Nicholas," Redman spoke over the communicator. "You two are coming up on your first target now. I remind you that you are strong, and can heal at an accelerated rate, but you are not bulletproof. Understood?"

The Gemini began to slow and came to a stop on a street corner. There were no police on the scene yet, but several bystanders surrounded a storefront, staring inside. Nick scanned the scene for any signs of the Blades or their symbols. Nothing immediately came into view. Nick and Megan exited the Gemini and cautiously approached the store. As they got closer, the bystanders' attention shifted from the robbery to the costumed duo.

"Get back," Nick ordered them. Most moved away, but some only took out their phones and began to snap photographs. Nick sighed.

"I hope it's Matthew in there," Megan said, not turning away from her target. Nick nodded and nudged her arm.

"Just try to keep your cool, alright? I know this guy hurt you. I know you want revenge, but we need him. He might be our only chance at finding the Blade Leader." Megan didn't say anything, so all Nick could do was hope she understood.

They reached the entrance to the store, and a voice could be heard within, shouting and making demands. Nick glanced at Megan.

"We go in fast and take control of the situation," he said. "Keep it clean, okay?"

"I know what I'm doing," Megan snapped.

Nick grabbed the handle and nodded to Megan. He

ripped the door open and ran in, with Megan right behind him.

"No one move!" she yelled. A man turned away from the counter and pointed a gun directly at Megan. He had it carefully aimed at Megan's head, without so much as a shiver in his hand. Nick and Megan put up their hands, choosing their next moves very carefully.

The man had dark skin, and his black hair was arranged in corn rows. He had a low brow with several piercings over his left eye. His chin was broad but well defined. Each movement he made was deliberate and sharp.

"Who the hell are you?!" he demanded. He switched his sights from Nick to Megan and then back again, each time moving the pistol along with it.

"My name is Nuclear," Nick replied, "and this is Reactor." The man slightly lowered his weapon. He raised his eyebrow and cocked his head to the side.

"What the hell kind of names are those?" he asked, "and what the hell are you wearing? What sort of freaks are you guys?"

"Just put the gun down," Megan snapped. "No one here needs to get hurt." Megan wanted to defuse this situation, but the more time she spent here, the more she realized this had nothing to do with the Blades. That being the case, Megan was finding it hard to concentrate on this situation as a whole.

"No!" he yelled, lifting his gun back into place. "I'm

getting the money I came here for! If you take a single step, I will put a bullet straight between your eyes. You got that?!" The man turned back to the cashier and pushed the barrel of the pistol into his chest. "Now keep going! I'm running out of patience, which means you're running out of time!" Megan sighed and shook her head.

"This is a waste of time," she said to Nick.

The room grew silent after that. Nobody made a sound. A few seconds later, the man slowly turned his head back, staring directly at Megan with his dark black eyes.

"What did you just say?" he hissed.

"You're not who we came here for," Nick replied. The man removed the gun from the cashier and put it down next to his hip. He took a few menacing steps toward Nick, lifting the gun slightly while he did. He pointed it at Nick once again and pulled back the hammer.

"Is that so?" he asked again.

Nick still had his hands raised, when the man noticed that one of Nick's hands was steadily getting brighter than the other. It was creating light all on its own.

"What the..." A fireball sprang into existence in Nick's palm and shot out, smashing into the man's hand. The gun flew to the ground and skidded across the tile floor while the man dropped to his knees. He yelled in agony, clutching his hand to his chest. Smoke was rising from his fingers, and his eyes were slammed shut.

Nick stepped in and threw his foot forward, kicking the

man in the chest and knocking him to the ground. The man desperately tried to suck in air as he fell to the floor. The cashier lowered his hands. He stared in disbelief at the marvel in front of him.

Megan didn't say anything but motioned with her head toward the exit. The cashier nodded rapidly and ran to the door.

Nick approached the robber cautiously. He knelt down next to him while pulling two small rings off his belt. He knew the gadget was designed to restrain criminals but was finding it difficult to remember everything from Redman's quick tutorial.

Megan knelt down next to Nick with a sigh. She took the rings from him and clipped them onto the man's wrists, causing a few small lasers to connect them, sufficiently restraining him.

"Uh, thanks," Nick said.

"Don't mention it," Megan replied. She stood up and made her way back to the Gemini.

"C'mon," Nick muttered, lifting the man to his feet.

"Who... who the hell are you?" he said between deep breaths. "No one does that to me! No one!"

"We're the Nitros," Nick quietly replied, escorting the man to the exit. "As long as we're around, that's gonna keep happening to people like you."

They exited the store, and Nick pushed the man down to the curb. He could see blue and red lights off in the distance getting closer to their location.

"Doesn't matter what big shot you used to be." Nick continued to look into the distance but spoke loudly and clearly. "Compared to us, you're nothing."

The man growled and tried to push himself off the ground, but with his hands tied he couldn't manage it. Megan was already back at the Gemini and climbing inside. "Redman," Nick called over the communicator, "the robbery is taken care of. What's the story with this guy? Is he a Blade?" Redman typed on his console, having accessed the security cameras in that area.

"No, he's not," Redman replied, "but he *is* a wanted criminal. Quite a list he has here. Everything from petty theft to attempted murder... of his own family."

"What a saint," Nick muttered, sarcastically.

"His name is Mac Sampson," Redman continued. "The authorities have already been alerted of his capture. You two did a good thing, Nicholas. It was only a matter of time before someone ended up dead because of that man." Nick nodded and started toward the Gemini.

"This ain't over, Nuclear!" Mac yelled from the sidewalk. "You hear me?! You two aren't seeing the last of me!" Nick smiled and shook his head. He turned to look at Mac.

"You're right," he said, calmly. "Maybe we'll come visit you in prison sometime."

Police were now beginning to arrive on the scene, and officers started peeling Mac off the sidewalk to load into a squad car. As Nick turned away, he noticed another vehicle coming up and beginning to slow. The car stopped in front of the store, and the window slowly slid down.

"Hi Nuclear!" the passenger inside shouted. Nick squinted and leaned in to get a better look.

"What the hell... Thomas?!" he asked in disbelief. "What are you doing here? You were supposed to go to the hospital."

"I'm fine," he replied, stepping out of his car. "I told them I was fine."

"Then I reiterate," Nick started, "what are you doing here?" Nick didn't enjoy the idea of being followed, especially if the man following him was putting himself in danger. Thomas was fidgeting with something in his hands, and bouncing nervously up and down.

"I heard you were coming here, so I wanted to come, too," he said shyly.

"But why?"

"Because I want to help!" he exclaimed, snapping out of his shyness. It was like he was releasing something that had been bottled up for years. "I'm telling you guys, I can be one of you! Maybe not fight and stuff, but I can do other things."

"Thomas..."

"Like... I'm a lawyer. I can help you guys out if something gets damaged in a super cool fight."

"I believe Redman has people for that, Thomas."

"Or maybe I can..."

"Thomas," Nick said. "Look, I understand you want to help, and that you probably want to get back at the Blades for what they did to you, but there's no place for you right now. I know what it's like to wish you could help and can't. Trust me, I appreciate all the help you've given us, but just let us handle it from here. The best thing you can do is just keep your distance." Thomas frowned and looked down at the road.

"But... but I..." He looked up at Nick, who didn't change the stern look on his face. Thomas sighed yet again and shrugged. "Okay. Yeah, I get it."

Nick nodded and started once again toward the Gemini. Thomas suddenly reached out and grabbed his shoulder, stopping him one more time. "But, please, take this." He handed Nick a small card. Nick took it from his hand with a small nod. He looked it over, seeing it had all of Thomas's contact information spread across it. His name, phone number, address. Nick closed his eyes, trying to avoid having the same conversation a second time.

"Fine," he agreed. He waved the card in the air next to his head a bit. "I'll take this, and if we need you, we'll call you. Okay?"

Thomas nodded happily and turned back to his car, never taking his eyes off of Nick. He got back in his car, which slowly started up and then made its way down the road.

Nick returned to the Gemini and climbed inside, muttering a few words to Redman as he did.

"What was all that about?" Megan asked. Nick handed her the card. He pressed his fingers against his temples.

"We have a fan," he said in a low tone. Megan chuckled as she read the info on the card.

"He *was* a lot of help with this whole Matthew thing," she stated. "You sure he couldn't help us out in some way in a more permanent fashion?"

"Maybe, but that's not what I'm worried about," Nick added. "I mean, think about this for a second. Thomas was supposed to die in that truck aimed for the lab, and we saved him. Then the guy gave us info on where Matthew might be. That's a lot of things the Blades most likely really don't want happening." Megan was confused for a moment, but then came to the same conclusion.

"The Blades are going to go after him aren't they?"

"With any luck," Nick responded quickly. Megan shot him a look, but Nick didn't look back. "I called Redman and let him know about the situation. We'll have surveillance on him. So if the Blades do come for him…" Megan smiled and nodded.

"We'll be ready." The Gemini sprung to life and pulled away from the store as Nick and Megan headed for the hotel.

Nick looked out of the window just in time to make eye contact with Mac Sampson who was being forced into the back of a squad car. The two didn't break eye contact until the car door shut.

CHAPTER 9: A DISEASE

Nick stepped out of the vehicle and looked up at the dilapidated hotel.

The roof was caved in, and graffiti lined the perimeter of the building. The building was massive. Nick could understand why they wanted to demolish it. They could make several new homes or businesses in its wake.

Megan walked around the Gemini and stood next to Nick, carefully scanning the cracks between the boarded-up windows for any signs of movement. Megan put a finger to her ear, listening to an incoming message, while Nick continued to observe the scene.

"Sounds like Matthew wasn't at the train station," she stated. "The three of them are heading for the apartment complex now."

Nick suddenly stopped and lifted his hand.

"Tell them not to," he said with conviction. "Matthew

is here."

Megan raised an eyebrow and again checked for any signs of life. However, she soon noticed that Nick wasn't looking at the building itself, but rather, at the alleyway next to it.

Nick walked toward it. It looked the same as he had seen it before. The cold brick seemed to be closing in on them the further into the alleyway they went. Garbage and dust circled his feet and spilled into the surrounding puddles. Finally, there, on the back wall, written in black were the words "What you built, we will destroy."

"This is that photo Redman showed us," Megan realized. "With the bodies."

Nick nodded, mostly to himself, but also so Megan could see him agreeing. Nick couldn't fully be sure Matthew was within the building next to him, but something in his stomach was urging him to continue. It was like the Blades were leading him to this alleyway to remind him exactly how dangerous the Blades were.

"Matthew is in there," Nick repeated.

That was all Megan needed to hear.

"Then we're going in," she stated. She turned on her heels and quickly made her way to the front entrance. Nick snapped to attention and chased after her.

"Wait, wait, wait!" he called out.

"What?"

"We have no idea what we're up against. If Matthew

really is in there, he could have twenty soldiers with him."

"Then I'll go through all twenty to get to him. Nick, when we eventually meet the Blade Leader, how are you going to feel? He's the one who took everything from you. He thought you were worth absolutely nothing, like complete garbage."

Nick sighed and looked toward the doors.

"That's what I'm feeling right now," Megan continued. "Of course, I'll help you take him down and stop the Blades for good, but this battle is mine. Matthew needs to pay for what he did to my Dad, and I'm going to make sure he does." Megan turned away from the conversation and put her hand on the thick front doors of the hotel. A small purple orb formed in her palm and began to expand. The doors exploded off of their hinges and flew into the hotel in a puff of purple smoke.

The interior of the main hall was dark and only illuminated by the thin streaks of light that still managed to sneak in through the boarded windows. Cobwebs hung from the ceiling and dust fell from above like snow. The floor was made of ornate, marble decorations and the light fixtures were complicated, yet beautiful.

Nick and Megan cautiously stepped inside, keeping vigilant for even the slightest movement.

"Keep your eyes open," Nick muttered. He could be anywhe…"

"Matthew Zealo!" Megan shouted into the building.

"We know you're in here. Show yourself right now!" Her voice echoed around the room, reverberating off every object. The echo faded, and the room returned to the same silence. The Nitros took a few more steps into the hall when a reply rang out in the dusty air.

"It isn't wise to chase a bear back into its cave," the voice spoke. It was high-pitched and nasally. Just like Megan's voice, it bounced off everything in the room, making it impossible to pinpoint where it had originated.

"Where are you, Zealo?" Nick demanded. Nick was doing his best to sound intimidating, but he didn't know how well Matthew was going to respond. Matthew was clearly a psychotic man, and putting him in a corner could easily be a mistake. "Putting up a fight isn't going to go well for you. I'm sure you've probably already heard about us. Knew we were coming, even."

"Ohhhh, yes," he replied. "I've heard all about you, Nuclear, and yet, I think I've heard even more about you, the lovely Reactor. Megan Sods." Megan ground her teeth together and kept her eyes darting around the room. "Our history goes so far back, doesn't it? All the way back to Memphis."

The memories were coming back to Megan again. She didn't want to lose control, but the voice of her father's killer was enough to make her sick to her stomach. "How did it feel, Megan?" Matthew continued. "I've always want-ed to know. How did it feel to see him fall? What washed over you when you saw him hit the ground? That's why I love doing what I do. If I had only known you were there that day, I would have made sure to see the look on your face the moment it happened. The moment I smiled at your old man before I gave him that one… last… push."

An explosion tore through the hotel lobby, knocking Nick to one knee. Purple smoke billowed out of a hole on the upper floor as debris showered down on the Nitros. Megan yelled and threw a second orb at another door on the balcony. The eruption tore metal and wood from its place. Screws shot like bullets through the air. The balcony ripped away from the wall and crumbled to the ground in a heap of dust and splinters.

"Where are you?!" she screamed. "Show yourself!!!" She loaded up another orb but stopped when Nick grabbed her forearms and held them tightly to her sides. She fought against him, overpowering him and throwing him away from her. Nick hit the floor, but immediately got up and ran to her again.

"Get away from me!" she yelled at him. He grabbed her arms yet again, in a hopeless attempt to calm her down.

"Megan!" he yelled. "Listen to me! He's in here! We have him cornered! If you kill him now, we may never find the Blade Leader."

Megan was breathing through her teeth and her chest was pumping in and out with each erratic breath. As she went to push Nick away again, a set of double doors at the end of the lobby slowly started to open. The creaking noises filled the room and caught the attention of both Nitros.

Megan writhed her way away from Nick, with her eyes fixed on the doors. The sign next to them read 'Ballroom.' A dim orange light was coming from within, casting a thin line along the ground.

Nick chased after Megan as she picked up speed toward it. She burst through the doors and into the ballroom, which again was massive. The marble floors continued into here but were now damaged and deteriorating. The orange light was coming from sunlight feeding through giant, stained-glass windows. The room was empty, except for a solitary figure standing in the center of the floor.

He was wearing black jeans, combat boots, and no shirt. The tattoos Nick remember from the photo were now beginning to fade from the years that had passed. Matthew was gently rocking back and forth and kept his eyes on Megan. He had a sinister grin etched across his face, and his fingers were twitching into the side of his leg.

"Well, now," he began. "I'm glad you could finally..." Megan jumped forward and threw an orb directly at Matthew. He gasped and put out his hand to stop it. As soon as there was impact, an explosion buried Matthew in smoke.

"No!" Nick yelled. He ran toward the smoke as it began to clear. Fearing the worst, Nick was somewhat relieved when he could hear Matthew's screams coming from within the cloud.

The dust began to settle, revealing Matthew down on one knee, gripping his shoulder with his other hand. As Nick got closer, Matthew pulled his hand away, revealing the horrific aftermath of the explosion. His right arm was completely gone, with only a few scraps of skin and bone hanging down from his shoulder.

"Oh my god," Nick whispered to himself. "We need to call for help, now!" Nick turned to Megan and saw her standing still with her hands covering her mouth. Tears were welling up in her eyes, and she was shaking her head.

"What did I do?" she asked herself. "What did I just do? What the hell is wrong with me?" Nick stepped closer to her as she moved her hands from her mouth to her hair, gripping it tightly. "I shouldn't have done that. How could I do something like that?"

"Reactor!" Nick yelled in an attempt to get her to focus. "We need to get him help. Get outside, get reception, and call the others. Tell them we need medical teams here right away. I'll stop the bleeding as best I can for now, but I…" Nick trailed off as he noticed Megan's expression change. "Reactor?"

She was staring at something behind Nick, something that was causing her tears to stop and her mouth to hang open. Nick slowly turned around and saw Matthew forcing himself back to his feet.

The skin on his right shoulder began to boil and crawl around like it had a mind of its own. It gripped into his bone and pulled away from his body. It began seeping from his torso, forming a new appendage right before Nick's eyes. Matthew grunted as his new skin grew into the shape of an arm, sprouting fingers at the end which curled and caused each knuckle to crack. Matthew lifted his new hand into the air and turned it around in front of him, examining it closely. Finer details like nails and wrinkles faded into place just before his hand closed into a fist.

"Ahhh," he exhaled. "Looks good as new, doesn't it?"

"What… what the hell is this, Matthew." Matthew snickered and lowered his hand again.

"This, Nick… this is what real power looks like." Matthew's skin started to move once again. The color began to fade to a dirty green, and his tattoos began to disappear. He started to laugh as the skin on his lips connected across his mouth. It was as if he was melting. Soon, where his mouth used to be was now just a solid layer of green. A slimy substance oozed out of every pore in Matthew's skin, like he was bubbling and boiling. Nick stepped away and took his spot next to Megan as Matthew's transformation came to a finish. His body was now completely coated in that bright green slime, with stripes and dots of red floating around within it. The red cracks would form, grow, shrink, and then disappear back into the green sludge. His eyes were two black beads

Jeremy Dooley

staring soullessly at the Nitros. He tilted his head sharply, cracking his neck and rolling out his shoulders.

"But... but how?" Megan asked, looking at the monstrosity in front of her. Matthew chuckled. He lifted his arm and ran it slowly across the air in front of him like he was painting a picture for the Nitros.

"It was almost a year ago, now," he started, in a voice that was muffled and seemed to split into several different pitches as he spoke. "I was tasked with infiltrating a lab, like your own, and eliminating a man who had promised the Blades the world and had given us nothing. He ran, like all pigs do when they smell the slaughter. Unfortunately, he knew his way around the building like a trained animal. A filthy animal... and yet, I was the one who ended up locked in a cage.

I found myself in some sort of chamber. I thought I was alone in there... but I wasn't. Some sort of experimental bacteria was in that air. It bonded with me, infected me, and turned me into this."

Matthew's fingers started to melt together until they were one single shape that began growing toward the floor. It became a point, and the rest of his forearm sharpened into a deadly blade. Matthew scraped the tip against the floor, carving a line into the marble as he took a step toward the Nitros.

"I'm like you, now," he explained. His head was still tilted to the side as he approached. His voice sounded calm, like the way you would speak to a little child so they'd feel like everything was okay. "I'm not a human anymore either. You two became Nitros. And me? I became a Germ."

Nick put both his hands in front of him and a ball of fire formed in his palms.

"I'm warning you, Matthew!" he ordered, "stay back!" Matthew didn't stop his slow approach. His bladed arm was scraping on the ground behind him as he went, filling the room with its horrible screech.

The fireball spread out to Nick's fingers and erupted forward in a cone of flames. They circled the Germ and buried him inside the fire. The light from the inferno reflected off the stained-glass windows and danced around the room in an incredible light show. As the fire faded away into smoke, the Germ emerged, walking at the exact same pace. The slime around him churned and boiled. Each popping bubble released a puff of steam into the air.

"You know," he croaked, "I haven't had a good kill in a long time." The fingers on his other hand were twitching against his leg, tapping away. "I'm starting to get the itch."

Nick pulled his hand back as lines of fire spun around his fist. He ran forward and threw a punch into the Germ's chest. Green slime exploded out of his back and coated the floor behind him. Nick was up to his elbow in the Germ's chest, with his hand hanging out of his back.

The Germ leaned in, getting his face right up to Nick's.

"Ow," he muttered. The slime on his mouth began to stretch and pull away from itself, revealing a giant pitch-black mouth underneath. "The pain is unbearable." He lifted his bladed arm off the ground as Nick furiously tried to pull his arm free. The Germ went to swing downward, just as a purple orb collided with his elbow.

Nick was launched away from the explosion and slammed into the ground. The Germ groaned and snapped his head toward Megan. Once again his shoulder was a webbed mess of green slime, with no arm attached.

"Leave him alone, Matthew!" she yelled. "This is between you and me." The Germ's arm sprouted from his shoulder and grew back to its original form. When it was finished, he exhaled and stood up straight again.

"You really should not have done that," he grunted. He threw his hands forward, launching his fingers off of his body. They sharpened as they went through the air toward Megan. She quickly ducked to the side as they passed by. One of them sliced through her hair, leaving a few strands to flutter to the ground. They embedded in the wall behind her as she regained her balance.

The Germ was already charging at her and unleashed several punches and kicks, all of which Megan managed to block in time. Megan forced her elbow forward into the Germ's chin, knocking him back a step. She cupped her hands together and pushed them into the Germ's stomach.

A purple orb formed and only moved a few inches

before erupting just below the Germ's sternum. His upper body evaporated into smoke and splatters of slime. His waist and two legs were left standing for a few seconds, before going limp and collapsing.

Megan took her moment to run to Nick. He was pushing himself off the floor, groaning while he did.

"Are you okay?" she asked. Nick nodded and put his hand on her shoulder. His ears were still ringing, and his vision hadn't quite cleared up yet. "I'm sorry about that. I panicked. I know I probably should have…"

"Look out!" he yelled, pushing Megan to the floor. Five more projectiles launched across the room and sunk into Nick's arm. Nick stumbled backward and leaned himself up against the wall. He slid a few inches down, falling to one knee. Blood was leaking down his arm and dripping onto the floor. A small pool began to form underneath him. The orange from the stained glass windows reflected off of it and cast a dark red around the area.

The Germ menacingly walked closer to Nick, forming his hand into a blade once again.

"I heal real fast," he laughed. "Let's see how long it takes you to grow a head back!" Nick could see a small purple light glowing inside of the Germ's chest. A second later, green slime splattered across Nick's face and body. He could see straight through a large hole in the Germ's torso to Megan standing behind him.

The Germ sighed and lowered his arms. "You're just

not getting it, are you?" he asked, condescendingly. Megan stepped back, preparing herself for another attack. The Germ turned his head over his shoulder to look at her. Then a horrible crack rang out in the ballroom, followed by another, and another as the Germ's head continued to spin. The turning only stopped when he was staring directly behind him at Megan. As the hole in his chest began to fill in, his feet spun around as well. His back remolded itself and became a chest and stomach instead, while his elbows snapped the other way, and his thumbs slid across his palms to the other side of his hands. He walked toward Megan, having turned completely around without taking a single step.

Megan continued to walk backward out of fear. After seeing the abilities Redman had given her and her teammates, Megan never thought someone could surprise her. Now, having seen what Germ was capable of, she wasn't just surprised... she was terrified. She instinctively shot another orb at the Germ's leg, blowing it off at the thigh and dropping him to the floor. He managed to crawl another few feet forward as his leg regenerated. As the process finished, he exhaled and got to his feet.

The Germ lunged forward and took a swing with his bladed arm, which Megan managed to duck underneath. She threw a powerful uppercut into the Germ's jaw. His entire head spun upward until his chin was where his forehead should have been. His eyes slid down his face and took their rightful place once again as his head reshaped back to the normal.

"How do I...?" she said quietly to herself.

"Stop what you can't hurt?" the Germ finished. "Contain what isn't solid? Kill what is barely alive?" He slashed again, this time missing to the side and cutting a solid line into the marble floor. "It's really simple. You don't."

Megan couldn't step out of the way of a follow-up backhand which slashed across her shoulder, ripping through the suit and leaving a bleeding cut behind. She stumbled from the attack and fell to her backside. The Germ raised his hands high over his head and came swinging down. Megan quickly fired an orb upward, severing both of his arms at the elbow. She rolled to the side and away from him, knowing he would regenerate by the time she regained composure. However, when she turned and put up her hands, she found his forearms still slowly growing back. His hands formed sluggishly, with each finger taking a moment to arrive. When the regeneration was finished, the Germ exhaled and sucked in a large breath of air.

Megan's eyes widened. "It's feeding off of him," she realized. "That bacteria on you is a living thing, right Matthew?"

The Germ whipped his arm around, launching another round of projectiles at Megan. She barely managed to avoid them. She fired off another orb, which lopped off half of the Germ's torso. It slowly grew back, rib by rib. The Germ was straining to reform, and the green slime began to break in certain spots, revealing Matthew's pale white skin.

"It needs energy to survive. So it feeds off of you," Megan continued.

The Germ became whole again, but couldn't stop himself from wavering a little while trying to stay standing.

"It isn't some sort of gift." Megan stepped forward, throwing another orb, which ripped the Germ's shoulder off his body. His arm dropped to the floor and melted into a puddle of goo. "It's a parasite."

The Germ's arm grew back again, but this time it was no longer covered in the green slime. The Germ's mouth pulled apart, and his black eyes were replaced with Matthew's blue ones. The bacteria tried to keep crawling over the Germ's body, but there just wasn't enough left to do it.

"What is this?" he groaned as he fell to his knees. "What have you done?" Megan approached him and formed another orb in her hand. Once she reached the Germ, she reached down and grabbed his neck with one hand, turning his head up, so he was looking at her.

Megan knew this was her chance to bring this to an end. She didn't know exactly how much punishment Matthew's body could take, but she also needed to make sure he couldn't attack anymore.

"Now that you're little tricks are finished," she started, leaning in, "this is one for my Dad." She forced the orb into the Germ's chest, letting go of his neck when she did. The explosion didn't break any parts off of the Germ and instead launched him from the floor. He careened upward and slammed into the wall, shattering two of the stained-glass windows on impact. Colored shards of glass danced through the air as sunlight poured into the ballroom. The sparkling particles fell past Megan and bounced across the floor. Glints of light reflected off of every piece. The refractions bathed the room in thousands of tiny lights. The Germ stuck to the wall for another few moments, before peeling away and collapsing to the ground.

Megan took a deep breath in and lowered her arms. She relaxed her entire stance. The Germ made a few light noises as he tried to reach forward, but he had nothing left. He dropped his hand back to the marble floor and laid flat on his stomach. The last pieces of green crawled back into Matthew's skin and disappeared. All traces of the green slime in the room melted and faded away, including the shards in Nick's arm. Nick pulled away from the wall and gripped his arm tightly with his other hand.

"That was..." he started, "that was uh... very... you know, I just wasn't expecting that. I'll say that. I was not expecting that when I showed up here today."

"You okay?" Megan asked.

The door to the ballroom flew open again, and Dante,

Steven, and Diego ran in. Dante had an ice sword on his forearm and blindly started swinging it around.

"Get away from my cousin!" he shouted frantically. He examined the scene and saw Matthew lying on the ground in a sea of orange glass. He turned his eyes to Megan and Nick. The ice melted away, and he threw out his hands. "And the day was once again, saved by Dante Bruno." He slapped his hand against Steven's chest and pointed toward Matthew. "Look at him. Passed out just from the *thought* of fighting me."

"Jealous," Steven added, "I wish I could shut down every time I heard you coming."

Diego pushed his way past those two and got to Nick. He pulled some bandages out of one of the compartments on his belt and began to wrap up Nick's arm.

"You just carry that stuff around with you?" Dante asked.

"Well, I'm the only one here with any previous medical training," he stated. "Did some training in the army after I moved to America. Redman told me it might be my most important role on the team."

Dante squinted at Diego and folded his arms. "I realize now… I know very little about you."

Megan never turned her eyes away from Matthew. She took a deep breath and slowly approached him.

CHAPTER 10: A TARGET

Megan grabbed Matthew off the floor by his shoulders. His back hit the wall as Megan threw him into the corner. He winced at the impact. Small cracks split into the wood behind him, crawling up the wall like insects. Megan put her boot against his chest and pressed him further back. He gasped for air, desperately grabbing at her leg, and trying to move it away.

"You're a scumbag, Zealo," Megan said. "What you did to me and others like me will never go away, but at least knowing that you're rotting away in jail will give me some closure. Especially the fact that I put you there."

Matthew giggled to himself as he writhed around on the ground.

"You think a cell is gonna hold me?" he chattered. "The Germ will come back to me, soon. It always does. When it comes back, nothing is going to be able to keep me contained."

Megan ground her teeth together and jumped toward Matthew. She had an orb in her hand and pressed it right against Matthew's face. He braced for the explosion, but nothing came. When he opened his eyes again, the orb was stopped just in front of his chin. Another inch of movement and that would be the end of it. Without his bacteria to protect him Nick could see a look of fear in Matthew's eyes for the first time.

"Who?" Megan demanded. "Who is the Blade Leader?"

"Shotgun, okay?" Matthew yelled. "L… look, lady. I get you're still worked up, but take it up with him? I just follow orders. That's all any of us do. I never knew your old man personally. I was just supposed to get him out of the picture."

"Shotgun?" Nick asked, approaching the two. "His name is Shotgun?"

Megan pulled the orb away, giving Matthew a chance to breathe. Matthew took in a huge breath and coughed a little blood onto the wall next to him. He wiped his mouth and talked downward, to the floor.

"That's the guy you're all looking for," he replied. "He's been in charge of the Blades for years. Anything going on is a direct order from him."

"Where is he?" Megan interrogated. "Where can we find him?"

"I don't know."

"What's his real name?" Nick tried.

"I don't know!"

"Well, what does he look like?!" Megan shouted, leaning closer to Matthew.

"I don't know, okay?! He wears some sort of body armor. Kevlar, armor plating, and... and a mask. Covers up his face. I've seen him get shot a bunch of times. The guy just kind of walks it off."

"You have no idea what he looks like under all that?" Dante attempted. Matthew slowly lifted his head and started to lightly tap it against the wall behind him.

"He's got... these eyes," Matthew said, closing his own. He was taking himself back to the last time he and Shotgun met. The rhythmic tapping of his skull against the wood seemed to be helping him. "That's one of the only parts of him you can see under the armor. They change when he talks. Sometimes they look normal, but other times they... I don't know... they look alive. Like they're glowing."

"Glowing?" Nick asked, trying to understand. He wanted to think what Matthew said was bizarre, but Nick also just saw a man covered in a living bacteria. At this point, anything seemed believable.

"Yeah," Matthew said. "They glow bright green. I swear I can see it leaking out of his eyes sometimes when he's ordering me around. I never keep staring for too long. Offending him isn't high on the list of things I want to do." Matthew shook his head and slowly pushed himself to his knees, holding his ribs along the way. "The guy's an enigma, alright? He just sort of… showed up one day and took control of our gang. We were already a collective that was hunting the Otrolium, but he made us into an army. No one is more powerful than this guy. Definitely not any of you."

Nick leaned down, so he was closer to Matthew.

"We were good enough to take you down," he muttered. "That must mean something."

Matthew started to laugh again, spraying blood onto the ground. He tried to stand but ended up falling back to the ground against the wall.

"You really think that matters when it comes to him?" Matthew asked. "If I was anything compared to that guy, why do you think I'd take orders from him?"

"What makes him so strong?" Steven questioned. "What does he have that you, Hard-Drive, and Stunner didn't?"

Matthew put his back to the wall and lifted his hands, turning them slightly. It was like he was pretending he had Shotgun's abilities. He stared at his own hands.

"He can make this… green light from his hands," Matthew stated, "and he's like a sponge for energy. He can turn a human into a skeleton just by touching them."

Nick's eyes widened as fragmented memories and images flashed through his head. The photograph in the alley. The bodies lying across the pavement shriveled up and falling apart. Nick could picture Shotgun standing over them, holding a victim tightly in his grasp until they fell apart into dust and disappeared in the wind.

"High amounts of energy," Megan began listing off. "Green light." She turned back to the others. "Everything here is pointing to the Otrolium."

"That's what they say," Matthew groaned. Megan tilted her head while returning her gaze to Matthew.

"What who say?"

"Everyone. Shotgun lives in a world of legends and rumors. No one knows where he came from or who he was. The best anyone can do is speculate. A lot of rumors say he used to be a member of the R.A.N.T. before it disbanded. The only detailed story we've heard from before he was... well... what he is now, is about his father. Apparently, the guy was a real scumbag businessman. He taught Shotgun the best way to take down your enemies was to get as close to them as possible, so you could do more damage... like a shotgun. Everyone assumes that's where the name came from."

"Is he using the Otrolium to fuel himself?" Nick asked. "We've heard the Blades are stealing the Otrolium for a weapon. Maybe Shotgun *is* the weapon."

Matthew started shaking his head and was clearly drifting in and out of consciousness.

"He isn't using the Otrolium on himself," he coughed, "He doesn't like to go near the stuff. Probably because of its ties to Redman. If he really was part of the R.A.N.T., he'd already have a real dislike for that guy. No... rumors started spreading that his powers are somehow related to the Faraday Center exploding. He didn't show up until after that. It just seemed like too much of a coincidence."

"How is that possible?" Diego asked. "If he was anywhere near the explosion he would have been killed like everyone else, right? I mean, entire bodies were vaporized from that eruption."

"Maybe he was exactly the right distance away," Matthew suggested. "Who cares? It's all rumors anyways. Most likely a load of bullshit. There are only two people in the Blades that would know any real info on the guy. They spend the most time around him."

"Name them, now!" Steven ordered.

"My sister is one of them," he explained, "but good luck finding her. She's been off the radar longer than I can remember."

"Miranda," Nick muttered. "Redman had no luck finding her, yet."

Matthew smirked. "Heh, already know her name?" he said. "Figured Patrick would spill as soon as he got the chance. No one backstabs quite like a Zealo."

"Yeah," Nick said, "you're a family of saints. Who's the other person who knows where to find Shotgun?"

"Shotgun's personal bounty hunter. The guy's an expert when it comes to killing, and he does real clean work."

"Why does Shotgun need a bounty hunter when he has you?" Megan asked. "I thought you were his little pet assassin."

"Again," Matthew said between clenched teeth, "he does clean work. That isn't my style. This guy does his research, he plans out his attack, and he strikes without warning. Wouldn't be surprised if Shotgun went ahead and sent him after you soon."

Nick stared at Matthew while getting lost in his own thoughts. After only a few minutes, Nick now knew the Blade Leader's name, that fact that he had devastating powers, and that a skilled bounty hunter was most likely already on their tail. Catching Matthew should have made the Nitros' job easier, but instead a countless amount of hurdles simply made themselves known.

Nick sighed and turned away from Matthew. He nodded to the others and put a finger to his ear.

"Redman, you there?" he asked. There was a pause.

"Yes, I'm here," he replied. "Special forces are in route to your location to contain and lock up Matthew Zealo. Even his Germ won't be able to help him out of that one."

"Good. He gave us an identity for the Blade Leader. Guy goes by the name Shotgun. Anything you've heard before?"

Redman typed for a moment before responding. "Unfortunately, no," he replied. We'll crosscheck what Matthew gave you against the database when you get back.

If that name has come up in any police records before, we'll know about it."

"Got it. Also, try looking for any reports of a bounty hunter operating in the area. The guy is supposed to be really good, so digging into suicides and unsolved murders might be worth your time. If we get to him, he might know where we can find Shotgun."

"Roger. I'm on it. Good work stopping Matthew."

"Yeah," Nick agreed, "we probably got him just before he left town."

Matthew's head lifted up after the sentence, despite his obvious growing weakness. He fought to continue the conversation and avoid passing out.

"Left town?" Matthew asked. "What the hell are you talking about?"

Nick looked at Megan, who was now wearing a look of concern on her face.

"That's what Thomas Hessen overheard while you had him captive," Megan told him. "He said Shotgun gave you express orders to leave town, instead of attacking your target."

Matthew looked at each Nitro like he was nervous about being the butt of a joke. He shook his head.

"Thomas?" he asked. "I don't... I don't know who..." Matthew's head was still shaking, but it was moving slower and slower. His eyelids started to sink down over his eyes. His chin dropped to his chest, and he fell completely silent.

"Matthew?" Nick asked. He knelt down next to the fallen Blade and tapped him on the shoulder. He shook Matthew a little, before sighing and standing up. "He's out cold. Damn it!"

"How could he not know about Thomas?" Megan asked. "The guy was a captive for at least five days. Matthew would definitely know if he was having meetings within earshot of him."

"And why didn't he know anything about skipping town?" Steven added.

"Maybe Matthew wasn't the one Shotgun was talking to?" Diego suggested. "Could have been the bounty hunter."

"That wouldn't make sense either," Dante replied. "As far as we heard, Matthew went over his three hiding spots later in that same conversation. That's the only way we managed to find him. It *had* to be Matthew that Thomas overheard."

Nick looked around the room, collecting his thoughts and reimagining everything Matthew had said.

"The best way to take down your enemies is to get as close to them as possible, so you can do more damage," Nick whispered to himself. He envisioned Thomas standing next to him, clasping his hands together.

"I want to help! I'm telling you guys, I can be one of you!" Thomas yelled within Nick's memories.

"Rumors started spreading that his powers are somehow related

to the Faraday Center exploding," he could hear Matthew saying again. The words echoed in his head for a few moments, before his eyelids popped open.

"The Faraday Center!" Nick yelled, turning back to the others. "The explosion. That's how the Blades are claiming Shotgun was made, right? What turned him into what he is?"

"Yeah," Diego agreed, having just heard Matthew explain it, "but we talked about that, man. Anyone remotely near that explosion was killed instantly. You saw the papers. Your Dad was there that day, Nick. I'm sure he told you about it."

"But then what did Matthew say?" Nick quizzed. "Maybe Shotgun was the perfect distance away from the explosion to be affected the way he was, but not be killed. A distance no one else would have been."

"You seriously think he was the only one that perfectly far away?" Megan asked, unconvinced. "Those are pretty slim odds, Nick. There were over a thousand people in the Faraday Center that day. The only line we saw there was the line between dead and injured."

"But what if it wasn't how perfectly *far away* he was?" Nick asked. The other Nitros looked at one another, all equally confused. "What if it was how perfectly *close* he was?"

Dante was rubbing his chin, picturing the scenario. He was only left with one question. The same one that Nick was working the other Nitros toward.

"What if he's the one who caused the explosion?" Dante asked, completing the thought. Nick put his finger to his ear again and spoke very clearly to Redman.

"Redman, I need you to find everything you have on Scott Cells!" he demanded.

"Scott Cells?" Redman asked. "The man who robbed the Faraday Center?"

"Yes."

"Nicholas, he was killed in the explosion. There's no way someone could have walked away from a meltdown like that. Otrolium erupts at an extremely high..." He stopped talking. Nick waited for a response. A noise. Anything. It felt like years of silence.

"Redman?" Nick called out, checking that his connection hadn't dropped. Redman's voice did eventually return, but it was quiet and shivering.

"Nicholas..."

Nick sighed and closed his eyes.

"He didn't die in the explosion, did he?" Nick asked, solemnly.

Redman was staring at the screen where a photograph of Scott Cells had just popped up. There, looking back at him, was the face of Thomas Hessen. "It's Thomas," Redman barely mouthed out. Nick shook his head.

"We have officers following him, right?" he asked.

"I'm checking right now, but it looks like the officer we

sent to watch him lost visual over an hour ago." Nick growled and looked back to Dante.

"Thomas Hessen is Scott Cells," he announced. "He's the one who caused the Faraday Center to explode. He was so close to the explosion that the Otrolium must have fused with him somehow." Nick shook his head in anger. He was dumbfounded by his stupidity as reality washed over him. The man he had been searching for was standing right next to him, talking to him, and Nick had no idea. "He's not a fan. He's the one we've been looking for this entire time! He's Shotgun!" Nick reached into the pouch on his belt and pulled something out, looking it over carefully. "We have to find him, now."

"But Matthew has no idea where he is," Dante admitted. Nick held the item in his hand up to the light. It was a business card with contact information filling almost every square inch, including an address.

"No," Nick began, "but trap or not… I think I know where we can start looking.

CHAPTER 11: A MONSTER

"Not what I was expecting to find," Dante stated. The Nitros cautiously stepped out of the Gemini. Redman had piloted the vehicle to the location printed on the card. The only thing there, however, was an empty lot. A chain-link fence surrounding dirt and crumbled concrete.

Nick stepped through the open gate in the fence and walked slowly across the barren space.

"I mean, maybe I shouldn't judge too quickly," Dante continued. He lifted his hands and began pointing in different directions. "Put a couch over there, a fridge in the corner, maybe a skylight?"

"Redman's getting us more info on this place," Diego announced. "Apparently there used to be some sort of complex here. The company went under, and it was green-lit for demolition two years ago."

Nick scanned the area for any signs of life, but the only

movement came from scraps of paper fluttering by in the breeze. He sighed and looked down at the card again. He flipped it over and examined it further, but no new information came into view.

"There's nothing here, Nick," Megan stated. "Our best bet is heading back to the lab. If we search through enough police records, I'm sure we'll come across something. With how much Shotgun has done, there's no way he can stay hidden."

Nick looked up from the card, knowing Megan was right. There was nothing there for them. Nick shrugged and turned away from the lot, preparing to return to the Gemini, when Steven called out from the middle of the open area.

"I hate to suggest it," he started. Nick turned back around. Steven was standing over a metal grate leading down into the Lattice Light sewers. He was shaking his head and looking down into the murky darkness. He knelt down and grabbed the cold steel, pulling it out of its setting and tossing it to the side. It hit the ground with a heavy thud, sending dirt scattering in all directions. "Maybe we aren't in the wrong spot."

Nick approached Steven and stood on the edge of the pit downward. He held out his hand and formed a small fireball in his palm. He dropped into perfectly in the center of the hole. It fell into the shadows, illuminating a long tunnel with a ladder, before hitting a floor sixty feet down.

Nick squinted at the fireball, seeing it reflect off the surface beneath it.

"Is that metal?" Nick asked, kneeling down to get a better look.

"Sure looks that way... but that wouldn't make any sense," Megan stated, walking up to the two. "New Exeter was a pretty old city before it became Lattice Light. Which would suggest the sewer lines should be concrete... not metal." Nick looked at Dante who sighed and folded his arms.

"Whatever, dude," Dante began, "but you're going in first. If anything under your foot goes 'squish,' I'm leaving."

Nick nodded and stepped down onto the ladder. He carefully lowered himself in and began climbing down. The ladder was extremely rusty. Each rung released a loud creaking sound into the gloomy air. Nick continued to descend for what felt like a mile before he finally reached the floor. The tunnel was dark, filling Nick with a deep sense of dread. He felt vulnerable, and everything in his brain was convinced this was some form of trap. Why would Shotgun willingly give up a location to the Nitros? Nick looked back and forth, assessing the situation before letting go of the ladder.

"Coast is clear!" he yelled up the ladder to the others. He stepped off into the hallway and cleared the way for the next one down. Dante was next, followed by Megan, and then Diego. Once they were all in the hallway, a black portal opened next to them, and Steven stepped through.

Diego let go of the ladder and turned to Steven. "Show off," Diego muttered.

Down one end of the hall was nothing but a metal wall. The dead-end wall seemed shinier than the others around it. It simply seemed out of place. Down the other end of the tunnel was a large opening with a light shining through. The tunnel was on a downward slope leading toward it, cutting off any visual they could have from their current position.

"Doesn't look like any sewer I've ever been in before," Dante muttered. Megan raised an eyebrow as she turned and looked at him. Dante didn't look back at her but quietly continued. "I had a weird childhood, okay?"

"It looks like there might be a room up ahead," Nick stated. "Power's on in there, too. Good chance someone's home."

"Dude," Dante cut in, stepping up next to his cousin, "what if this is some super-secret underground base for the Blades? How cool would that be?"

"A secret base that they gave us the address to?" Steven asked. "A secret base disguised as a sewer drain? You're an idiot."

"No, you're ridiculous!" Dante yelled back. He paused and then significantly lowered his voice, whispering to Steven. "Umm, can you say that again, but end it with 'that's ridiculous?'"

"Maybe after we clear this place out, we can make it our base," Diego whispered to Dante. Dante grew a massive smile and nodded his head furiously.

"Yeah, yeah!" he yelled. "With a periscope that looks up above us at the common folk."

"And a tube that we can send stuff down in, like sandwiches," Diego continued while mimicking a vicious bite into an invisible sandwich.

"Guys, we have a base, remember?" Megan asked, interrupting the fantasy. "Honestly, if you really think about it, one of its best qualities is that it's above ground."

Dante and Diego stopped smiling, and both folded their arms.

"Spoken like a true land-lover," Dante groaned while shaking his head.

"It's land*lubber*," Megan corrected, "and it means someone who is unfamiliar with the sea, not someone who loves the land. Also, you're underground... which is still land."

"I would argue that anyone unfamiliar with the sea probably also loves the land," Diego added. "Therefore, there is no difference between what he said and what you said."

"I wasn't joking when I said they were insufferable," Steven said to Nick as the two walked toward the opening.

"Dante will grow on you," Nick stated. "Just give him

a chance. Diego is also just trying to be your friend, man. There's nothing wrong with trying to have fun, even during a bad situation."

"No," Steven said, "but there *is* something wrong with losing your focus mid-mission. I'm not here to be friends with anyone, and I don't think you should, either. Redman wants you to be the leader? Fine. Just keep your head in the game and focus on what really matters."

"And what's that?" Nick asked.

Steven kept his eyes forward. "Getting revenge for everything we've lost."

The two reached the end of the hallway and looked out toward the light. The metal floor of the hall transitioned into a concrete one and poured out into a giant room. The room was cold and damp, with moss growing on the concrete walls. The enormous chamber was surrounded by metal bars, like a giant cage. Some of them were rusted and looked like they were on the verge of breaking. The area outside the bars was elevated, so anyone standing there could look down on whoever was inside.

Nick and Steven stepped into the room, taking in the incredible sight. Nick couldn't fully bring himself to believe this place existed. It was a marvel of construction and hidden deep underneath the city. If the Blades had the ability to hide something like this, Nick was dreading to think what else they could have hidden. Especially whatever weapon Shotgun was planning on creating.

"Is this some sort of prison?" Steven asked. Nick shook his head and continued to examine the room.

"I don't think so," he began. He went to continue his thought when something caught his attention. A difference on the floor he only noticed out of the corner of his eye. Nick snapped to attention and ran to the object on the ground.

"Nuclear?" Steven asked. He also turned and saw Nick kneel down next to the body of a man. Nick grabbed the man's shoulder and rolled him onto his back.

The man was skinny, with pale, white skin. He had no hair on his head, including eyebrows. His body was covered in bruises and cuts. Nick and Steven could only assume they were fresh, as blood was still leaking from the wounds onto the ground below him.

Nick put his hand over one of the wounds and tried to hold in some of the blood. Nick knew this could just be a trap set by Shotgun, but the only thing he was concerned about was this man's life.

"Diego!" Nick shouted back at the hallway. "We need medical, now!"

Without hesitation, the other three Nitros came running from the hallway and into the room. Diego slid on his knees to Nick and began reaching for his medical supplies. Dark crimson was leaking out between Nick's fingers. The man was feeling colder and colder to the touch with each drip. Diego quickly began bandaging the man's shoulder, but couldn't stop himself from asking an obvious question.

"What is this guy wearing?" he asked.

The man had a black mask on his head that covered his nose and mouth and buckled on the back of his neck. A metal plate extended upward off of that and floated in front of his forehead. The entire helmet shook anytime the Nitros moved the body like it was several sizes too large. Other than the helmet, the man only had black pants and boots. The pants seemed to be made of a similar material to a Nitro uniform. Flexible, yet didn't have a single hint of damage, despite the man's injuries.

"Shotgun wanted us to find him," Nick assessed. He thought for a moment and then nudged Steven in the shoulder. Nick motioned his head toward the door. "Let's take this guy and get out of here. Whether or not this place is a prison, it definitely feels like a trap."

On cue, a loud rumbling echoed throughout the chamber. Unable to pinpoint the source, all the Nitros could do was cover their ears and search for what was happening. It was far too late when Nick saw the shiny metal wall from earlier in the hallway slide into place over their exit.

Nick lowered his hands and ran to the wall. He placed his hands flat against the surface and pushed with all his might, but it didn't budge. Repeatedly he smashed his fist into it, but it was too thick and sturdy. The Nitros were sealed inside the prison.

"I can still get to the other side through the Void,"

Steven called out. "Maybe there's a mechanism over there that can open it again."

"I assure you, there isn't," a voice replied. Nick slowly turned away from the metal wall and looked out beyond the bars around him.

Standing on the other side, six feet above the floor, was a man. He was wearing a black combat vest adorned with scratches and tears. The suit underneath only covered his arms down to the elbow, and Nick could see the veins in his wrists glowing a faint green color as they traveled up his arm. His hands were inside gloves that were missing the fingers, so his touch would be unavoidable. His head was hidden inside a mask that only left his eyes exposed.

Nick recognized them immediately. His eyelids were hanging lazily over his eyes like he was tired. He paced slowly back and forth, never taking his stare off of Nick. He was like a tiger, stalking his prey and picking a moment. He finally came to a stop and folded his arms behind his back, lowering his chin a bit while he did.

"Shotgun," Nick growled. This was it for Nick. The moment he was finally coming face-to-face with the man he'd been seeking. Unfortunately, Nick was standing on the opposite end of Shotgun's trap. Nick was hoping to enter this battle on top, but instead, Shotgun was in control of the entire situation.

Shotgun slowly turned his eyes to examine everyone standing on the floor below. Every movement he made was slow and calculated. Not a single muscle in his body seemed to move if he didn't want it to.

"Looks like you've found yourselves in quite a predicament," Shotgun hummed.

Nick was about to respond when Steven put a hand on his chest and forced him backward, away from Shotgun. Steven stuck out his hands and began moving them in circles. Blackness crept out of the air in front of him and formed a portal, while the air behind Shotgun began to twist and move as well.

"Explosion, don't!" Nick yelled, getting his balance back. "Not by yourself!"

Steven's teeth were bared, and his eyes were locked on Shotgun's. Not a single word from Nick was making it into Steven's brain. His anger was focused, and it was the only thing driving him.

"You!" he yelled. A fire was lit inside of Steven that the other's had never seen before. It was like every emotion Steven usually didn't display burst out of him in one moment. The portal behind Shotgun was still forming, but he seemed to be refusing to turn and look at it. "You son of a bitch!" Steven lowered his arms and took a step back.

Nick went to grab him, but couldn't reach him before he took off in full sprint toward the darkness. "You killed my brother!" Steven screamed. He jumped into the portal and erupted out of the one behind Shotgun. Shotgun expertly slid to one side and dodged the initial attack, without ever removing his hands from behind his back. Steven's fist hit the metal bars where Shotgun used to be, bending the metal inward.

Without missing a beat, Steven spun around and threw his other arm at Shotgun's head. Almost faster than Steven could see, Shotgun's left arm rocketed upward and stopped Steven's fist dead in its tracks. The impact caused dust to fly from the ground around them. Shotgun stared into Steven's eyes as the two stood, locked together.

Shotgun shook his head, and his eyelids slowly began lifting up. His pupils turned a bright green and shined in the shadows. Small wisps of green light leaped from his eyes and into the air around his head.

"So quick to anger," Shotgun mocked. "You should listen to your friends more often, Steven. Otherwise, you could get hurt." His right palm rushed forward and jammed itself into Steven's chest. There was a bright flash of green as the strike connected.

Steven took off like a rocket away from Shotgun and slammed into the concrete wall. Cracks spider-webbed out from the point of impact and dislodged several rocks, which toppled to the floor below.

Nick watched helplessly as Shotgun dismantled his teammate. He should have been angry that Steven disobeyed a direct order, but was too overcome with the fear that Steven wasn't going to be okay. Also, after watching Shotgun singlehandedly dismantle a Nitro, Nick wasn't exactly feeling confident that he could take the Blade Leader in a fight.

Shotgun slowly lowered his arms and turned to look at Nick once again. Nick didn't know why, but Shotgun almost seemed to be singling him out. Before he could determine the reason, Steven was already back to his feet and running at Shotgun once again. Without taking his eyes away from Nick, Shotgun raised his hand and effortlessly caught Steven's fist. Steven froze and growled as he tried to push his fist further toward Shotgun's head. Veins were popping out of Steven's neck. He was using every ounce of his strength, and yet, made no progress. Then, slowly and steadily, the edges of his vision began to blur out. Shotgun's veins began to glow an even brighter green as he turned back to Steven.

The light leaping from Shotgun's eyes began to change from a vibrant green to an ominous black. Steven dropped to his knees and gasped for air, unable to remove himself from Shotgun's grip. Shotgun held onto Steven for a few more seconds, before letting his limp arm fall to the ground. Steven collapsed in a heap and didn't make a single move.

"Steven!" Diego cried. There was no response. Not even an attempt to show any signs of life. "What did you do to him?! You monster!"

"He's alive," Shotgun reassured as he slowly lifted one of his hands. He looked down at his palm and moved it carefully in a circle. A few moments later, blackness began to fold out of the air around him and melt into existence. The Nitros watched in horror as a portal formed next to Shotgun, with the other one nowhere in sight. "Though, his power is truly remarkable. The Void is without question a magical thing."

"You stole his power?!" Nick yelled, astonished.

Shotgun reached toward the portal and put his hand through.

"Temporarily," he replied, without turning to look at who he was addressing. "It will last me until this is over."

"Until what's over?" Megan questioned. Shotgun gave a single chuckle and shifted his eyes to her.

"This place isn't a prison, Nitros," he stated. "It's an arena." He raised one of his arms and motioned to the metal bars surrounding the Nitros. "When Blade members don't meet expectation... they wind up here."

Nick finally took his eyes away from Shotgun to look around the room again. He could envision hundreds of Blades standing around the bars shouting and pounding their fists on the metal. Those less fortunate were locked inside, left to fight like gladiators. Nick looked at the body that Diego had temporarily stopping aiding.

"Is that what happened to him?" Nick asked. "You had him fight?"

Another cold laugh escaped Shotgun's lips.

"Yes."

"So, where's the winner, then?" Shotgun shook his head and took a step into the portal. He cocked his head toward the arena floor again.

"He's lying right there," Shotgun replied.

The rest of the Nitros turned their attention back to the man on the ground. After a second, his chest leaped upward as he inhaled a massive breath of air.

Shotgun pointed at Diego. "And Diego," he called. Diego looked up at Shotgun as he turned away and walked into the portal. "If you really think I'm a monster... you haven't seen anything, yet." Shotgun disappeared into the blackness, which faded out and collapsed into nothingness behind him.

Nick had no idea where Shotgun could have gone. It wasn't worth deciphering at this point. Several more important issues had taken charge. Getting to Steven and getting him out alive was priority number one, and priority number two was seemingly waking up just across the chamber.

Diego slowly turned his attention back to the man on the ground as he began hyperventilating, trying to get enough air into his body. The man rolled himself onto his stomach and slowly pushed himself to his knees. His eyes blinked open.

"No," he muttered in a high-pitched voice. He sounded scared, and his words began to get more frantic. "No," he said again. "I can't have... I didn't." He lifted his hands off the ground and stared at them. He turned them back and forth, looking from his palms to his knuckles. He closed his hands into fists, and he worked his way to his feet. He began erratically feeling his own body. He ran his palms over his shoulders, sometimes even sinking his fingers into the still open wounds in his skin. After several seconds of doing this, he lowered his hands again. His fists were shaking, and his eyes were now clamped shut. "That should have been the one! He said that would be the one!"

Diego slowly reached one of his hands out toward the man and spoke as softly as possible.

"Listen," he began. The man snapped his head up and stared at Diego like he didn't know anyone else was around him. He looked at each Nitro in the chamber and took a step back.

"No!" he yelled. "Not more!" He pointed a finger at Diego and took a second step away. "I don't care you who are! I don't care what you did or didn't do! Shotgun told me the last round was it!" The man whipped around and grabbed the bars, shouting into the empty area behind them. "You hear me?! Shotgun! You said you'd cure me!" The man gripped the bars even tighter. He violently shook them with enough force to make the entire wall of them rattle around. "Shotgun!!!"

"We can help you!" Diego yelled. The man lowered his head to the bars and started to shake back and forth. Diego could hear him whimpering and groaning to himself. "Just

Jeremy Dooley

tell us what's wrong and…"

"And what?!" the man shouted as he cracked his head over his shoulder, letting one of his eyes meet Diego's. His voice was a significantly lower pitch than before. The man's pupil started to grow until it began filling his entire eye with a horrible blackness.

"No," he said as his voice continued to drop. "Not again! Please!" He turned his head away from Diego again. With one swift move, he smashed his forehead into the metal bar. It dented inward like it was straw. "Run! He's coming!" The man's body began to shake more violently, and he pushed himself away from the bars. He fell to his hands and knees, causing Diego to quickly move away and regroup with the others. The man pounded his fist against the ground like he was fighting away a tremendous pain. "He's coming! Razor's coming! Run away!"

Sounds of cracking and ripping began to emanate from his body as every one of his veins began to inflate under his skin. His body began to grow, one muscle at a time. His skin began to fade to a dim gray, before taking on a blue tint. The gauze Diego had applied to the man's shoulders tore along the center as jet black spikes grew out of the man's skin. The same spikes erupted from his forearms and the top of his head. The man's shouts of agony transformed into animalistic roars. His head grew until the mask fit tightly in place, and his skin was now a dark shade of blue. He slowly looked upward and made eye contact with

Diego with his soulless black eyes.

Dante gulped away his fear. "Ummm… I'm going to assume Razor's here, guys," Dante whimpered.

Razor slowly rose until all nine feet of him was standing tall. He clenched his fists and threw them away from his body, roaring loudly into the air.

"Have any plans going into this one?" Megan asked, turning slightly in Nick's direction.

Nick had his hands up in front of him. One at a time, they were surrounded by a bright, red fire.

"Throw everything you have at him," Nick replied. "That's pretty much all I got." Nick wished he had more information for his teammates. A better thought out plan or some kind of elaborate play to ensure victory, but he didn't have that. All Nick could do was take each situation at face value and try to pick the best solution. Staring at the monstrous being in front of him seemed to only leave one option.

Razor finished roaring and dug his foot into the ground, right before taking off at a full sprint toward the Nitros. He raised his fist into the air and slammed it down at Dante. Dante managed to jump out of the way, causing Razor's fist to hit the concrete and embed into it like it was sand.

Nick threw two fireballs at Razor's back. They hit his leathery skin and puffed away into smoke without leaving a single scratch. Razor snorted at the attack and latched onto a fistful of concrete. He spun around and hurled the chunk at Nick. It careened through the air, dropping pebbles onto the ground behind it. The boulder then started to slow down and came to a full stop only inches away from Nick's face. It hovered there for a moment, and then reversed direction.

Diego had both his hands out, controlling the object as he launched it back at Razor. The chunk hit Razor in the chest and shattered into debris and powder on impact. Razor flinched slightly but didn't seem damaged at all once the dust had settled. He leaned his shoulders down and went to step forward, but was tripped up and stumbled before regaining his balance. He snapped his head to look down at his leg as ice crawled up off the ground and surrounded his knee. Razor roared and kicked his leg forward, tearing his leg out of the ice and scattering shards of it across the floor.

"Well… that didn't work," Dante muttered to Megan.

"It looks like ice isn't going to hold this guy," she added. "I think it's safe to assume containing him isn't an option."

Dante nodded and pointed his hand at the floor. "Take him out, then. Got it!" Dante shot a sheet of ice out in front of him and ran to get a moving start. He jumped onto the ice and skated across its surface. He reached the monster and jumped into the air, spinning around and whipping his back foot into the side of Razor's head. The crack of the impact echoed throughout the chamber.

Razor's head snapped to the side, but the rest of his body remained completely motionless. Dante used Razor's shoulder as a foothold to push himself backward. He landed on the ground and nervously rubbed the back of his head as he stepped away from Razor.

The beast slowly turned his eyes down to meet Dante's. He straightened his head back to center with a menacing slowness. Dante couldn't believe the monster's durability. It was like attacking a brick wall.

"So, ummm, I thought that was going to do a bit more than it did," Dante admitted. He shrugged and held out his arms. "How about we just start over?" He put out his hand and planted his other firmly on his hip. "Hi, I'm Blast. That shade of blue is just lovely on you. Really brings out your…"

Razor hurled his arm across his body and smashed his forearm into Dante's chest. Dante shot like a rocket from his footing. He hit the metal bars, embedding into them for a few seconds, before peeling away and falling to the floor. He attempted to push himself up, but collapsed shortly after and remained motionless.

"Dante!" Megan yelled. As she looked at his body, the ground below her began to shake. She only had a few seconds to assess the situation before having to quickly roll to the side, dodging Razor.

The giant barreled past her, unable to stop himself. He hit the metal bars and ripped through them like they were twigs.

Razor grabbed one of the broken bars and turned around, throwing the bar at Nick. Nick jumped backward as the bar stuck several feet into the ground in front of him. Razor lined himself up and got ready to charge once again. Nick looked back and forth between the bar and Razor a few times. He lunged forward and grabbed the bar with both hands, trying to pull it from the ground like Excalibur. Razor lurched from his position and sprinted in Nick's direction. Nick continued to try and pry the bar loose. Razor was getting closer by the second, and right before making contact, Nick managed to tear the bar from the ground and swing it across his body like a claymore.

The bar cracked off the side of Razor's head, causing him to temporarily lose focus and divert from his original path. Razor lost his balance and fell to one knee. Like a meteor hitting the Earth, a ring of dirt and dust flew from the ground around the beast.

Before he could regain his footing, Nick swung the metal weapon upward into the bottom of Razor's chin. Nick quickly changed his momentum and ripped the bar down again, crashing it into the top of Razor's head. He continued to take blows to the head, each one making it harder for him to stay off the ground. Nick raised the bar over his head and prepared to strike again when a voice cried out to him.

"Nuclear, wait!" Diego shouted. Nick stopped and

turned his head to his teammate. "You saw what Razor was before he became that thing." Diego never took his eyes off of Razor as the behemoth took in some heavy breaths. Diego looked sympathetic, like the only thing he could see was someone in pain. "We need to figure out how to change him back."

Nick turned back to Razor and slowly lowered his weapon. "If we don't knock him out, how are we going to stop him?" Nick asked. "We'll find out how to help him later. I need to end this, now." Nick hoisted the bar back in the air and swung down with all his might. Just before colliding with Razor's skull, the blue monster's giant hand shot up and caught the bar.

Razor snapped his head to the side and glared angrily into Nick's eyes. Razor growled and threw a massive punch into Nick's stomach. Nick tumbled backward and crashed into the ground, flipping a few times before skidding to a stop. His hands were gripping his chest as he desperately tried to breathe again. He pressed the side of his face into the dirt. The edges of his vision began to fade to black, and his eyes rolled back a bit before his eyelids slowly closed.

Razor rolled his head, loosening his neck. He slowly turned his sights to Diego. The monster took a few steps, squaring himself up with the green Nitro.

Diego clenched his hands into fists and widened his stance. Razor was preparing to charge again when a bright purple light emanated from behind him. Razor turned to see Megan jumping into the air with an orb tucked tightly between her hands. She yelled and forced her arms forward, jamming the orb into Razor's chest. The orb erupted, sending Megan hurdling from the smoke like a bullet. She smashed into the wall and slid down to her backside.

Razor was buried in the light of the explosion, his roar barely audible over the massive bang. He swung his arms wildly, flailing away the smoke, before falling from the dust and collapsing onto the floor. He had dark lines of smoke tracing off of his sizzling body. A large crater remained where the detonation took place. Every few seconds another small rock would tumble from the outer ring of the crater and roll down into the center.

Diego relaxed his stance and took a careful look around the room. His friends were sprawled across the ground, motionless. Dust and pebbles rolled across the concrete. Metal bars were torn and dented like they were made of splintered wood. The final thing to drop into Diego's vision was Razor.

The behemoth pushed himself up onto his knees. He placed his palms flat on the ground and released a few small growls. He shook his head a few times, clearing his brain. There was a thick tension in the air as Razor managed to stand up. He set his sights on Diego with a blank, remorseless stare.

The two stared at each other. Neither made a move. Razor's breath started to quicken like he was a shark smelling blood in the water. He growled and smashed his fist into the ground, scattering cracks across the concrete.

Diego didn't flinch. He slid his foot back and put up his hands. "I know there's an innocent person in there somewhere," Diego spoke, quietly. "Maybe Redman can fix you." Diego's fingers bent slightly. He focused everything he had on Razor and slowly exhaled. "But first I have to stop you."

Razor's veins were beginning to flex through his skin as his movements became more erratic. He curled his head down, took in a massive breath of air, and then snapped his head backward, roaring into the air. A shockwave of dust tore across the floor away from him from its sheer intensity. Razor leaped off his back foot and charged at Diego.

Suddenly, his chest snapped forward and slammed down into the ground. Razor's head cracked off the concrete with a loud snap. He shook off the hit and looked at his foot, which was now covered in concrete that was crawling off the ground and around his calf. Razor growled and ripped his leg out of the rock, shattering it to bits. He quickly pushed himself up again, but barely took two steps before his foot became trapped a second time. Razor forced his foot through the rock, trying to continue forward. More concrete leaped from the ground and wrapped itself around Razor's shoulders, trying to pull him backward. Razor gripped his fingers into the concrete around his shoulder and tore it off of him. With each step, more and more concrete would crawl onto his body and hold him back.

Razor furiously ripped the rock away as he pressed forward, his eyes never leaving Diego's. Chunks of concrete were rocketing off his body as he tore them away. Diego stayed locked in his position. Any rocks that were thrown his way would divert path and curl around him at the last second like he had an impenetrable bubble protecting his body.

Razor was only five feet away when the concrete began to connect to itself and harden around the beast. Razor reached his massive hand forward to grab Diego. His fingers stretched and extended as far as they could. They ended up only inches away from Diego's unfazed face when Razor was finally frozen in place.

The only things peeking out of the rock were Razor's hands and head. He growled and roared, trying to wriggle himself free, but to no avail. Cracks would form in the concrete, but fill in and harden again quicker than they could form. Diego lowered his hands and took in a well-needed breath of air.

"I promise," he said in the silence. "We'll find you help."

CHAPTER 12: A WARNING

Diego stepped away from the frozen Razor and made his way to Nick.

Nick had crawled toward the bars and was now leaning his shoulder against them. He still had a hand laid across his chest, and one of his eyes had swollen enough to be completely shut.

Diego knelt down next to his fallen friend, reaching into pouches on his belt in the meantime. He fished out some medical equipment while assessing the damage.

"Atomic?" Nick barely mouthed out. He cringed as Diego added some alcohol to his wounds. "Where's Razor?"

Diego didn't speak right away. He turned his head to make sure Razor was still trapped in his concrete cocoon. The monster was struggling, but unable to break the rock around him.

"He's trapped and unharmed," Diego replied as he moved torn pieces of Nick's suit so he could properly apply bandages. "Hopefully Redman can come up with a way to change him back." Diego returned his gaze to Nick and put away a few of his supplies. "Once he's back to being human again, I'll leave it to God to determine if he's innocent or not. It's not my place."

Nick nodded and pushed himself away from the bars. He coughed a few times as he shakily got to his feet. Diego quickly grabbed Nick's shoulder and helped him stand.

"You a religious man, Diego?" Nick asked.

Diego helped the shaken Nick stay upright.

"Always have been," he replied. "My family and I are very close to God."

Nick coughed. His leg crumpled once again as his knee gave out. Diego caught him before he could fall and helped him remain standing.

"What about you?" Diego asked. Nick chuckled and shook his head a little.

"I'm too much a skeptic to follow a religion," he answered. "I'm sorry to say."

"It's understandable, and there's no need to be sorry. I've known a lot of incredible people that don't practice. I don't judge based on what you believe. I judge based on what you do. I like to think God does a similar thing."

"Well, for my sake, I hope so." Nick winced away some more pain and patted Diego on the back, letting him know he was comfortable standing on his own. Nick knew Diego was a good man, but never realized quite how good he was. Nick didn't just see Diego as a teammate anymore. He saw Diego as the best of them. He was a man the rest of humanity could only aspire to be. Nick felt like he could rely on Diego if he needed it, but now, he was certain that Diego would always be there for him.

Diego slowly stepped away.

Nick rolled out his shoulder with a few satisfying cracks. "But with everything that's happened to me in the past... I assume God turned his back on me a long time ago."

Diego nodded and closed his eyes. He sighed softly in understanding.

"I'm very familiar with the feeling, Nick," Diego added. "When my parents and I started our lives in New York, we had nothing. We worked our way up from the ground until we could finally afford a home just outside of the city. The American dream that we used to hear stories about in Mexico." Diego folded his arms, keeping his eyes closed the entire time.

Nick recognized the face he was making. He was convincing his mind to remember a moment it had spent years trying to forget.

"My parents were good people, Nick. They had too much love and trust in their hearts to turn anyone away. When we were driving home one night, we saw a boy walking down the side of the road. Couldn't have been any older than eighteen. He looked scared and cold. My father pulled over and tried to help. The boy said he couldn't go home, and he had no one to contact. My father couldn't bring himself to just keep driving. He invited the boy to come stay with us for the night."

"They just let someone they didn't know into your home?" Nick asked.

Diego opened his eyes again, slowly. "Yeah, but it's more complicated than that. My father brought him into the next room and talked to him. I overheard as much as I could. The boy said he had no parents left and was in town trying to find help for his sibling."

Diego looked up at the ceiling. "We didn't know the Blades were the ones he was running from. They tracked him down. All the way back to our house. He pleaded with them, but... words turned to fists, and fists turned to gunshots." Diego nodded a few times as a single tear traced a line down his cheek. "I was the only one who walked away from that place. They made the decision to leave me alive. As far as I know, they wanted me to tell this story. They wanted me to help spread fear and send a message about the Blades. The last one left alive was the boy we picked up. He was on the ground, and I was kneeling over him."

Diego looked down at the ground like he could see the boy in front of him. "He was the reason my parents were dead, but... he was just lying there and..."

Nick waited for the next words, but Diego refused to say any. It was like he was still confused over his actions.

"You stayed with him?" Nick asked. Diego sighed again and gave a slight nod.

"He was alone," Diego reasoned. "My parents were already gone. It just didn't matter to me what this man had done. I didn't want him being there by himself. So I stayed. I held his hand as he passed away while the men who killed my family watched."

"And do you regret doing that?" Nick asked.

Diego opened his hand and stared down at his palm. He slowly closed his fingers back into a loose fist.

"No," he answered, "because the last thing that boy ever got the chance to do, was apologize. Not just to me, but to everyone. His family that he was trying to help, his friends he was leaving behind, his parents that died too soon. I could tell it was a weight taken off of him that someone was around to hear it. That was enough for me. The Blades that invaded my home allowed me to live, but they took the boy's body with them. I was left alone until the police arrived."

"The world isn't good enough to deserve people like you, Diego," Nick stated. "It's what sets you apart from the rest. Keep that in mind."

Diego nodded and quickly shook away his thoughts.

"We have to get the others," he announced, snapping back to reality. "I'll go find a way to get to Steven. We need to get him out of here as soon as possible. You go check on Megan and Dante."

Nick went to respond but instead allowed his mouth to hang open in shock. A bright green light formed behind Diego and silhouetted his body. Diego turned around as the green light centered itself in his chest. Diego launched from his feet and shot across the floor, leaving a wake of dust behind him. He slammed into the bars and gasped for air. The green light was like a flashbang. Nick's vision was blurry and faded. He could barely make out the shape of a figure standing across from him.

"Touching story," Shotgun stated, calmly. The black portal through which he entered was still fading away behind him. Clearly Steven's powers hadn't yet left Shotgun. He turned his eyes to Nick and tilted his head downward. "But you and I need a moment alone."

Nick put his hands up on guard. His vision was slowly returning but seemed to be taking longer than usual. His fight with Razor had left him weak. Fire leaked out from the center of Nick's fists and surrounded his fingers.

"You don't scare me, Shotgun," Nick hissed. Shotgun didn't react to the threat and instead took a slow step toward Nick. Nick stepped away, pushing out his hand while he did. A ball of fire sprung forward and hit Shotgun in the shoulder. He continued walking through it, without flinching. Nick took another step back and attempted a second attack. Again, the fireball curled around Shotgun's armor, without changing his momentum at all.

Nick quickly moved his hands together and released a cone of fire into the air. The flames enveloped Shotgun, burying the Blade leader in a sea of blinding light. Rust began to flake and fall off the metal bars behind Nick as the flames grew in intensity. The ground started to blacken, and beads of sweat burst into steam off of Nick's forehead. As the flames were about to reach their hottest, two hands erupted out of the fire and grabbed Nick's forearms.

Nick's arms were thrown apart, breaking the fire and causing it to disappear into embers. Shotgun's armor was on the verge of glowing from the temperatures, but again he seemed completely unfazed. He pushed his hands into Nick's chest, sending a surge of green energy tearing through the Nitro's body.

Nick collapsed into the bars behind him, finding it almost impossible to remain standing. Shotgun reached out and gripped his fingers into Nick's head. Nick continued to sink against the bars. He could feel himself losing control of his limbs.

"Your strength is impressive," Shotgun complimented. "Redman must be so proud of his newest inventions."

Nick pushed his arm into the air, knocking away Shotgun's grip on him. Nick threw a desperate punch at Shotgun's stomach. He didn't know if it would hit, but he was willing to try anything at this point. His friends were still down from the fight with Razor, and Nick was getting more and more desperate.

Shotgun simply swatted the punch away like he was dealing with an unruly child. As soon as Nick was open again, Shotgun clamped both his hands into the sides of Nick's head. Nick ground his teeth together. It felt like the blood running through his veins was stopping. His muscles were quivering and giving out. The longer Shotgun held onto Nick's head; the less Nick could move, or even think.

"Shotgun... you won't," Nick growled, "you won't win!"

"What drives you to do this?" Shotgun questioned. "Why do you feel the need to help Phillip Redman?"

Nick fought to breathe. He slowly lifted his head and stared into Shotgun's eyes.

"You..." he tried, "you killed my family! You took them from me! It's... it's your fault they're gone!" Nick's arms dropped to his sides, and he fell to his knees in front of Shotgun.

Shotgun's eyes changed from fluorescent green to a deep red. He let Nick drop away from his hand and collapse onto the ground, barely conscious.

"Is that what you've been told?" Shotgun chuckled and held his palm out in Nick's direction. "This," he started, but then paused, "no. No." He pulled his hand away, shaking his head and closing his eyes. "No, not like this. It won't be like this."

Shotgun snapped back to Nick and knelt down next to

him. His eyes were still leaking red light as he placed his hand on Nick's head. "It would be so easy right now. Look at you. Defenseless. Weak." Shotgun pressed his hand harder against Nick, forcing his head down into the dirt. Just as the pressure became unbearable, Shotgun pulled back and returned to his standing position.

"But then you'd never know," he murmured. "Then you and Redman would never know the truth." Shotgun's eyes slowly closed, and when they opened again, the red light was gone. His eyelids were now hanging lazily over his eyes like he was tired. He looked away from Nick, setting his stare on the rock monolith in the center of the room.

Razor was still within its grip, desperately trying to free himself. Without Diego to continue containing him, the concrete was beginning to chip away and lose its hold on the monster.

Shotgun slowly approached him. He stopped a few inches away from the growling beast and reached out his hand. He gripped the side of Razor's head and instantly the monster grew quiet. His pitch black eyes widened, and he finally stopped struggling. The blue color of his skin began to fade away and return to its normal, pale tone. His frame began to shrink, and his limbs disappeared into the concrete. Soon he was just a tiny human lying within a giant hole in the rock. His head dropped down as he passed out once again.

Nick couldn't bring himself to fight against Shotgun. His body was disobeying every single command. He had never before felt so weak.

Shotgun pulled his hand away and sighed. "It's the only way he can return to his normal form," he spoke, calmly, "at least for now. Jason Powell. That was his name before all of this. He's just the product of an experiment by some very bad people, Nicholas. His energy needs to be controlled. Otherwise, his body will continue to produce it, and keep him as Razor forever."

Nick had fought to remain awake, and now had enough strength to push himself off the ground, but nowhere near enough to stand, yet.

"You're acting like I'm supposed to care," he groaned. Shotgun didn't turn to look at Nick and instead continued to examine Razor. Nick tried to get to his feet but ended up staggering and falling to his backside again. He slid himself away from Shotgun and pressed up against the bars. "Why didn't you kill me right there?" Shotgun didn't react, like he never even heard Nick's words. Nick was walking a fine line. He knew fighting Shotgun alone wasn't going to end well for him, especially in his current state. "You said if you killed me, I'd never know something."

"I did," Shotgun agreed. Nick rested his head on the metal, sucking in as much air as possible.

"So, get on with it," Nick demanded, trying to buy himself time. He pressed his hand against the wound on his chest, trying to will his body to heal. Shotgun sighed and slowly turned away from Razor.

"What do you know about us, Nicholas?" Shotgun asked. "What do you know about our mission?"

"I know you're stealing Otrolium so you can make some sort of weapon," Nick replied, "and I'm never going to let that happen."

Shotgun closed his eyes, not speaking again immediately.

"I'm guessing this is the part where you tell me I'm wrong," Nick guessed.

"Yes... and no," Shotgun corrected. "We are creating something, yes, but we aren't the ones who built the weapon. Redman is the one to blame. Otrolium has claimed hundreds of lives and was released onto this city by him. He needs to be stopped and what we're building will be the ultimate end to his reign."

Nick was now seeing that Kristen was telling the truth. Shotgun and the Blades really *did* hate Redman. Nick couldn't figure out how so many people could hate him and the things he's done. Nick couldn't help but wonder why he felt like the only one on Redman's side.

"Why?" Nick insisted. "What are you trying to prove?"

"I'm here to show Redman that everything he's worked for, everything he's created that makes him feel so superior and progressive can easily be turned against him. Just look at the street grid. The future of transportation, yet we still managed to route a bomb to his lab using it. We could send hundreds more if we desired. The technology Redman developed for the Hard-Drive Exo we have already duplicated and improved for my bounty hunter. The Void that your friend, Steven, harnesses without care, our top operative has been using for years."

Shotgun knelt down in front of Nick, so they were face-to-face. "You see? Everything your precious lab churns out is a weapon, and people only seem to care when that weapon is finally pointed at them."

Nick did his best to keep Shotgun's words out of his head. Shotgun was the bad guy here. Nick had to keep reminding himself of that. Unfortunately, Shotgun was right about Redman's accidental affinity for making weapons. As far as Nick could tell, he himself was the next weapon in this long line.

"You're a member of the R.A.N.T. aren't you?" Nick questioned. "You and the Blades are what's left over of them."

"Close," Shotgun returned. "The R.A.N.T. was a group of individuals who would have loved to see a gun against Redman's head. The Blades are an organization that is determined to pull the trigger."

"So this is about power?" Nick said through closed teeth. "You want to control all these weapons like Redman does? That's why you want the Otrolium?"

Shotgun sighed and looked down at the floor, like Nick

was making this difficult.

"I don't want Otrolium due to a need for power," Shotgun stated. "I have a need for power *because* of the Otrolium." Shotgun pushed himself up from the ground, turned on his heels and took a few steps away from Nick.

Nick saw an opening, but for some reason, couldn't bring himself to attack. Shotgun's words had his full attention. He knew it was exactly what Shotgun wanted, but at this point, he was far too invested in what the Blade Leader had to say.

Shotgun turned his head and talked back over his shoulder. "Did Redman ever tell you why it was marked as a failing project?" he asked.

"He said it gave off some kind of radiation," Nick replied. "That it was dangerous."

"And did he ever once tell you the effects of Otrolium radiation poisoning?" Shotgun continued to interrogate.

"What are you getting at, Scott?" Nick hurried.

Shotgun turned back around, so his body was now facing Nick. He lifted his arm and turned it slightly, so Nick could see the veins near his wrist glowing a bright green.

"You can call me a psychopath," Shotgun began, "or a monster, or whatever you might perceive. But, I was in the middle of that explosion at the Faraday Center, and gallons of Otrolium fused into my blood in an instant. I needed to know the effects of this poisoning, and Phillip Redman simply refused to ever truly test it and find out. So I *did*."

Shotgun turned and began pacing back and forth across the concrete floor. "Over thirty people have been taken by the Blades and exposed to this radiation. Every single one of them had the same reaction. Otrolium does not poison the body." He looked at Nick again and tapped the side of his mask. "It poisons the mind and gives you uncontrollable urges for power and control. You lose every sense of morality and honor that most humans take for granted."

"Are you saying that's what happened to you?" Nick asked. "That you can't control what you're doing?"

Shotgun stopped pacing and held his arms out to the sides.

"Shotgun controls everything that I do," he replied. "He lets me, Scott, speak from time to time, but I don't have the power to stop what he's doing."

"Fight it, then, Scott!" Nick interrupted. "It's still your mind, not his

"You're wrong about that, Nicholas. I fought him for as long as I could, but Shotgun finally won. Otrolium poisoning is a progressive disease and will not stop until you are fully transformed. There is no cure."

"So you're trying to convince me that me and my entire team are diseased?" Nick asked.

"No," Shotgun answered. "Just you."

Shotgun walked toward Nick again and knelt down, one last time. He placed his hand on the back of Nick's head, instantly taking his breath away.

"Why..." Nick fought to say, "why are you telling me this story? If... if Shotgun already won, then why not... why not just kill me and end it?"

Shotgun chuckled and shook his head.

"Because I've seen the plans for Project Nitro," he replied. "I've seen everything that went into making you. So this, my friend, was not a story." Shotgun gripped a hair on the back of Nick's head and pulled it away from his scalp. He brought his hand around, in front of Nick's face, and held the hair in between their eyes. "This is a warning."

Nick focused on the hair, before using every ounce of his strength to reach up and take it. Once the hair was taken, Shotgun stood up and nodded.

The metal door sealing them in the underground chamber shook and slowly began to slide away. Several Blade soldiers marched to the entrance and held their position, waiting for Shotgun to join them.

"You may want to ask your Professor a little more about what went into making you a Nitro. Right now, he is desperately trying to stop me. So, I can't wait to see how he plans to handle two of me." Shotgun turned away and walked to the exit. The soldiers had already marched into the center of the chamber to collect Razor. One of the soldiers threw him over his shoulder, before they ran back to the door and followed close behind Shotgun as they all disappeared into the darkness.

Nick was still trying to get his strength back, but his muscles simply refused to move. With all his strength, his lifted his hand once again and looked carefully at the hair. The same length as all the others, but still distinctly different.

"Nick!" a voice called out. Dante limped across the floor, holding his chest and barely staying on his feet. Clearly he had just come to and was fighting off the urge to pass out again. He got close to his cousin before falling to his knees. "We need to get the others and get back to the surface," he said. "The door out looks like it's open. What happened to Shotgun?"

Nick didn't say anything. His eyes were still locked on the hair. "Are you okay, man?" Dante asked.

"It's red," Nick replied, finally. He still didn't make eye contact with his cousin. "My hair is turning red."

Not able to make sense of what Nick was saying, Dante leaned in closer.

"What are you talking about, Nick?" Nick turned to look at him and shook his head.

"Something really bad might be happening…"

CHAPTER 13: A PLAN REVEALED

"Why wouldn't you tell me this?" Nick demanded.

Redman held out his hands in defense of himself. The other Nitros sat around the main chamber in the lab. They were covered in cuts and bruises, and several had large, blood-soaked bandages on them.

"You said the Otrolium in our enhancers wasn't dangerous," Nick continued.

"It acts as the binding agent," Redman responded. "That's what holds the Nitro enhancements to your DNA. Besides, the percentage of Otrolium in that formula is so astronomically tiny, that there's no way you could suffer the effects of Otrolium poisoning. I didn't lie to you, Nicholas. Especially not to the extent of Scott Cells."

"Then why is my hair changing to red?" Nick asked. "You told me right at the beginning that my formula had more of that binding agent than the others. Shotgun's

211

claiming the Otrolium is changing me, just like it did to him."

"Why would you believe anything that guy says, anyway?" Megan asked, jumping into the conversation. "All he ever did was lie to us. You don't have any reason to start listening to him now. He's just trying to get into your head and distract us."

"I talked to him, Megan," Nick snapped back. "It was like talking to two different people. When his eyes are all lit up, he's Shotgun, and when they're not, he's like a normal person. I really think he was telling the truth when he said the Otrolium split his mind. The guy is clearly insane, and that would help explain it."

Redman sighed and nodded his head.

"Fine, Nicholas," he reluctantly agreed. "If it will ease your mind, I'll run some tests and make sure nothing is out of the ordinary. The changing of your hair is just a minor side effect of the procedure. I can assure you right now that you have nothing to worry about, but I can't have this clouding your brain."

"Not when Shotgun has some kind of weapon in the works out there," Steven noted. "We don't know what the hell it is, or what it does. So, let's stop it with this stuff and just focus here."

"You're one to talk, Steve," Nick asserted. He pointed his finger at Steven and stepped away from Redman. "You went running in after Shotgun alone. You could have gotten yourself killed. We need to work together if we have any hope of stopping this guy."

Steven pushed himself away from his seat and stood closer to Nick.

"Then stop talking all the time!" he snapped back. "All you guys do is whine about strategy and planning when we should be taking action to stop this psycho! Redman might expect you to be our leader, Nick, but you're not. So stop acting like one! If I called the shots that bastard would already be in the ground!"

Diego ran between the two Nitros and put his hand on Steven's chest.

"That's enough!" Diego yelled.

"Why are you so damn pissed all the time?!" Nick questioned. "If it's because of what happened to you when you were younger, we get it. Okay? We've all lost people, but that's no reason to go pushing your friends away!"

"For the last time, you are not my friend!" Steven shouted. He grabbed Diego's hand and threw it away from him. "You all act like we're supposed to love each other. Sit down next to each other like a psychiatrist and spit out our problems. Well, I've had it with that! The only thing that matters to me is finding the guy who killed my brother and putting a permanent end to what he does."

"We're not going to kill Shotgun," Diego stated. Steven looked away from Nick and set his eyes on Diego. His eyebrows lifted, in a surprised manner. He turned his head to look at everyone else in the room, but they all remained quiet.

"Wait, wait, wait," he muttered through chuckles. He looked back at Nick and smiled. "You guys are serious aren't you?" Again, the others didn't say a word. "You're gonna let this guy, that murdered your family members for no God damned reason just walk away? Stick him in a jail cell somewhere and hope he learns his lesson?"

"None of us signed up for what you're proposing," Megan jumped in. "We're not here for revenge. We're here for justice. We're not killers."

"No, *you're* not killers!" Steven snapped, pointed his finger at Megan. "I want justice, too, but my brother is lying dead in the dirt right now! Where's the justice there?! You guys really want to know why I'm so pissed? You really want to know what's gonna make me feel better? I want Shotgun dead. That's the only thing on my mind, and it's the only thing that will make me feel accomplished. When my parents died, I had nothing left but my brother. He took care of me. He did everything he could to protect me. You see this scar?"

Steven pointed to the long red line across his light blue eye. "He saved me when I got robbed and cut up by thugs. He gave everything for me and then he was just gone. I never got to know why. I never got to ask him why he left me alone. He was just gone, and then the next thing I knew, he was dead. The Blades killed him under direct orders from Shotgun. He has to pay, and I'm going to make sure he does. You can try to take him alive, but you better hope I don't get a second alone with the guy."

"It won't fix anything," Dante assured, calmly. He was sitting at one of the tables and had remained silent for the entirety of the conversation. He wasn't looking at the others. "Good people can never feel happy about bad things. It will never leave you feeling accomplished. If anything, you'll probably feel worse than before."

"Well, Dante," Steven began, quieter than before. "Maybe I'm not as good a person as you thought."

"That's not true!" Diego exclaimed. Steven snapped his head at the outburst, staring into Diego's eyes. "You are not a bad person, Steven! I've been around you long enough to know that. You might be ready to give up on yourself, but I'm not."

Steven didn't have an immediate reply. He simply kept looking at Diego. Neither one of them made the decision to break eye contact first.

"Why do you care so damn much?" Steven questioned. "Why are you always on my case about this stuff?"

"Because I see a better person in you," Diego replied. "I see the goodness in you that apparently, you don't. My parents were exactly the same way. It didn't matter who the person was, they just saw the potential in them."

"Yeah, your parents thought like that," Steven butted in, "and look where that got them."

Everyone fell silent and darted their eyes back and forth between the two. Dante covered his eyes with his hand and leaned his head downward, trying to escape from the moment.

Diego continued to stare at Steven. In the middle of the tension, a thin layer of tears glazed over Diego's eyes.

Steven was finally the one to break the eye contact. He looked away and closed his eyes. "Diego… I didn't mean to…"

Diego put up his hand, stopping Steven. He slowly shut his eyes and attempted to collect himself.

"Maybe you're right," he said quietly. "Maybe everyone isn't who I wish they were." He turned away from the rest of the group and walked toward the exit of the chamber.

"Diego!" Steven called after him. "Diego, don't leave, I just…" The door to the chamber slid down into place behind Diego, sealing him away from the rest of the Nitros. Steven stared at the door like his mind wanted him to chase after Diego, but his body didn't know how.

"That was, uh…" Dante began, "kind of a dick move, dude."

Steven turned his head but didn't look directly at Dante. His eyes finally set on Nick. He shrugged and held out his hands for a few seconds.

"That was… I didn't mean to…" he tried.

"We get it," Nick finished. He turned to the others and spoke loudly. "Everyone here is clearly under a lot of stress at the moment, but we can't let that get to us. We've been through a lot, and we have a lot ahead of us. The best advantage we have is each other." He looked back at Steven. "So, let's not push them away, too."

Steven sighed and nodded his head. "Do I apologize, or…"

"Give him some time first," Nick replied. "Then yes, apologize. We need to stick together, okay?"

"Right. So where do we stand?"

"Well," Megan started, "we know Shotgun is building some sort of weapon using the Otrolium. It sounds like he and the Blades have a fixation on turning everything Redman invented against him."

"I'm sure he blames the Otrolium for what happened to him," Dante added. "I mean, I would if I was him. The guy's a freak."

"He has to have some sort of motive aside from that, though," said Nick. "Why else would he have left us alive? It'd be ten times easier to continue his operations if we were out of the way."

"To scare you and Redman," Megan replied. "He's trying to make you think the Otrolium in the Nitro enhancers is enough to turn you into him. It's would also be enough to distract Redman while he researches the problem. Shotgun is just trying to fragment us and divide our attention."

"But I reiterate!" Redman jumped in, "the percentage is

incredibly small."

Nick squinted as his brain began to process the information around him. He turned to Redman, holding out one of his hands.

"Redman, why do you keep saying 'percentage?'" he asked.

Redman thought for a second and then shrugged his shoulders. "Well, if you look at the actual *amount* of Otrolium, it's quite substantial," he replied. "Nearly fifty tanks per Nitro. However, the Nitro enhancers are so concentrated that we need to use that amount just to get a very tiny percentage in the enhancer. The rest of it is burnt off."

"That's a lot of Otrolium," Dante acknowledged. "I guess that's a good thing to know. There's no way the Blades have that much at their disposal."

Nick lowered his hand and tilted his head, thinking back to his previous fights with the Blades.

"But they don't need to steal that much," he said, quietly. He snapped around to the other Nitros. "They have the Converter. They can make as much Otrolium as they want if they have a good enough source of energy."

"There's no way the Blades have an energy source like that in their control," Redman stated. "It would take a massive generator to make the amount they're looking for." Nick fell silent again, trying to think as Shotgun would.

"I might be wrong here," Steven began. The others gave him their full attention. "But didn't you guys just recently fight a massive generator of energy? What if Shotgun is using Razor to create more Otrolium?"

Nick and Megan looked at one another, realizing the possibility.

"Woah, woah, woah," Dante interrupted, throwing his hands in the air. "Are you guys suggesting that Shotgun is trying to make a Nitro?" He held up his fingers and began pointing to them as he counted off. "Number one, it takes two years for a Nitro to even finish cooking. Number two, the machinery Redman used is one of a kind. There's no way he'd be able to replicate it. And number three, all the plans for Project Nitro are in this room. Not with him."

"Kristen worked here for years," Nick stated. Dante perked up at the fact, listening carefully. "She easily could have given him the plans for the machinery if she understood them well enough." Nick looked at Redman, who had his eyes closed. He let out a long sigh and shook his head.

"She helped me construct them," he admitted. "If there was ever a person besides me who was familiar with the machinery, it was her."

"And then after we stopped the bomb," Nick reminded everyone. "Shotgun was in here. We invited him in. The two paramedics that took him away? Blades. It would have been the perfect time to take anything he wanted without us noticing." Nick pointed at Redman. "Where are they?" Redman looked back and forth.

"Where are they?" he asked back. "What are you…"

"The binders, Redman!" Nick yelled. "The binders for Project Nitro, where are they?"

Redman didn't say another word and snapped right to attention. He ran to his desk and ripped open one of the drawers, fishing through the contents within. He quickly pulled out the binders and threw them onto his desk. Nick could hear him muttering to himself.

"Nuclear," he listed, softly. "Blast. Reactor. Explosion. Atomic." He looked up from his desk and held out his arms. "They're all here."

Nick approached the desk and glanced down at the files. The names of the Nitros printed on the front of the binders glistened in the light of the chamber. Nick sighed and closed his eyes.

"No, they aren't," he said, solemnly. "Subject Uranium is missing."

Redman looked back down at his desk. Nick was right. The binder for the sixth Nitro was nowhere in sight. Nick turned and set his stare on the tubes that once held the uniforms for the team. He looked up and down the unlit blue suit that sat alone with no owner.

"Shotgun wants to turn everything Redman made against him," Nick echoed. "That's his final goal. His weapon is a Nitro."

"But Project Uranium is unstable and untested!" Redman exclaimed. "Does Shotgun really think he can find someone to undergo, let alone survive, that process?"

As Redman's mouth closed, a siren sounded off in the chamber. The map of Lattice Light City painted across the screen, with a red dot flashing one of the streets several miles away.

"What's going on?" Dante asked, standing up from his seat. Redman ran to the computer and began typing.

"There's an attack on a police convoy across town," he quickly replied. "Police are already claiming it's the Blades."

"Then we need to get there, now!" Nick ordered. "What are those officers transporting?" Redman shook his head as his fingers desperately tried to keep up with what he wanted to type.

"I don't have that information, yet. Whatever it is, the Blades are after it." Nick nodded, turned, and pointed his finger at Steven.

"Go get Diego. Everyone else, let's get to the Gemini."

"Me?" Steven asked.

"Yes," Nick said without hesitation. "I'm not telling you it's time to say sorry, yet, but it's worth letting him know your goal isn't to shut him out completely."

Steven sighed. He turned away from Nick and left the room.

"Nick," Megan stopped. "What if Shotgun is there?"

Nick continued to catch his breath and nodded his head.

"I'm expecting him to be," Nick replied. "He might want to spring another trap on us, but we might finally get the chance to team up on him. Which means we'll finally be able to take him down."

CHAPTER 14: A RAID

Cars slowly moved out of the way as the police vehicles traveled smoothly down the street. Their sirens were flashing, and they stayed in a tight formation. Two cars in front, an armored van third, and another car bringing up the rear.

Officer Ferguson sat in the passenger seat of the van, with his foot up on the dashboard in front of him. He had a thin chin, big teeth, and short blonde hair poking out of the top of his head.

The driver was Officer Tavis, a heavy-set man with red hair and a face covered in freckles.

Ferguson held a coffee in his hand, blowing on it slightly before taking a large sip. He sighed in relief, before motioning it toward Tavis.

"You want a sip?" he asked.

Tavis put up his hand and shook the coffee away.

"No," he snapped. "Let me focus. This isn't supposed to be some leisurely drive. Once we finish the transport, then we'll go out. Beer will be on me, okay?"

Ferguson chuckled and took back his coffee, resting it on his knee. "Relax, dude," he began. "I know you haven't done this before, but it's super routine. Besides, the damn thing drives itself. You're here for 'emergency situations' only. We're essentially just along for the ride." He knocked his hand against the metal grate behind him leading into the back compartment of the van. "We get this guy to his brand new hotel and then call it a night. Sound good back there?!" Ferguson's voice echoed into the rear of the van.

A prisoner sat on one of the benches with his hands cuffed to a bar below him. He had his head lowered and made no attempt at acknowledging Ferguson's joke.

"Yeah, with those Nitros around, there ain't no room for you in Lattice Light," Ferguson taunted. "They got a little too good at locking up punks like you. Already got two of the Zealos behind bars."

The prisoner lifted his head up at the mention and stared straight ahead.

Ferguson leaned forward and pointed out the windshield. "Imagine how much worse this convoy business was before the grid was a thing."

"Driving isn't exactly the hardest activity in the world," Tavis said, quickly. "Also, quit talking to that guy. He creeps me out."

Ferguson took his foot off the dash and leaned forward a bit. "Dude, enough," he started. "He's back there, and we're safely up…"

A massive explosion tore through the air as the front car in the convoy erupted into flames. It shot into the air and flipped end over end across the length of the other cars, landing several feet behind them. Like a comet coming to Earth, the car buried itself into the ground. A ring of smoke and flames shot out from the impact.

Ferguson dropped his coffee to the ground and slapped his hands over his ears. His heartbeat skyrocketed as he was ripped out of his relaxed state into a mindset of pure panic. He could barely hear after the explosion, and his teeth felt like they were cracking from how hard they were clenched together.

"What the hell was that?!" Tavis yelled. He slammed on a red button on the dash, giving him manual control of the vehicle. As he looked back up through the windshield, the police vehicle in front of him began to dip and roll to the side like it was floating on water. It tossed and turned as the officers inside desperately tried to jump out before the car fell into the Earth and disappeared into a black portal. The screams of the officers instantly went from piercing to silent. The last thing to disappear into the darkness was the hand of one of the officers inside who almost managed to crawl out.

Tavis stomped onto the gas pedal and ripped the wheel

to the side, avoiding the massive black hole in front of them.

As they passed, Ferguson stared in amazement at the swirling pit of black and purple. It faded in and out of reality like it wasn't even really there. Ferguson pulled the radio off the dash and screamed into it.

"This is transport vehicle 227!" he shouted. "We need back up! Now! There's something attacking the convoy, and…" He shook the radio in his hand. "Hello?" He banged it against the dash a few times, but still, nothing came back. "Damn it!" he yelled.

As he threw down the radio, two heavy thuds rang across the hood of the van. Tavis sat forward and could see two dents form in the metal in front of him. A faint glow emanated from the dents, but nothing seemed like it was there to make it. Then, out of nothing, a figure took form, standing on the hood. His metal suit reflected the glare from the streetlights as they passed them. The man lifted his arm and took a massive swing at the windshield. Two huge, metal blades, attached to his wrists, cut through the cab like paper and sliced the roof clean off. Wind tore into the front seats and pulled the hats off the officers' heads.

Tavis ducked and ripped the wheel to the side once again, trying to shake the figure off the van.

The man stayed locked in place and simply turned his head to the side. The van was barreling toward a wall, and without hesitation, the man jumped from his position and took off into the sky like a rocket. Soot and ash covered the front of the van from his launch and dusted across Tavis's eyes. The van smashed into the brick wall, sending shards of metal and shattered glass in all directions. Tavis's head cracked off the wheel in front of him, instantly blacking him out.

Tavis eased his eyes opened, but his vision was extremely blurry. It was impossible to know how much time had gone by. Was he unconscious for a few seconds, or a few days?

He couldn't hear anything but a high-pitched whining noise. As his vision began to sharpen, he could make out Ferguson laying his head down on the dashboard. A thin stream of crimson was leaking down from under his cheek and his eyes were locked open in shock. Small shards of glass were embedded in his face like tiny blemishes. The fresh blood made it obvious to Tavis that he indeed was only out for a few seconds, meaning he was still in danger.

Tavis pushed himself away from the steering wheel and managed to fight open the door. He dropped out of the van and collapsed onto the pavement. His brain couldn't form complete thoughts, or lead itself to any final actions. He wanted to grab his pistol out of its holster, but his arm refused to land in the right place. He was simply rubbing a limp hand around on the asphalt.

Tavis whimpered, trying to cry out for help. The more

he tried to speak, the less noise seemed to escape him. He could hear footsteps around him as several people gathered around his body. Tavis turned his shaky head upward as two heavy black boots landed in front of him.

Shotgun stood over his body, shaking his head in disappointment. Before he could speak his first words, a hand reached out and grabbed hold of his ankle. Shotgun tilted his head and looked down.

Another officer, barely alive, was holding desperately onto Shotgun's leg. Blood was trickling out the officer's nose, and every movement he made was slow and helpless.

"Please," he begged, "stop this. We need help."

Shotgun continued to stare down at the man, unfazed by his haggard appearance. Shotgun slowly knelt down, resting his forearms on his knees. He leaned in closer to the injured officer.

"Please… I have a son," the officer pleaded.

Shotgun nodded to the officer, very slowly and peacefully. Shotgun's hand left his knee and was carefully placed over the officer's face. Shotgun's grip tightened slightly, and he spoke in a low, calm voice.

"There's no need to worry," he hummed. "I'll help you." Shotgun rubbed his palm against the officer's forehead like he was trying to soothe him. "You've served your department well, in the time that it's been necessary, but let's be honest with one another..." Shotgun suddenly rose back to his feet. His hand gripped tighter onto the officer's face as he was ripped from the ground. Shotgun held him firmly by his temples.

The officer screamed and clawed at Shotgun's forearm, trying to release himself.

"You've seen the superhumans that patrol these streets thanks to Dr. Phillip Redman," Shotgun growled. "You know the power they possess." Shotgun's veins started to glow a bright green color.

The officer's screams began to exhaust and turn into muffled gasps. His skin grayed out and shrunk around his bones. His struggling began to slow as the last of his energy seeped into Shotgun's blood.

As Shotgun's grip tightened, another noise became apparent. A small voice that Shotgun found all too familiar, scratching at the back of his mind.

"Let him go," the voice commanded. "He's done nothing wrong." Shotgun sneered. "He's just an innocent man. A father."

"No one is innocent," Shotgun growled. The two Blades with Shotgun looked away from their Leader. They knew exactly what was happening within Shotgun's brain, and trying to interfere was just suicide. "Everyone in this city is either an enabler or a message waiting to happen."

"Please, this isn't me," the voice pleaded. "This isn't who I am."

Shotgun kept his eyes locked on the man in his clutches. He spoke even louder than before, making sure the struggling officer could hear him clearly. "You would never be able to protect your son from the Nitros... or anything that man has released onto this city. Redman created the perfect weapons to fight his war. He claims what he made can never be defeated."

The officer's arms dropped to his sides. His skin was wrapped so tightly around his skeleton that it started to tear like paper.

"This isn't who you *were*," Shotgun whispered to the grating voice within his own head. He grunted and crushed his hand into a fist. The officer's skull shattered like brittle stone, causing his body to drop from Shotgun's grasp. It hit the ground and erupted into dust and fragments of bone. Shotgun looked down at the pile of dust in front of him. A small smirk came across his face. "This is who you are, now."

Tavis wasn't aware of what noises he was making. Gasps and whimpers at the horrors happening in front of him. He was trying to push himself away from the situation, but his body seemed to refuse every command he gave it.

Green light danced out of Shotgun's eyes and folded back into the small gaps on his helmet. "I find it hard to argue with Redman. He knows how to make a weapon. After all..." Shotgun turned his head to stare down at Tavis once again, "he made me."

A second figure stepped up next to Shotgun. "What do

we do with this one?" asked the female voice above Tavis.

There was a long silence as Tavis awaited the answer. He tried to push himself off the ground and barely made it to his hands and knees when Shotgun's voice spoke softly in the air.

"He's no use to us," he solemnly replied.

"When does it end?" the voice within Shotgun asked once again. "When does the killing stop?" Shotgun exhaled through his nose.

"Soon," he replied. "Very soon." Shotgun turned and nodded to female alongside him. "Kill him."

The following scream pierced into the rear of the van, where the prisoner was on the floor, with his hands still cuffed to the bar next to him. His wrists were bloody from the impact, but the restraints were probably the only thing that saved him. He got back to his feet just as the doors at the back of his chamber tore open.

Three figures stood in the opening and stared inward at him. Shotgun motioned his hand forward, ordering the man with him to enter the vehicle. The man leaned down next to the prisoner and grabbed his restraints. With a loud, sheering noise, two metal blades flew from his wrist and sliced clean through the chains. The man then stood up straight and turned his back on the prisoner, slowly exiting the vehicle again.

The prisoner stood up and rubbed his wrists a bit, trying to make the pain go away. He stumbled toward the exit and cautiously put up his hands, preparing for a fight. Outside the van were the charred remains of the police vehicles, with several bodies lying on the ground next to them.

"This the right guy?" the man leaving the van asked.

"Mac Sampson," Shotgun called out.

The prisoner looked up as he stepped completely out of the van and down onto the ground. "Who the hell are you guys?" he asked, still on the defensive.

"I'm the only thing standing between you and decades inside a cell," Shotgun calmly replied. "I know you aren't from around here, but Lattice Light doesn't exactly view crime as passable. They were nearly crime-free before the Blades came into power. A combination of a heavy police force and Redman's grid tracking almost every vehicle made it much more difficult. Its rarity meant punishment for crime became more severe. Now you're looking down the barrel of that inflation."

Mac's hands lowered. "You're here to help me?"

Shotgun smirked under his mask. "Yes, but only if you can help me. See, I hear you had a run-in with the Nitros."

Mac perked up, now completely fixated on what Shotgun was saying. "But you didn't stand a chance against them, did you?"

Mac didn't respond, but Shotgun could see his teeth starting to bare. Shotgun snickered to himself and shook his head. "Well, I'm determined to change that, Mr. Sampson," Shotgun began.

"Quit beating around the bush!" Mac hissed. "I've seen the Nitros and what they can do, even if you haven't. You'd need a really big gun in your hand if you plan on going after them." Shotgun stepped toward Mac and lowered his head.

"Oh, there's no need to be concerned with that," Shotgun reassured. "I have the plans for a weapon that will wipe those Nitros off the map entirely."

Mac's eyes widened as Shotgun piqued his interest. However, his shock quickly transitioned into condescending laughter.

"Right," he mused, "a weapon that can stop a man that can literally make fire. Don't take this the wrong way, freak show, but you don't exactly strike me as someone who could make something like that."

"I assure you, I can. In fact, everything is in place for its construction, apart from one final piece."

"And what exactly is that?" Mac asked.

Shotgun slowly tilted his shoulder back and extended his hand out to Mac. It floated for a moment in the air between them. Mac looked down at the offer and then back up to Shotgun's eyes.

"Well, that's simple, Mr. Sampson," Shotgun began. "It's you."

CHAPTER 15: A BOUNTY HUNTER

"What happened here?" Dante asked in a hushed tone.

The Nitros stepped out of the Gemini and into the scorched remains of the police convoy. The vehicles themselves were nothing more than charred shells casting deep red flames into the air. The black smoke billowing off of them was visible for miles. The pavement was covered in a thick veneer of rainwater and blood, which rolled down the edges of the sidewalks, illuminating brightly when positioned over the lights of the grid. The crimson dripped into various sewer drains and disappeared, like the lives of the officers melting away.

Diego was already kneeling next to the first corpse, checking for any signs of life. Nick simply surveyed the scene and set his eyes on the van embedded into the side of a building.

"This was a massacre," Steven whispered, mainly to

himself. Steven had spent so long trying to convince the other Nitros to use deadly force against Shotgun, that he had forgotten exactly what deadly force looked like. This scene was hard enough to take in, and Steven couldn't even begin to imagine how it would look if he were the one who caused it.

Nick stepped toward the van but stopped when a loud crunching noise echoed out from under his foot. He looked down and lifted his foot into the air, tilting it to examine the bottom of his boot.

A fine gray powder danced off his red padding and floated away into the wind. A large pile of the powder traced a shape on the ground under Nick. He followed the lines as they led to a body.

The body was reaching both its arms out, and its mouth was wide open like it was gasping for air. Its skin was gray and stretched tightly over its skeleton. Its eyes were a dark black, and its teeth had begun to rot. The gray dust led to the body's legs, which were falling apart into nothing. The more Nick stared, the more dust came into view. What seemed like a countless number of bodies were lying in the middle of the road. Almost all of them were either crumbling or already drifting away in the breeze. Memories of the photograph Redman originally showed Nick dropped back into Nick's mind.

Nick had seen this before, and it could only mean one thing.

"Shotgun has been here," he said under his breath.

"The Blades are thorough," Diego stated. He stood up from another corpse with his eyes closed tightly. "They didn't leave anyone alive."

"Why would they?" Nick asked. "They clearly were after whatever was in that van. Chances are they got it. Anyone left alive would just be a liability to them."

"So, is that it?" Dante called out. "Are we at a dead end, here?" Dante sighed. "Excuse the poor choice of words."

Nick looked up into the sky, squinting his eyes at the night. He slowly shook his head, while listening closely to the wind.

"There's no way the Blades would make this much noise and not expect us to show up," Nick determined. "There has to be something else here."

"Good call," a voice added.

The Nitros quickly snapped around and bunched up.

A man stood across the street from them, with his head lowered and his arms folded in front of him. Most of his features were hidden in the shadows of a damaged streetlight, but it was evident that the man was wearing some sort of suit that covered his entire body. It reflected the light of the fire around them and made it seem like the man was made of flames. He was shaking his head and speaking in a very calm manner.

"You just couldn't leave this all alone, could you?" His voice was modulated like it was running through several filters before exiting his helmet.

"Who are you?" Megan demanded.

The man didn't reply and instead raised his head to meet her eyes. His eyes blinked to life. The bright red light of them pierced through the darkness and sent a chilling hush over the Nitros. The streetlight began to flash as it desperately tried to regain functionality. The beams of light revealed that the man was wearing a full silver, metallic suit. The helmet was a bright white and molded into the shape of a skull. Two large devices were strapped to his wrists and stopped halfway up his forearms. He was also wearing a backpack-like device that was blinking with red lights. He uncrossed his arms and dropped them to his sides.

"I'm just a man who was hoping it would never have to come to this," he replied. "You seem like good kids, really, and this is just one of those times that bad things have to happen to good people."

"Is that a threat?" Steven growled.

"No, no. I'm afraid it's worse than that. See, I've never missed a kill. I've never had a target walk away from me, and you certainly aren't going to be the first on that list."

"So, that's who you are," Nick surmised. "You're Shotgun's bounty hunter."

The man held out his arms and nodded his head like he was giving a slight bow.

"You can call me, Slicer," he introduced.

Nick clenched his hands into fists as the other four

Nitros stepped into line with him.

"How do you fit into all this, Slicer?" he asked. "What do you get when Shotgun brings down this city?"

Slicer widened his stance and hunched downward a bit. "The only thing that matters," he replied. "Money."

"You're willing to let Shotgun get away with creating a Nitro?" Diego questioned, shocked by the answer. "Hundreds, maybe thousands, of people will die! You're prepared to let that happen for money?"

"It's a bit more complicated than that," Slicer began, "but to put it simply… yes."

"We beat Hard-Drive, you know," Dante stated, "and now there's all five of us, against one of you. Are you sure you want to do this?"

Slicer brought his fists in toward his chest for a moment before throwing them back out to his sides. As they snapped to a stop, two sets of twin blades fired out of each wrist and extended two feet beyond his hands. The ends of them glistened from the flames. Slicer tilted them down and dragged them forward, letting them cut into the asphalt below. Sparks flew in all directions, and the noise was nearly unbearable. He lifted his arms back into position and rolled out his shoulders.

"Oh, I'm sure," he snickered. "Five on one sounds pretty good to me. Wouldn't want an unfair fight, now would we?" Slicer dug his back foot into the ground. The lights on his backpack began to glow even brighter, and two small ports on the bottom of the device sparked to life. Fire rocketed out of the bottom of the jetpack and launched Slicer forward. He wound up a strike at Nick and took a swing.

Dante quickly jumped in front of his cousin and crossed his arms in front of his head. Ice sprang out of his hands and surrounded his forearms. Slicer's blades collided with the ice and cut a massive shard away.

Slicer continued on his path and flipped over Dante and Nick, landing expertly behind them. He threw his boot forward, slamming it into Nick's back and making him crash into his cousin, knocking them both to the ground.

As Slicer went to take another step forward, Megan's fist smashed into the side of his helmet. Slicer stumbled back but kept enough awareness to block the next swing. He threw Megan's arm away and slashed again. Megan spun away from Slicer and fell to her knees. A large slice across her shoulder began leaking blood onto the pavement.

Slicer ran toward her and hiked his fists into the air. Before landing, Megan turned away from the ground and threw her hands forward, forcing a small purple orb into Slicer's chest. A blinding light engulfed the area before burying Slicer and Megan in a torrent of smoke.

Slicer careened away from the impact. His back hit the brick wall of a building, shattering the stone and dropping pebbles to the ground. Almost instantly, Slicer gripped his fingers into the brick and pushed himself off the wall. He shook off the impact and brushed some dust off his suit. Some of the fabric under his armor was torn and shredded. The fingers of his right hand were now visible and scratched up.

Before he could fully recover, his helmet began to beep and flash. Red lights illuminated at the edges of his vision, alerting him of incoming danger. Slicer quickly looked to the side.

Two pillars of rock sprouted from the ground and positioned themselves to close in on Slicer. Diego's hands were out in Slicer's direction. He threw his arms together, causing the rock slabs to rip from the street and continue on their colliding path.

Slicer lifted his gauntlet and hit several buttons below his hand. His entire frame blinked out of existence a few times before he faded away into nothing. The rocks slammed into each other, shattering into debris and spreading across the road.

"What the...?" Nick whispered. He thought he had seen everything up to this point. Men turn into monsters, robotic suits, gauntlets that fire light, and a human-sized bacteria, and now here he was, faced once again with something new. Nick was turning his head in every direction, hoping he might have just temporarily lost track of Slicer. However, no sign of the bounty hunter ever came into view.

"He's gone invisible!" Megan yelled from the street. Blood was still trickling through her fingers as she fought her way back to her feet. "He must have some kind of cloaking device."

The Nitros pushed their backs together, trying their best to pinpoint his location. Diego squinted as a small glint cause his attention. He stared across the street, waiting to see if the anomaly would return.

"Guys," he started, in a whisper, "I think I saw..." Diego's head ripped to the side as an invisible force rammed into his cheek. He fell to his knees. A series of coughs from him threw splatters of blood onto the pavement.

Dante knelt down next to Diego. "Are you okay?" he asked. A noise rang out down the street, making Dante snap his head up in attention. He saw ripples fading away in a small puddle like something had just charged through it. Dante raised an eyebrow while the ripples faded away. He jumped back up and put out his hands.

"Everyone bundle up!" he shouted. He moved his hands apart, causing ice to spring out from underneath him and slide across the pavement. It quickly snaked around everyone's feet and covered a large area around them. Puddles on the street instantly froze into a fine sheet. Frost crawled up the light-posts and buildings, stopping a few feet off the ground. The ice extended in an even layer until it encountered any disturbances. Eventually, two shapes became visible in the smooth ice.

"There!" Steven called out. He moved his hands in circles, forming a portal next to him and one next to the spot Dante determined.

Slicer blinked back into reality and pointed his fist at the growing shadows next to him. He fired a glowing red device into the portal. Within a second it burst out of the darkness next to Steven and hit him in the chest. The device ripped Steven off his feet while extending into a glowing red net. The net pierced into the wall behind Steven, holding him firmly within its grasp. Electricity began pulsing through the fibers of the net, shocking Steven to his core.

"Redman!" Nick yelled through his communicator. "We need help, now! What can you tell me about this guy?!"

"Nothing," Redman begrudgingly reported. "I have no idea who he is. You have a scanner in your belt. If you can manage to get any sort of DNA or identify mark logged in it, maybe I can find a match."

Nick searched through the different pockets on his belt, eventually landing on a square device with a large blue screen. A steady pulsing light was its only feature. Nick glanced back up at Slicer as he jumped back into battle with Dante. He could see the tears in Slicer's clothing, including his glove.

"How about a fingerprint?" Nick asked.

Redman was silent, but Nick could almost hear the wheels in his head turning.

"That could be all we need," Redman finally replied.

Nick nodded to himself.

Dante extended his ice gauntlet into a sword and began swinging at Slicer. It clashed off his blades, splitting off pieces of ice every time. Dante went for another slash, but Slicer managed to stop his attack against the back of his blades. He pushed Dante away, making him spin around and face his back to the bounty hunter. Slicer took another swing, cutting a deep gash into Dante's back. Dante fell forward to his knees and screamed in agony. He dug his fingers into the pavement in an attempt to fight the pain.

Nick jumped in over his cousin and threw a punch into Slicer's chest. Slicer stumbled back and put up his hands.

"Atomic!" Nick yelled, without taking his eyes off Slicer. "Help the others! I'll deal with this guy."

Slicer chuckled to himself and tilted his head. "You think that's a fight you can win?" he queried.

Nick smirked and motioned his head toward Slicer's stomach. "Looks like you have a hole in your suit, there."

Slicer glanced down. The missing pieces of his suit immediately became the center of his attention.

Nick stepped forward and pushed out his hands. A cone of fire grew in front of him and crawled its way around Slicer. The exposed parts of Slicer's skin had no protection from the inferno as it grew in intensity.

Slicer jumped from the flames and rolled across the ground. His blades retreated into his gauntlets with a loud swish. Slicer held a hand against his stomach in an attempt to cool the singed flesh.

Nick threw his hands apart, dissipating the flames. He ran for the fallen enemy and grabbed his arm. Slicer growled and quickly pushed himself to his feet. He wrestled against Nick as the red Nitro wrapped his entire body around Slicer's forearm. He struggled to move Slicer's hand down onto the device and hold it there long enough to help. Slicer's bare finger pressed onto the screen, which lit up brighter upon contact. Nick managed to hold it there for a few seconds before the sound of Slicer's blades extending again pierced the air.

Nick pushed away from Slicer, but couldn't dodge the first attack. Slicer's blades ripped across Nick's arm, leaving a long cut down his shoulder. Nick fell to the ground and scrambled to roll onto his back. He had the information he needed, but now he wasn't sure if he had enough time to use it. Slicer was ready to end this and Nick wasn't prepared to stop him.

Slicer was menacingly moving forward. Every attempt at standing was met with Slicer's boot as he kicked Nick back to the ground. Slicer slammed his boot into Nick's shoulder, making him flip onto his stomach. Before he could correct himself, Slicer planted his foot down on Nick's back and held him to the ground.

Slicer's blades scraped across the concrete. Nick could feel the sparks dance against the back of his neck. He was set up for an execution.

"Nicole Hollands!" Redman screamed into the mic.

"What?" Nick grunted back. He tried pushing himself up but to no avail.

"Just say it!" Redman insisted.

"You guys messed with the wrong group," Slicer moaned. "I'll do you a favor, though. I'll make this one quick." Slicer lifted his arm into the air. His blades glistened in the light, now sporting a thin veneer of blood.

"Nicole Hollands!" Nick yelled.

Slicer's swing was interrupted by the words. His arm hung in the air. It shook in anticipation, but couldn't bring itself to move another inch. It was like his body refused to accept the commands from his brain.

Redman continued to speak into Nick's ear on the assumption his original advice has worked.

"What did you just…" Slicer began but was quickly cut off.

"Nicole Hollands. That's why you do what you do," Nick said quietly. His face was still pressed against the pavement, and a pool of blood was now forming under his shoulder.

Slicer growled. His blades retracted into his forearm with a piercing, scraping sound. "Shut up!" he yelled. He pulled his foot off of Nick and knelt down next to him. He rolled Nick over onto his back and grabbed his lapels, pulling him in. Slicer's face was only inches from Nick's.

"You'd better shut your mouth right now!" Slicer shouted. "Don't talk about what you don't understand!"

"This isn't the only way to get the money to save her, Jed," Nick reasoned. "We can help you. We can help her."

"You have no idea what I've done for her!" he yelled, even louder. He began to shake Nick as he spoke. "The things I've sacrificed for her!"

Slicer stood up, taking Nick with him. With one big motion, Slicer ripped himself around and threw Nick into a brick wall. Nick cracked off the rock and crashed down onto the sidewalk with a heavy thud.

"The blood I've spilled!" Slicer continued. "The lives I've taken! It was all for her!"

Nick gasped for air. He pushed himself back to his hands and knees, still trying to talk Slicer down.

"I know," Nick tried. "I know she's sick. I know you think this is your only option."

Slicer's breath was audible through his helmet. Nick swore he could hear Slicer's heartbeat getting faster. The tension between them could only end in one of two ways. Nick was praying it was the one that kept him alive.

"What happens once you have enough money?" Nick asked. "Do you seriously think Shotgun will just let you walk out of this?"

"I have my plans, kid," Slicer responded, quieter than

before. "Shotgun gets his city, and I get my baby girl the help she deserves."

"No, you don't."

Slicer lowered his head but kept his eyes locked on Nick.

Nick slowly rose to his feet. His movements were all slow and deliberate in an attempt to not agitate Slicer. "Shotgun knows your weakness. He knows by using her, he can get you back whenever he wants."

Slicer finally looked away from Nick. He stared off into the distance. Without being able to see his expression, it was impossible for Nick to tell what he was thinking. Slicer seemed so much less like a monster. Despite the things he had done, Nick saw him as just another person. A father who made all the wrong decisions for all the right reasons.

Slicer helmet scanned the area, pinging every time it locked onto a new target. It highlighted each body on the ground. His helmet would scan them for a moment, and then spell out a cold word next to them. DECEASED. However, before turning back to Nick, a standing figure caught Slicer's attention.

He focused on her. Even though he knew she wasn't there, her presence alone made Slicer's blood run cold. He could see his daughter standing in the blood. Nine years old. Her blonde hair was tied back, and her face was dotted with freckles. She didn't look happy or relieved to see her father. Instead, she looked scared. Her eyes never left his mask. Her image started to fade away as her eyes left her father. Eventually, Slicer found himself staring at an empty stretch of pavement.

"Nicole," he spoke quietly.

"What would she think, Jed?" Nick asked, solemnly.

Slicer looked down at his hand. Trickles of blood traced eerily familiar lines down his glove. He slowly closed his hand into a fist. The blood forced its way out through every single crack in his fingers. The harder he tried, the less blood he was able to hide.

"What do I do, then?" he questioned, still not returning his gaze to Nick. Nick looked around.

Diego had released Steven from the net. Dante and Megan were barely on their feet, but watching the confrontation between Nick and Slicer from afar. They seemed ready to jump in if things were to turn bad.

"You help us take Shotgun down," Nick replied. "That's the only way you'll ever be done with him."

Slicer squinted his eyes, weighing his options carefully.

"Help you?" he repeated. Slicer turned back to Nick and tilted his head. "And what if I refuse?"

Slicer could feel his feet getting colder. Ice crawled up from the ground and surrounded his lower half. He turned his head to see the other four Nitros in various states of getting back to their feet. As they collected themselves their eyes never left the bounty hunter.

Slicer chuckled. "Fair enough." He looked back at Nick

and nodded. "I think we can make a deal."

CHAPTER 16: AN INSIDE JOB

"So, that's it then," Slicer finished. "I help you now, leave with my daughter, and you," Slicer pointed his finger at Nick, "never hear from me again."

"Only if you lead us to Shotgun," Nick snapped. "You have a lot of blood on your hands, Hollands. I want you to know, we're not letting you run away with that. You can stay with your daughter, but you're on extremely thin ice. One wrong move, and we won't hesitate to track you down and lock you away from her for good."

Slicer snickered to himself as he folded his arms.

"You can hunt me for the rest of your life," he said, grimly. "I can promise, you'll never find me." He stepped closer to Nick.

Nick returned the gesture, without a second of hesitation. The two stood face-to-face for a moment.

"Do you think I'm scared?" Nick asked. Another

chuckled slid through Slicer's teeth.

"Of me?" he returned. "No. I *know* you're scared of me. Let's not forget, the only reason you're still alive is the fact that I allowed it." Slicer lifted his hand into the air between the two. He held up one finger and shook it gently. "But I've seen the look on your face before. You're scared of something else, too. Scared you're up against something stronger and more dangerous than you are. I can tell. I've been there." Slicer was the first to break the eye contact and shot a glance to Steven.

"You," Slicer called out.

Steven raised an eyebrow in anticipation.

"His name is Explosion," Nick hissed.

"Sure it is," Slicer laughed as he returned his eyes to Nick, "Nicholas."

Nick took a deep breath and unclenched his fists. Slicer was giving a grim reminder of how much the Blades knew about the Nitros. Nick wasn't going to ignore that.

"Now, Explosion," Slicer began again. "You're the key to finding Shotgun. Fact is, he has a base somewhere in Lattice Light, and there are only two people on this planet that know where."

"You and him, right?" Megan interrupted.

Slicer closed his eyes and shook his head slightly.

"No such luck. Shotgun rarely dealt with me in person. When he did, it was in a predetermined location of his preference. Never his own base. That's where he's building his weapon. Chances are... that's where he is right now."

This was just another example of how powerful the Blades had become over the years. They had their own base, and after seeing their arena buried underneath the city, Nick was certain this base could be hidden anywhere. However, through all of the pessimism and despair, there was a glimmer of hope. It finally seemed like the Nitros had Shotgun on the ropes. Nick was all to eager to finally come off the defensive and be the ones to attack.

"Well, then we need to get there," Diego stated. "We have to stop Shotgun from completing Project Uranium. The last thing we need in our way of taking down the Blades is another Nitro."

"We've got time, dude," Dante jumped in. "A Nitro takes years to cook. Shotgun just got the plans for Uranium recently. It's gonna be a long time before that new Nitro is a delicious golden brown. We just have to get to him before that."

"Not necessarily," Slicer interrupted. He lifted his gauntlet to his face. Slicer began typing on small buttons, which emitting a tiny beep with every press. Information displayed on a screen on Slicer's gauntlet. The bright red words reflected off his mask and bathed the area in a faint red glow. "I've been keeping tabs on Shotgun's operations as best I could. Between his previous thefts, and the successful acquisition of the Matter Converter, he has a massive stockpile of Otrolium at his disposal."

"Redman told us he'd need a lot," Nick admitted. "It's not shocking that he's been saving it up for this project of his."

"That's just the thing," Slicer interjected. "I've seen the documents for Project Nitro, and I know how much Otrolium is needed to make one. My calculations are showing Shotgun could have two, maybe three times that amount ready to administer into his test subject. Kristen was in charge of modifying the Project Nitro equipment so it could withstand the heavier doses."

Nick looked at the ground. His thoughts were running marathons, trying to come to a reasonable conclusion. He wanted to find a justification for all of the Otrolium Shotgun planned on using. How could he think anything would happen other than Mac's death. Before Nick could reach a final thought, Megan decided to break the silence.

"Why would he increase the Otrolium dosage in Uranium?" she asked. "He knows how dangerous that stuff can be. Better than anyone, really."

"Because Otrolium is the binding agent," Nick answered, without looking up from the ground. He stiffened his lip and sighed. "That's what Redman told us. Nitros take so long to create because the binding agent needs time to adhere the enhancers to our DNA. Shotgun isn't willing to wait that long. He knows we're here, and he knows he has limited time."

"Increase the amount of Otrolium," Diego took over, realizing where Nick's statement was heading, "decrease the amount of time it takes to bind."

Nick looked back up. He and Diego stared at one another for a few moments.

Diego nodded and turned to Slicer. "He's trying to churn out a Nitro as fast as he can," Diego finished.

"And I believe he has the resources to do it," Slicer finished. "I don't know how much acceleration the boosted Otrolium will cause, but that's what makes this situation so dangerous. Uranium could already be here for all I know."

"So, he already has a test subject?" Nick asked.

Slicer nodded. He turned his head to examine the remains of the police convoy, still burning behind him. He remained silent as he absorbed the sight. The remains of the fallen officers were almost completely gone at this point. Bits of them were blowing away with even the slightest breeze.

Nick took a step forward, so he was standing shoulder to shoulder with Slicer. He spoke quietly, but firmly, and without ever turning to face Slicer.

"Those officers probably had families, you know," Nick stated. "Children... just like you."

Slicer didn't need to acknowledge Nick's words. His silence was a bigger statement than anything that could have left his mouth. Without looking away from the scene before him, Slicer carefully reached a hand up to his head. He pressed a series of small buttons on the back of his helmet. A hissing sound was followed shortly by Slicer's mask lifting from his face and folding back over his head.

His face was lined with tiny scars from past fights. His short blonde hair was cut neatly and showed no signs of ever being stuffed into a helmet. His eyes were a light green and sported an unmistakable veneer of sadness and regret.

Slicer's calm, unmodulated voice finally broke the tense silence.

"I didn't personally kill any of them," he reasoned. It wasn't like he was arguing with Nick. It seemed more like he was assuring himself.

"You also didn't stop the ones who did," Nick argued. "If that were me, I wouldn't be able to call myself 'innocent.'"

Slicer took a deep breath. He shifted his eyes back to Nick, but the Nitro seemed to be refusing to return the gesture.

"You're right," he whispered.

Nick finally turned to him.

"You're right, Nick. I'm not innocent." Slicer looked up at the sky like he was deciding whether or not he had a place there. "To be honest, that isn't what matters. What matters to me is my daughter. She's the innocent one. I'm not helping you with the expectation that you're going to forgive what I've done. I'm doing it, so my daughter will have a fighting chance."

"If you want to help us," Nick began, "then do it. Tell us what you know."

Slicer lowered his eyes again, pulling them away from the stars.

"A prisoner," he called out, louder than before, "being transferred to a maximum security facility outside of town. That's what was in this convoy. Shotgun plans on using him for his project. The guy's name is Mac Sampson."

The name instantly pulled Nick's mind back to the liquor store robbery. Mac waving a gun through the air, threatening innocent lives, and standing up to a Nitro. The look in Mac's eyes as the police locked him in the cruiser. His dead stare that tore right through Nick.

"Sampson… but…" Nick couldn't find the right words, "why would he…?"

"Shotgun is completely insane!" Megan yelled. "Mac Sampson is a criminal. Who knows what he's capable of? Giving him that kind of power could end up killing people. There's no way Shotgun could ever control him."

"Then we're wasting time standing here," Steven exclaimed. "Hollands, you said I was the key to getting to Shotgun. Spill it."

Slicer darted his eyes to Steven after his outburst. He snickered to himself, shaking his head slightly while he did.

"Well, if you're so eager," he said, mockingly. "As I said, there's only one person who knows the location of

Shotgun's base other than himself. Miranda Zealo. She's his second in command. Been with Shotgun since his days in the R.A.N.T."

"Her brother already spilled the beans on her," Nick snapped, lifting his arm into the air. "He said no one's seen her in years."

"That's because she floats around Shotgun most of the time," Slicer began. "I don't know her exact location, but Explosion's powers could help you find her."

"Go on," Steven urged.

"Miranda would do anything to please Shotgun. It's like she was addicted to the guy after the first time she met him. Shortly after scientists began to understand and experiment with the properties of the Void, Shotgun knew he had to tap into that power. He kidnapped some of the city's leading scientists in the hopes they could somehow help him harness the Void's power. They produced a serum that would link the test subject's brain directly to the Void, or so they hoped. Shotgun deemed the experiment too risky to undertake himself, but the bastard had no problem volunteering Miranda for it. Like the blind believer he trained her to be, she accepted."

"I'm guessing the serum worked?" Dante asked. "Seems like it'd be really boring to end that story with 'and nothing happened. The end.'"

"They call her the Shadow, nowadays," Slicer finished. "Her link to the Void is extremely similar to Explosion's."

"So, how do you expect me to find her?" Steven questioned. "The Void is massive. The size of our entire universe, in fact. Finding her in there is no different than finding her in the overworld."

"Possibly," Slicer agreed, "but what I understand, after hearing her drone on about it, is that disturbances in the Void are very easy to detect once you're inside. She uses the Void like a dumpsite. If there's something she doesn't want in our world, she throws it into that one. We're talking machinery, scrap... even humans." A tense silence hovered over the group. "Yeah, I know. She's a menace. Shotgun knows too much about me and my family. If I tried to stop her, there's no way I'd be able to protect Nicole. That's why I'm hoping Explosion will be able to enter the Void and see where she's set up this 'dumpsite.' It's going to get you to her, which will get you to Shotgun."

Steven never took his eyes off Slicer. Slicer nodded to the black Nitro. He started to walk, passing close by Nick. His mask flipped back over his head and fastened tightly into place.

"Where are *you* going?" Nick snapped. Slicer took a few more steps past him before turning his head back over his shoulder.

"I'm getting that head start you promised," he responded with his modulated voice. "There's nothing else I can give you. Now my only job is to get my daughter as far away from this place as possible. She doesn't know the danger she's been in this entire time. She doesn't just deserve to be free from it, but she deserves to never know it existed in the first place." Slicer's jetpack sparked to life. The thrusters powered up and started to glow.

"Jed!" Nick shouted before Slicer could take off. "You know we can't let you leave with that suit."

Slicer let out a few small laughs. He lifted his hand out to the side and spun his finger around.

"You know, Nuclear," he started. "I've been over those Nitro documents more times than I can count." Slicer turned around, fully facing Nick one last time. "But nothing listed in there made me believe you could take my suit if you tried."

Slicer's jetpack spun up and fired two bright columns of fire into the ground. Nick had to take a step back and shield his face. The bounty hunter shot into the air, and within a second was no more than a small white dot buried in an endless sea of stars. A thin line of white smoke traced his path through the sky.

Nick slowly lowered his arm and stared upward. He sighed.

"Well," Dante began, cutting into the silence, "he's got a point."

Nick flashed a glance over to his cousin, who was still staring at the stars.

Dante looked back down and shrugged. "I mean… I can't do that."

CHAPTER 17: AN INFILRATION

Steven sucked in air through his nose before slowly exhaling out through his mouth. Steven was about to spend more time in the Void than ever before. Redman warned him about the dangers and uncertainties of doing the exact thing he was gearing up to do. His hands lifted into the air, hanging motionless in front of him. One at a time, they began moving in circles.

A small, black hole formed in front of his chest. Darkness leaked out into the air from the opening. It crawled into existence and started to grow larger. It was an eerie feeling for Steven. Nothing was more uncertain to him than forming a portal, without predetermining an exit. Even with his powers, the Void was a dangerous place. Simply having its presence around you was like being watched by a thousand eyes. The weight and uncertainty. The portal grew to six feet in diameter before stopping.

The edges were wisps of black that were flowing in an imaginary breeze. The center was nothing but darkness and mystery.

Steven turned around to face Nick.

"I don't have an extremely wide radius of awareness in there," he stated. "If I don't sense something immediately, I'll have to keep moving until I do." Steven slowly returned his gaze to his portal. "No matter how far away that might be."

"Radio us when you come out the other side," Nick instructed. "Redman can't track your position while you're in the Void, but as soon as you step back out, he should be able to pinpoint your location."

Steven nodded and reached toward the portal. His hand dipped into the blackness like a thickened water. Nick watched Steven's hand vanish. Nick sighed and looked at the floor.

"Look," Nick began. "We haven't always seen eye-to-eye, but you're my teammate, Steven. We've both been through a lot, and we need to be in this together to the end. I need you to think this through and play it safe."

"We just finished fighting a mechanized bounty hunter," Steven stated. "I think 'playing it safe' was out the window a long time ago." Steven looked at Nick. "I'm going to get us to Shotgun's base, and we're going to end this… together."

The ripples from Steven's touch flowed toward the

edge of his portal. Each time one of them reached it, the wisps escaping from the edges would grow longer and become slightly more erratic.

"Steven," Megan called out.

Steven didn't look but perked up his head in acknowledgment.

"Redman warned us about the Void," she continued. "Remember? He said even you couldn't stay in there for a long time." A long silence followed. It was a combination of everyone knowing the danger, but also knowing how necessary it was to brave it. "All I'm saying is… be careful."

Steven reached further into the portal and took one last breath of fresh air. His brain forced his body to take that final step forward. Steven disappeared into the darkness. The portal began to swirl with brilliant flashes of deep purple and blue, before shrinking and finally fading away. Steven glanced behind him just in time to see the portal officially close.

"Okay," Steven quietly spoke to himself. "Disturbances are easy to detect. That's what Slicer said."

He began walking forward. Each step resonated out across the darkness like ripples on the surface of water. He could still see the outlines of the other Nitros, talking to each other and pointing toward where the portal used to be.

Steven thought deeply about the words both Nick and Megan said to him before he entered the Void. His brother was the only person who ever really showed Steven any concern or affection. He wasn't used to the idea of other people being concerned about his wellbeing. If Steven had these new teammates in his corner, maybe they were right. Maybe Shotgun didn't have to die for everything to be okay again. Maybe Steven's life could be fixed because of his new friends.

Steven returned to the mission at hand, finally turning away from the other Nitros. Nothing in the Void made a sound. It was the loudest silence he could ever imagine.

Steven scanned the area around him, looking for anything that seemed different. It was just an endless maze of dark outlines fading in and out of existence. Buildings that would appear only when Steven looked directly at them. As soon as he moved his eyes, they would drift back into nothingness. The edges of his view seemed to be dotted with distant stars that were ever changing. He didn't know exactly what he was looking for. As far as he could guess, when he saw it, he would know.

Steven continued to turn and found himself struck when a massive object appeared just in front of his face. He almost tripped over himself as he frantically stepped away.

"What the hell?!" he yelled. The police cruiser spun in the air, floating for eternity. Two figures were hanging out of the vehicle's windows, desperately trying to escape. Smashed pieces of the car floated in the air next to it, like it was in a frozen state of crashing.

"Must be from the convoy," Steven reasoned as he caught his breath and tried to slow his heart. He approached the car, examining the men inside. Their skin had faded to a purple color, with lines of black constantly dripping down every contour like ink. Their eyes and the inside of their mouths were an empty black. It was if they were hollow, or filled with nothing but the Void itself.

Steven grimaced and looked away. He continued to scan across the city. The police cruiser stuck out like a sore thumb in the darkness. Steven was hopeful something else would do the same. Something that would lead him to wherever Miranda had set up her dumping ground.

Then, through the edges and angles of the city, he could see something floating in the distance. It turned slowly through the air, floating without a purpose or destination.

Steven picked up his pace and started running toward the object. He was running through buildings, sometimes even through the people standing inside. The object Steven was seeing never seemed to get any closer. It was still spinning, helpless and lonely.

Suddenly, a small tingle crawled its way up Steven's hand. He didn't stop running, but looked down, expecting to see something attached to his arm. There was nothing. He grabbed the top of his glove and rolled it up. Everything seemed fine for a few seconds. Then Steven could make out the smallest traces of black lines swirling over his skin. The lines curled around his arm and darted in and out of his pores. Breathing was getting more difficult as the effects of the Void began to take their toll on his body. His skin was turning more and more gray by the second and the black lines were becoming more and bolder.

Steven shook away the thoughts. He rolled his glove back down and looked back toward his target. As soon as his eyes centered, he saw nothing. The object was gone.

Steven skidded to a stop, sending a wake out in front of him across the Void. His chest was pumping in and out. However, the more Steven tried to catch his breath, the thinner the air around him seemed to get. He knew he had been in the Void too long, and whatever he had seen was gone.

Steven lifted his hand and tensed his fingers. Slowly, but surely, a portal started to form. The Void began to bleed into the edges of his vision. Steven closed his eyes, trying to get the blackness to go away. Once he opened them again, he found himself staring deep into two black, soulless eyes.

Steven snapped his hand back as the corpse floated down in front of him. Its mouth was locked open like it was screaming, but again, inside was nothing but darkness. Its skin was that sickening purple color and was beginning to dry up and flake apart. Specks of skin that had fallen off were tumbling in the air around it.

Steven slowly lifted his head to examine the entire body. However, one object dancing in the air in front of him had become many. A sight he was dreading had faded into view.

"My... God..." he muttered with whatever breath he had left. Dancing in the air above him were nearly twenty corpses. All of them were as horrifically decomposed as the one he had seen before. Some were so old that they were simply black skeletons that were also beginning to deteriorate. They were all moving in a tornado formation over his head, amidst scraps of metal and broken machinery. The corpses were all in different states of fear or torment. Every one of them was screaming, and some were even reaching out like they were desperate for someone to save them.

Steven fought against a sudden churning in his stomach. He closed his eyes and turned his head away from the horrible scene. All Steven wanted to do was leave. He wanted to get out of the Void and convince himself what he was seeing wasn't real. He lifted his hand once again and moved it in small circles.

Suddenly, a pounding sensation started in his head. It felt like a vice was starting to clamp down on his temples. Steven's eyes shot open as the same pressure collapsed in on his chest. He gasped and coughed. With each cough, more and more black fog erupted from his mouth and spread out into the Void, like Steven was feeding it.

Steven had spent too long within the Void's boundaries. He continued to try and move his hand, but his portal sputtered and blinked in and out of reality. He could barely focus. His vision started to blacken, and his knees gave out. His brain started jumping to the worst scenarios. When was the time limit? Could he even still escape? He tried harder and harder to focus and form a way out. The portal in front of him finally opened. Steven crawled on his hands and knees toward the swirling darkness. He reached for the event horizon and made one last push forward.

Steven fell out of the portal and collapsed onto a metal floor. He gasped for air, filling his lungs with fresh oxygen and expelling more blackness out into the room. His vision slowly returned as he fought to stay conscious. Steven rolled his head to the side, taking in whatever he could see.

He was in a small storage room. The floor, ceiling, and every wall were made of rusted, old metal. Wooden crates lined the walls. Water dripped from above and formed a small puddle on the ground next to Steven.

He slowly reached his hand up to the communicator on his ear and spoke in a rasped, almost inaudible voice. The noises that came out of his mouth could hardly be called words.

"Nuclear," he attempted. There was a silence on the communicator. Steven closed his eyes, trying to quell the spinning in his brain. B… Bruno? Diego? Someone?" Still, there was nothing. Steven painfully rolled his way onto his stomach and pushed himself up onto his hands and knees. He crawled to one of the crates and used it to brace himself. He clawed his way to his feet but didn't dare let go of the crate. Again he brought his finger to his ear.

"Can anyone hear me?" he tried. "Anyone?" After a few more seconds, the sound of voices tore their way through the static. He was desperate for any response. He didn't want to be alone anymore. He felt real fear for the first time since becoming a Nitro.

"Steven?!" Nick shouted. "Steven is that you?!"

Steven coughed again. His knees were still shaking as they struggled to support his entire weight.

"I'm out of the Void," he reported. "I'm in some sort of storage facility. Not exactly sure where, yet."

"Are you okay, dude?" Dante asked. "You've been in there for like… an hour."

Steven's eyes widened.

"What the hell are you talking about?" he asked. "I was only in there for a few minutes."

"Steven, we didn't know where you were," Megan jumped in. "We were starting to fear the worst."

Steven looked back at his portal as it faded out of existence. He took some deep breaths and shook his head. He knew that no matter what, he couldn't let the others know just how scared he was. He collected himself and spoke in a low tone.

"Whatever," he muttered. "I'm fine. Just tell Redman to

hurry up on tracking my location. The sooner you guys get here, the better. I saw some real bad stuff in the Void outside of this place. Miranda must be close by."

"Roger that," Nick spoke. "We'll be there as quickly as we can. Just hold tight."

Steven glanced up from his crate. His eyes locked on something across the room. He stared at it, choosing his next move very carefully.

"Easier said than done, chief," Steven grumbled. After a moment's silence, Nick responded.

"Why?" Nick asked.

Steven pushed himself away from the crate and balled his hands into fists. His legs were shaky, but he did his best to stand tall.

Steven replied firmly and deliberately. "She's here."

CHAPTER 18: A DARKNESS

The figure standing in the doorway of the room slowly stepped down onto the metal floor. She was wearing an armored, black suit that left her arms, legs, and some of her torso exposed. The skin that was showing bore the unmistakable signs of too much time in the Void. Black stains dripped down her skin and traced its way along her veins. She had a mask covering her face. It hid every feature except her eyes. They were sunken into her head, with countless wrinkles wrapping around them. Her pupils looked like they were bleeding out into the white. She had her stare locked on Steven and carefully made her way forward.

"Miranda Zealo, I presume," Steven muttered. Steven wasn't exactly sure what to expect with Miranda, but at the very least he had a good idea of her abilities. He was going into this confrontation knowing more than he did about

Slicer or Shotgun.

Miranda tilted her head. She came to a stop across the room from Steven. Like an animal stalking its prey, she slowly began to pace back and forth, turning her head while she did so her eyes remained on Steven's.

"You shouldn't be here," she said, calmly. "How did you find this place?"

Steven rolled out his shoulders. He slid his foot back and put his fists up.

"I've seen what you've done in the Void, Shadow" Steven announced, ignoring her question. "How could you send all those people to their deaths in there?!"

Shadow's eyes never changed. It was like she was incapable of showing any emotion.

"They had all seen too much," she replied. "They all ended up in a place they should have never been." A light humming filled the room around them.

Steven looked over her shoulder to see a giant portal forming in the air behind him.

"Just like you," Shadow hissed. In an instant, she leaped forward and rammed her boot into Steven's chest. He flew off his footing and disappeared into the portal. The blackness spiraled and collapsed in on itself. Shadow stood in the stillness of the room, staring at her work. However, after another moment, a second portal formed behind her.

Shadow snapped around just as Steven rocketed out of the portal and rammed his knee into her chest. Shadow fell to her back and rolled onto her feet. She was on one knee, with one hand planted firmly on the ground. She slowly looked up, meeting Steven's eyes.

Steven put his finger back to his ear.

"Shadow's here," he announced. "There's no way I'm letting her get out of here."

"Wait for us, Explosion!" Nick ordered. "Get away from her and hide out until we arrive. We're still getting a lock on your position, and we'll get there as soon as possible. Remember, never engage someone like her alone."

"She has the same powers that I do," Steven continued, without acknowledging Nick's request. "I can take her. She's not anything new."

Shadow slightly widened her stance and threw her hands out to the sides. The floor between Steven and Shadow began to shake and spin. Twelve small black portals swirled to life across the metal ground. One at a time they blinked into existence. The portals opened and immediately started to bubble like boiling water. The portals bowed outward before exploding up in a series of black tentacle-like structures. They angled themselves in the air and pointed at Steven. They seemed to be made of the Void itself. The ends were sharpened, and their mass was made of a swirling torrent of black and purple, with an infinite amount of stars dotting the surface.

"Uh oh," Steven muttered.

"Something new?" Dante asked over the communicator.

"Something new," Steven confirmed. Steven didn't know what to expect from this new attack, but he knew it couldn't be good.

Shadow pushed her hands forward, commanding the army of black tendrils. They shot toward Steven with deadly intent.

Steven opened his palms, creating a portal on the wall behind him. He kicked off his footing and launched back into the portal. It sealed closed just as the tendrils hit the wall and horrifically mangled the metal that comprised it. Another portal opened on the ceiling. Steven dropped through, safe from the initial attack. He dropped to one knee and looked backed over his shoulder at the carnage he just avoided.

He turned back to Shadow and leaped off his back foot. An overhead chop was blocked by Shadow's forearm. She met Steven strike-for-strike. Each swing was instantly blocked and thrown away. Steven quickly pointed his hand downward, forming a small portal under Shadow's foot. She stumbled to catch herself, giving Steven an opportunity to land a solid strike across her mask.

Shadow spun away from the hit and dropped to her knee. Bits of her mask fell to the floor like dust. She lifted her hands and forced them together. Two small portals opened on the walls next to her. They fired out small black projectiles that attached themselves to her hands. The darkness covered her glove and turned into gauntlets made of pure darkness. She swung her hand back around and rammed it into Steven's chest.

He careened across the room and smashed through one of the crates, reducing it to splinters and shattered boards. Steven began to push himself up. He spat onto the floor and sucked in some air.

"What the hell is that?" he groaned. "What are you doing?"

Shadow slowly made her way across the room. She was moving her shoulders back and forth like a snake as she approached, looking down at Steven.

"So, you figured out how to enter the Void?" she asked. She lifted her hands into the air. A swirl of darkness formed on the ceiling over Steven. The edges leaked onto the metal and the Void began to crawl out of it. "But it looks like you never learned how to bring the Void... to us."

Shadow ripped her hands downward. The Void came flooding out of the portal and dropped on top of Steven. The massive pillar of darkness hit the floor, crushing everything in its way. The remains of the crate were eviscerated.

Shadow lowered her chin. She stared at the destruction without so much as a blink. She slowly moved her hand back up. The pillar raised off the ground to reveal...

nothing. She darted her eyes around, looking for signs of Steven.

Before she could prepare for the inevitable assault, Steven came flying out of another portal to her left. He shoulder-checked Shadow into the wall with a massive thud. Immediately after, he grabbed her lapel and threw her to the floor. Shadow skidded to a stop on her back.

She growled and gripped her fingers into the ground. A portal grew around her, and she slowly sank into the darkness. As soon as she was completely enveloped, the darkness faded and disappeared.

Steven knew a resurgence was on its way. He quickly switched channels on his communicator and spoke clearly.

"Redman," he yelled, "Shadow has control over the Void. We're talking enough control that she can bring it back into our world."

"Really?" he asked. "That's fascinating."

"I'm not here to tell you how great she is!" Steven snapped. He continued to rip his head around, desperately trying to predict Shadow's next move. "How is she doing it? Is there something different about her serum than mine?"

"I've been looking into that very serum. While you were in the Void, I did research on who was taken by the Blades and what knowledge they had of our link. Science has progressed since then. The facts seem to suggest that your link to the Void should be much more powerful than hers."

"What?"

"The serum that was used on Miranda Zealo was sloppy and crudely put together," Redman reported. "The scientists responsible for it had a vague understanding of the Void at best, and I'm sure they weren't working in the best of conditions for Shotgun. Your link is much more refined and advanced than hers. The only thing she has over you is time with those powers."

Steven's brain started to churn away at an idea as soon as Redman's words finished.

"Time," he repeated, quietly.

Steven then noticed the walls in the room begin to get taller. The ceiling was getting higher and further away from him with every passing second. He looked down to see a portal underneath him, swallowing him whole. Steven fell through the portal and immediately back out of another portal on the ceiling. While he was falling between the two, Shadow flew from a third portal on the wall and kicked him out of the air, knocking him backward. His back smashed into the cold metal, causing drips of water to rain down off the leaking ceiling.

Shadow quickly ran to Steven and smashed her forearm into his chest. The wall behind Steven dented inward from the impact. Shadow held up her hand, allowing the Void to crawl out of her portal and surround her palm.

"Shhhhh," she started, in a comforting tone. "This will all be over soon." She slowly reached toward Steven's face, preparing to smother him.

Steven ground his teeth together and clenched his fingers. Just as Shadow's hand reached his face, a small portal opened up on the wall above his head.

Shadow glanced up and was struck in the face by a cascade of darkness. Steven forced the Void out of the portal, knocking Shadow away from him. Without a moment's hesitation, Steven pushed himself off the wall and charged toward Shadow. He wrapped his arms around her and lifted her off the ground. Carrying her like a sack of potatoes, Steven continued on his path toward the opposite wall. A portal opened, and Steven carried Shadow into the Void.

They tumbled into the darkness. Steven fell onto his stomach, while Shadow was thrown several feet away. She rolled back onto her feet and stood at the ready. Then, her mood began to shift. She slowly looked around, taking in the sight of the Void surrounding her. The familiar sights of the fading outlines and changing shapes flooded her mind.

"This is your plan?" she asked.

Steven got to his feet, holding his stomach and trying to fight away some pain.

"Well, part of it," he replied.

Shadow took a few steps toward Steven. Each step sent ripples across the darkness. The ripples would reach Steven's feet, split apart and continue off into the distance.

"Do you understand what you've done?" she continued. "You started to fight a wasp... and then chased it back into its nest."

Steven didn't move. His eyes stayed locked on his target.

"Do you think you have a chance at fighting me in here?" Steven smirked and shook his head.

"My goal isn't to fight you in here," he stated. Shadow stopped walking. "My goal is to keep you in here."

Shadow tilted her head and squinted her eyes.

"I know the signs of someone who has spent too much time in the Void," Steven explained. "I've seen them. You have those markings."

Shadow looked down at her arm. The black, ink-like substance was crawling across her skin, and her veins were turning black underneath.

"You might have more experience in the Void than I do... but I'm designed to function in here better than you. You can try to kill me in here all you want," Shadow looked back up at Steven, meeting his eyes, "but you have very limited time to do it."

Shadow lowered her brow. She spun to the side and stuck out her hand, forming a portal next to her. Steven quickly reacted and bent the Void beneath it. Shadow's portal shot up into the sky out of her reach. By the time she turned back, Steven was already on her, throwing fists.

Shadow managed to counter almost every strike but

remained on the defensive. She jumped away and threw her arms apart. As she did, her body evaporated into a black mist. Steven took another swing, which collided with nothing but empty air.

"You think you can fight me in here?" Shadow's voice echoed through the darkness. It had no defined origin. It was like her voice was coming from every direction. "You can't control the Void like I can. I *am* the Void!"

Steven turned around and watched in horror as the corpses floating overhead began to descend. One at a time, their extended arms jolted and then slowly started to return to their bodies. The blackened skeletons started to creak and snap back and forth. Their heads turned to look at Steven as they reached the floor.

Like something out of a nightmare, they began to hobble toward him. Their arms were outstretched, reaching for him. Their bottom jaws hung off of their skulls like they were constantly screaming.

Steven pushed his hands forward, launching pillars of the Void into them and shattering them into bones. Their numbers seemed to increase as they got closer. Another attack shattered several more of the demons, but the bones would simply float away and then drop down to form the skeleton once again. Unable to fight them all, the skeletons eventually reached Steven. They were grabbing at his arms, pulling him to the ground and moaning in his ears.

Steven was desperately throwing punches, trying to

keep them away. Their numbers were too much, and Steven found himself completely overwhelmed. A black mist danced around the air behind the monsters and slowly formed into Shadow. She moved her arm in a circle, opening a portal behind her.

"I warned you," she commented, "but you refused to listen. I know your friends are on the way. I doubt you'll be completely dead by the time I'm finished with them. Maybe you'll be lucky enough to see them get thrown in here. You'll get to watch them become new corpses in my collection."

Steven ground his teeth together and balled his hands into fists. He was fighting as hard as he could against the forces around him. He knew if he couldn't break free, this was the end for him, the Nitros, and possibly the entire city. He was scared, but more importantly, he was getting desperate.

Shadow gave one last nod before turning to her portal. As she went to take a step, the Void ripped from the ground below and surrounded her leg. She pulled against it, nearly falling to her knees. She snapped her head back to Steven.

He threw his arms apart, causing several tendrils to fly from the floor of the Void and begin attacking the skeletons surrounding him. The tendrils tore apart their ribs and ripped the skulls from their necks. Bones were thrown around in an eruption of blackness.

Steven leaped from his position and tackled Shadow. The two tumbled to the floor. Steven gripped his hands into Shadow's arms and pinned her to the ground. The Void began to crawl up the sides of her mask and creep into the holes left for her eyes. The cracked pieces of her mask started to groan. Her mask buckled and crinkled until it shattered off of her face.

Miranda's face looked like it was stained gray. Her skin was smooth, apart from her horrifically wrinkled and scarred eyes. She gasped for air. Her pupils began to bleed further into her eyes, and her skin faded to an even darker gray.

She coughed and tried to force Steven away from her. He could feel Shadow growing weaker and weaker by the second. Her veins looked like they were going to explode out of her skin with black ink. Then her mouth slowly opened, and a black fog cascaded out of her lungs. Steven looked deep into her eyes, growling to himself.

"The people you've killed deserve justice," he hissed. Shadow's eyes were now almost completely blackened. Steven closed his eyes. His brow furrowed, and the ground beneath Shadow began to swirl.

A portal opened, and the two dropped back into the overworld. Shadow and Steven fell to the metal floor. Steven pushed himself away from Shadow and fell onto the ground next to her. Her eyes slowly closed and her head tilted to the side. Black mist continued to float from her mouth but was lessening. Her chest pumped in and out as clean air once again filled her lungs.

Steven coughed out a few black drops as well, but luckily, did not sport any of the same scars that Miranda did.

"Damn," a voice spoke. Steven turned his head to see Dante standing behind him. "Is she…"

"No," Steven interrupted. "She'll live… I think. The Void seems to have weakened her quite a bit. She knew as well as I did that she couldn't stay there. Don't know when she'll come to, but slapping those dampening cuffs on her should help. I hope locking her up will be enough for the families of the people she's killed. It wouldn't be for me… but I feel like that's not my decision to make here."

Dante knelt down next to her body and placed a device on her chest. Tubing snaked out of the device and fastened together on her back. Dante grabbed her hands and buckled them into the device as well. Once fully connected, blue lights began to pulse around the restraint. It emitted a low humming noise that echoed in the small chamber.

"Redman says this thing will break her tie with the Void," he stated. "I'm not gonna question him. If he says it'll work… the thing probably works."

Steven nodded and continued to catch his breath. Nick dropped down through a hole in the ceiling and fell to one knee to absorb some of the impact.

"Steven," he called out as soon as his eyes landed on his

teammate. "What the hell happened? Are you okay?"

Steven put up his hand, stopping Nick.

"I'm fine," he replied, calmly. "Shadow's done using the Void for quite a while. I guarantee that." He turned his head and looked up at the hole Nick had come through. "So you guys managed to track me, huh?"

Steven leaned forward and looked up through the hole. Tons of dirt and metal comprised its wall as it went up into darkness. "And you... tunneled here?"

"Yeah," Dante answered. "Wasn't easy to find you, though. Signal gets pretty fuzzed up when you're this far underground."

Steven squinted and tilted his head.

"Underground?" he asked.

"Yeah," Megan added as she dropped down through the hole as well. "Atomic made us this tunnel just to gain access. This place is nearly a mile deep. Whatever it is, it's siphoning electricity from a power plant nearby. The city thought the place was shut down."

"That doesn't make any sense," Steven stated, getting to his feet. "Why would the city assume a functional power plant was out of commission? They don't really just shut those places down."

"It was evacuated years ago," Nick responded. "Too much radiation." Steven turned to face Nick. Nick was picking his next words, not looking directly at Steven. He was just staring off into the distance.

"We should have guessed it sooner," Nick continued. "We're back where everything started, Steven."

Steven looked up through the hole again and sighed. His eyes closed in realization.

"We're underneath the Faraday Center, aren't we?"

CHAPTER 19: A DIFFERENT PERSON

Nick stepped through the doorway leading out of the storage room. He peered down the long metal hallway, searching for any signs of life. The long corridor was completely empty. Puddles were on the ground, and the lights flickered in a desperate attempt to stay lit.

Nick exhaled. He motioned toward the others and made his way into the hall. Almost immediately, his communicator started to beep with an incoming transmission. Nick put his finger to his ear and spoke in a low, quiet voice.

"Go ahead," he prompted. There was a plume of static on the other end. Mumbles of a voice were barely audible in the background. "Redman?" Nick asked. The static changed and then started to fade.

"Nicholas," Redman began, after another few seconds, "can you hear me?" His voice sounded frantic like he couldn't get the information out fast enough. "Are you at the base?"

"We just got here," Nick replied. "Explosion's fine. Well… he's alive anyways. Not sure what kind of fighting condition he's in if we run into danger. Talking him down was worthless. We're making our way deeper into the base. Hopefully, we can track down Shotgun and…"

"Nicholas, please listen to me," he interrupted.

Nick stopped walking, leaving the others to continue in front of him. "You need to get out of there, now."

"Is there a trap?" Nick asked, worriedly. "Damn it. I'll get the others and we'll…"

"No, this isn't a message for everyone. This is just you. You are in danger."

"Me?" Redman sighed and turned to his computer.

"I've been running tests on the hair samples we took from you. Almost every test came back inconclusive. None of my machines were able to compare your red hair and your brown hair accurately."

"What are you saying, Redman?"

Redman lifted his hand, staring down into his palm. A single strand of red hair traced along a line of his hand. He slid it up to his finger and carefully held it between his pointer finger and thumb. He was staring at it, like looking longer would give him more information than any of his machines.

"The machines couldn't accurately compare the two…

because they aren't from the same person," he finally spoke.

Nick's brow lowered. He stood in the middle of the hallway, unsure what his next move should be.

"The red hairs and brown hairs from your head have two completely different sets of DNA. The brown hair matches Nicholas Bruno's DNA perfectly, but the red hair..."

"Isn't Nick's," Nick finished. He brushed his hand through his hair and brought it back down in front of his face. A few hairs dotted his glove, including one that was a bright, unmistakable red. "It's Nuclear's."

"We never could have predicted something like this would happen."

"Because you aren't Shotgun," Nick interjected. Nick never took his eyes off of his hand. "Shotgun was willing to use human test subjects to prove his suspicions about the Otrolium poisoning. Without that, we never would have seen this coming." Nick did everything in his power to convince himself this was just a mistake. Assuming Redman was being reckless or knew more than he let on wouldn't help the situation now. That was for another time when Shotgun wasn't the main threat.

"I simply don't understand," Redman continued, nearly out of breath. "Why would Shotgun warn you about this. If he had kept it hidden, your mind could be at serious risk."

"Shotgun didn't warn me to try and help me," Nick replied. He closed his eyes and leaned his hand against one the walls. "It did it because he's sure that you can't fix it. He hates you, Redman."

Redman didn't speak. Nick looked ahead at the other Nitros, now stopping and turning around to see why Nick wasn't with them. Nick lifted one finger, telling them to hold on for only another second.

"That's the only thing we can be completely sure about with him," Nick continued. "He hates you. He found out something was wrong with me and refused to keep it to himself because he knows it will hurt you more if you know. He wants me to turn into what he is, and he wants it to be your fault."

"The Otrolium might be affecting your system, but the rate at which it's doing so doesn't seem to be at a dangerous point at the moment. Unfortunately, we can't be sure of when that dangerous moment will occur. We also don't know the *extent* of the Otrolium poisoning in your blood. The Faraday Center is covered in leftover radiation from the explosion. You can't be there absorbing more of it. You need to come back before your exposure to the Faraday Center accelerates this condition."

Nick looked back down the hallway. The other Nitros were getting smaller and smaller. He glanced down to the hairs on his hand once again. One at a time they turned bright orange at their ends and slowly dissolved into embers and puffs of smoke. He closed his fingers around the ashes. They sifted through his fingers and floated off into the air.

"I can't leave, Redman," Nick quietly reported. "The others need my help. If Shotgun is here, I can't allow him to get away."

"That is unacceptably reckless behavior!" Redman scolded as soon as Nick finished speaking. "You came to me concerned something was wrong with your enhancer. Now we know the truth. Something *is* wrong with your enhancer. That is fact! Knowing that, you're willing to put yourself in danger of worsening it? This poisoning of your DNA isn't aiming to kill you. It's aiming to destroy your mind and make you something you're not."

"He killed my family!" Nick yelled into his communicator.

Redman remained silent.

"Shotgun is responsible for the deaths of hundreds, including the people closest to us," Nick stated. "We need to stop him, and according to you... we're strongest when we work together. Besides, if I leave because of this... then Shotgun's plan worked perfectly. I refuse to give him that satisfaction."

Nick didn't know if Redman had hung up or simply didn't know the right words to say. Assuming the former, Nick continued to move down the tunnel. His communicator dove into static again as he marched further underground. Just before the static became unbearable, a clear voice cut through it.

"Please... end this quickly."

CHAPTER 20: A NITRO

Nick caught up to the other Nitros and fell into line with them. They were in a large room with metal tubing snaking in all directions overhead. On the opposite side of the room was a raised platform, sporting a giant machine in the center. The machine had a solid metal panel on the front, and all the tubing was leading directly into it. Clear sections of the tubes reveal Otrolium was flowing directly into the device.

"Well," Dante began, "that thing looks important."

"Let's find a way to shut it down," Megan suggested, "but we need to be careful about it. That much Otrolium will turn this place into a crater if it's ignited."

"No need to evacuate anyone overhead," Steven noted. "This area has been barren ever since the Faraday Center went up."

Nick added nothing to the conversation and kept his

eyes set on the device.

"You okay, Nick?" Steven asked.

Nick didn't respond. He knew his situation was bad and possibly even worse than he already imagined. However, breaking more bad news to his teammates in this environment wouldn't help anything. It would only distract them from their current objective. Nick reasoned waiting to tell them would be a better option for everyone.

Nick took a few steps forward when a sound echoed throughout the room. A sharp, repeated noise that bounced off almost every surface. Two hands slapping together, applauding the Nitros' efforts.

From the shadows behind the device, Shotgun stepped forward, clapping ever so slowly. His eyes were glowing with a faint green.

"Simply incredible," he complimented. "Over a mile underneath the Faraday Center, undiscovered for years… and yet here you are. You truly are Redman's greatest creation."

"This ends now, Shotgun!" Nick called out. "No more games. No more Blades to toss in our way. It's just you and us."

Shotgun stopped clapping and folded his arms behind his back.

"Is that so?" Shotgun's eyes floated over to Nick. He noticed Nick wincing and beads of sweat dripping down his forehead. Shotgun tilted his head and then slowly looked up toward the ceiling. He noted the many pipes overhead. The Otrolium sloshed and churned as it ran through them. Shotgun nodded with a small chuckle.

"Is there something wrong, Nicholas?" he asked, returning his gaze to the red Nitro. "It seems to me like you know how little time you have left. How long do you think you have down here before things get bad for you? An hour? A few minutes?" Shotgun lowered his chin down into his chest. His eyes were barely visible under his brow but remained locked on Nick. "Or maybe… it's already too late."

"Nuclear," Diego spoke, quietly, "what is he talking about?"

Shotgun laughed again. He unfolded his arms and motioned one hand toward the Nitros.

"Should have guessed," he mused. "Haven't broken the bad news to your friends, yet, have you?" He dropped his hand back to his side. "You'll be happy to know there's no reason to be afraid. I've been in your position before. Sure, it hurts for a while, but eventually," Shotgun lifted both hands and spread them apart, like he was drawing a fantastic image in the air in front of him, "everything becomes clear, and the man you really are, takes the control he wants so much."

"Nuclear, what is he talking about?" Megan asked. Nick bared his teeth in Shotgun's direction. Ignoring Megan's question, he made a loud announcement.

"That's it!" Nick shouted. "Enough talk from you, Shotgun! This is over! We came here for one reason, and that's to finally stop you!"

Shotgun's laugh grew until it was loud enough to echo off the walls, sounding like he was standing everywhere at once. Shotgun shook his head and carefully placed his hand on a panel next to the device.

"You just haven't figured it out," he announced, triumphantly. "You five are going to *have* to kill me," Shotgun's hand dropped down onto the panel, striking a large red button, "because you're way too late to stop me."

The device sparked to life, and a horrendous buzzing filled the room. The Nitros covered their ears and backed away. The Otrolium overhead stopped flowing into the device. The ends erupted into steam as they separated from the machine and dangled helplessly from the ceiling. The lights were flickering and small pebbles dropped from above as the very structure of the room was compromised.

The metal covering on the front of the device pushed away. It slowly began to slide upward, groaning and creaking along a rusty track.

Shotgun never shifted from his position. He watched in pride as the Nitros desperately tried to remain in formation. The panel revealed a blinding light within the device.

Nick held his forearm in front of his face, unable to look directly into the machine. The panel reached the end of its track and fastened into place with a loud crack. The light within the machine began to fade. The Nitros managed to get their first view inside the device, and it was exactly what they were all fearing most.

A figure stepped out of the machine, holding tightly onto whatever he could reach. He stumbled forward, eyes slammed shut. Nick instantly recognized him. He was larger now and had bright lines of blue crawling through every vein. Mac Sampson lifted his head, causing a series of cracks to echo across the floor. His eyes slowly eased open, revealing they were now a brilliant blue. Wisps of blue danced out of the edges of his eyes and rose up into the air.

"Uranium," Shotgun spoke, solemnly, and without setting eyes on his creation. "Kill them."

Uranium growled and took a massive step forward. His boot hit the ground and instantly shattered into a torrent of water. Uranium dropped from his position and fell to the floor below. He caught himself, but not without disintegrating another one of his hands into a puddle.

"What the hell is happening?" Dante asked, astonished.

Uranium started to yell, using every ounce of strength to try and stand. His face began to slide off of his skull. His teeth were melting, one by one, and falling from his jaw like water droplets. The pigment on his arm faded as it dissolved into water and dropped to the floor. The water oozed back under him and swirled into the air, forming a new leg. Again and again, body parts would melt and fall away, before crawling upward and reforming.

"No," Shotgun murmured. "This can't be…"

"You knew the formula was unstable, Shotgun!" Diego yelled. "Look what you've done to him!" Diego ran forward. He reached for Uranium's shoulder, desperate to help. Uranium was turned away, still shouting in pain. "We're going to get you help, Mac!" Diego shouted. "Just come with us and…"

Uranium let out another yell and snapped his body around to square up with Diego. He threw his arm forward, hitting Diego in the chest with a column of water. Diego rocketed across the room and slammed into the wall. Uranium's body parts continued to reform but were now decaying at a much slower rate.

"You know," Uranium started, roaring as loud as he could, "I was dreaming about doing something like that on my entire trip prison!" His voice was garbled like he was underwater. Each word coincided with a spray of water erupting from his throat.

Uranium lifted his chin and stared directly at Nick. His bared teeth eventually twisted into a sickening smile. His body was now completely solid, and he was standing without issue. His shoulders were raised up, swallowing his neck completely. Nick could barely see his eyes underneath his thick brow.

"Take them down, Uranium," Shotgun ordered. "Your

DNA makes you superior to them in every way. Redman created them in an attempt to stop me, and now... you, another one of his creations, will destroy everything he fought so hard to protect."

Uranium's smile faded. He looked down at his hand and slowly closed it into a fist. "I'm not just better than them," he growled to himself. Water leaked out through his fingers. A veil of water surrounded his hand as he turned over his shoulder to meet eyes with Shotgun.

"Now," Uranium lifted his hand and aimed his palm toward Shotgun, "I'm better than you."

Shotgun's arms quickly unfolded, but not quick enough to intercept the cascade of water the rushed toward him. He was thrown backward and onto the metal, grated floor. Shotgun rolled to one side, shaking off the attack. He clawed his way up to one knee. His head raised and his bright green eyes landed on Uranium. Shotgun didn't say a word as he rose to his feet.

Uranium smiled and turned back to the Nitros.

Shotgun grunted. He looked to his side and quickly walked away from the machine. Nick followed Shotgun's moves closely. Shotgun got to a set of stairs and started to climb them.

"Shotgun's trying to escape!" Nick shouted. "I'm not gonna let him get away!" Nick took two massive steps forward. As his pace quickened, Uranium threw his hand out, causing it to extend into a pillar of water. It surged through the air on a collision course with Nick.

Nick stopped in his tracks and turned toward the attack. Just before impact, the water brightened in color and solidified in the air. Particles of frost floated off of its surface and danced into the air.

Uranium's eyes widened. He cracked his head to the side, taking in the sight of Dante with his hands extended.

"Go!" Dante yelled. "We'll handle Uranium! Don't let Shotgun escape!"

Nick nodded to his cousin and ran for the stairs. The frozen column of water hung in the air for a few seconds. It crackled and snapped before falling to the ground and shattering.

Uranium squared off with Dante. He let his arms hang by his sides like they were nailed to his shoulders. Dante glanced to his left and right at Steven and Megan.

"Three on one, right?" Megan asked with an unsure tone in her voice. "How bad could it be?"

Uranium clenched his fists and shouted into the air. The veins under his skin began to glow blue once again. Steam rising off the machine started to whip through the air and circle Uranium like a tornado before absorbing into his pores.

"Oh," Steven started, "it's gonna be bad."

CHAPTER 21: A TSUNAMI

"Got a plan?" Megan whispered to Dante. Uranium rolled out his shoulders as he paced back and forth, sizing up his opponents.

"Have I thought about how to fight the ocean?" Dante retorted. "No... no, I don't have a plan."

"He's just like us," Steven noted, taking a step forward. "If we get hit hard enough, we go down." Steven opened one of his hands. A portal bled into existence behind him and begun to swirl. "I bet the same technique works on him."

Steven jumped backward, disappearing into the darkness. He erupted out of a portal behind Uranium with his fist cocked behind his head. He took a swing, which collided with the side of Uranium's unaware neck. Steven's hand passed through like a hand moving under a water tap. Uranium's neck became water, while still holding enough rigidity to support his head. Steven watched in slow motion as droplets sprayed into the distance, but sucked back into Uranium's form before hitting the ground.

As soon as Steven landed, Uranium sprung forward and rammed his boot into Steven's back. Steven was launched off his feet and slammed chest-first into the floor. Uranium lifted both arms into the air. He threw them downward, transforming his fists into massive torrents of water. The water hit Steven with the force of a fire hose. His skin instantly turned a bright red from the burning sensation that came over him.

The water carried Steven to the opposite end of the room. He slammed into a large metal tank and dropped to the floor below. A large dent formed in the tank, followed by a small crack. A window in the tank revealed the glowing green liquid contained inside.

"Ohhhh… please be some kind of new soda," Dante pleaded upon seeing it.

"Is that entire thing filled with Otrolium?" Megan asked.

Dante turned to her and held out his hand. "I'm gonna put this as delicately as possible," Dante began. "If you use your powers in here… we're going to die."

"Figured that one out, Dante," she sarcastically replied.

Steven tried to push himself off the ground, but could barely make it to his knees. His body had taken too much damage from his fight with Shadow and was finally starting to give out.

"Explosion," Dante called out. "Don't worry about us. Get to Diego and make sure he's okay. We'll handle Poseidon, over here."

"You really think we can handle this?" Megan asked, under her breath.

"Well," Dante began, also as quietly as possible, "would you rather lose with confidence or win like a coward?"

Megan nodded and put her hands up on guard. "I guess you make a good point," she finished.

Uranium pushed off his back foot and took off toward the two. He expertly managed to avoid and block almost every attempted strike by Megan and Dante. Each punch was quickly pushed out of the way, and each kick was ducked or completely dodged. Uranium caught Dante's strike and turned with it in his grasp. He flipped Dante over his shoulder and threw him at Megan.

"Coming through!" Dante yelled as Megan ducked underneath him.

Megan charged in and punched Uranium in the chest, knocking him backward. She threw two more punches which collided with his shoulder and face.

"Coming *back*!" Dante shouted. Megan knelt down as Dante leaped over her. He kicked Uranium in the chest, throwing him to the floor.

Uranium rolled out of the attack and threw his hands apart. Like two tentacles made of water, he whipped his arms forward. The streams snaked toward the Nitros and wrapped around their legs. Uranium pulled back forcefully. Dante and Megan were torn off their feet and crashed down to their backs.

Uranium hiked his foot into the air and slammed it down onto the floor, shouting while he did. Two pillars of water erupted from underneath the two Nitros. They carried them into the air and crashed them into the ceiling, before disappearing and allowing them to fall.

Before they could hit the ground, Uranium had re-formed his hands and wound up for another attack. He punched his arms out, and another two torrents took Megan and Dante out of midair, carrying them across the room and smashing them into the wall. They collapsed down onto each other in a heap. Dante rubbed the back of his head and pushed himself to his knees.

"He's strong," Megan commented, rolling out her shoulder. Megan was hoping the botched procedure would have taken its toll on Mac's power, but that wasn't the case. She couldn't believe his strength and already impressive control over his abilities. It was like he was born to be a Nitro. The more thoughts like that that passed through her mind, the more frightened she became.

Uranium turned to his side and grabbed a railing behind him. He tore the metal bar from its setting and hoisted it over his head like a javelin.

"Incoming!" Dante called out. He kicked his foot into

Megan, pushing her backward. The metal bar missed her by inches and embedded into the wall.

Uranium growled and ran at the Nitros once again. Dante gripped the metal bar and stepped forward, tearing it from the wall and swinging it like a bat. It collided with the side of Uranium's head, which knocked him off course. Uranium fell to his knee and violently shook his head.

"Just die already!" Mac yelled. He stood up and fired a torrent of water at Dante. Dante put out his hand to block it. As the water reached him, it solidified into ice. The ice traveled up the stream until it reached Uranium's arm. The ice crawled up his arm like a creature.

Uranium tried to pull away but found himself locked in place. Dante lifted the bar again and slammed it down into the pillar of ice. It shattered to bits along its full length, including Uranium's arm. Uranium yelled in pain as his arm broke into pieces and erupted into shards on the floor. Water flooded out of his shoulder and quickly formed a new arm, which was already in a fist.

"Well," Dante said as Megan ran back to his side. "That hurt him. Let's do that more. Sound good to you, cupcake?" he yelled to Uranium.

Uranium bared his teeth as he lifted his hands over his head.

"That's it!" he yelled. He threw his arms apart, causing his entire body to turn into water and drop to the floor. Dante stepped back, shocked by the sight. The newly formed puddle whipped back and forth across the floor. It slithered at the Nitros and shot like a bullet in their direction.

The water slammed into Dante's leg, making him fall forward. The puddle came to a stop in the middle of the two. Uranium's entire form launched out of the puddle and into the air. He dropped down a massive elbow on the top of Megan's head. As she bent forward from the blow, Uranium landed and caught her throat in his hand. He ripped her off her feet and jammed her into the wall. Megan gasped for air and gripped at Uranium's arm.

"Hey, asshole!" yelled Dante. He ran at Uranium with the metal bar hiked high over his head. Uranium pushed away from Megan. His body became clear, and his features began to flip. His knees bent the opposite direction. The back of his head grew a nose and eyes. He reformed facing Dante and pushed out his arm. A cascade of water smashed into Dante's chest.

The bar left his grip and flipped through the air. Uranium caught it as Dante tripped onto his backside. With one swift motion, Uranium turned and struck Megan in the side of the head with the heavy metal bar.

She fell to the floor. Blood leaked down from the side of her head and pooled underneath her.

"Megan!" Dante jumped back to his feet. The last thing Dante was willing to do was to watch his teammate get hurt. He had to help. He started running toward Megan, his hand out to help. "Hold on! I'm…"

Uranium turned again and rammed the bar forward. Dante's sentence ended quickly. He stopped dead in his tracks only a foot from Uranium. His mouth shuttered, letting only a few gasps and muddled words escape.

Dante slowly looked down at the metal bar buried in his chest. Megan looked up from the floor in horror. Uranium smiled as he pushed forward again, making the bar slide out of Dante's back. Dante reached one hand up and gripped onto the metal. Blood was dripping from his mouth with every breath.

Uranium leaned in and slowly shook his head. "Consider yourself lucky," he spat in Dante's face. "You're the first. You won't be forced to watch all your friends die, too." Uranium lifted the bar, pulling Dante off his feet. Dante slid a little further down the metal, getting even closer to Uranium. Like a corpse on a pike, Dante was skewered in the air in front of Uranium. "What's wrong? No little quips to throw around now?"

Dante gulped and shook his head.

"Just… just one," he barely spoke. "I told… told the others this was cool." Uranium squinted and lowered his brow. "What… do you think?"

Uranium quickly shifted his eyes down. Dante's forearm was surrounded by a gauntlet of ice. Dante quietly hummed out a sound effect as a spike of ice extended off the end of the gauntlet. It shot forward and buried itself in

Uranium's chest. Uranium stared at the spike before slowly lifted his gaze back to Dante.

"Are you… an idiot?" he asked. The area of Uranium's chest around Dante's spike was now clear and rippling.

"Not the first time… I've been asked that," Dante reminded him.

"You don't seem to be understanding. I… am… water." Dante smiled and gave a small nod.

"I know."

Uranium's eyes shot open. His entire body jerked. He pulled the metal bar back, yanking it out of Dante and letting him fall to the floor. Uranium stumbled backward, grabbing at the spike in his chest. Slowly, ice began to crawl out of his chest and onto the rest of his body. The ice crystalized his liquified body, freezing him in place.

"No," he started, frantically. "No!" The ice snaked over his arms, locking them in place.

"Reactor!" Dante yelled as clearly as possible. "Do it!"

Megan looked down at her hand and then back up to Uranium. "Are you insane?" she asked Dante.

"Not important right now!" he replied. "Just do it!"

"But this entire facility will…"

"Reactor!" another voice cried.

Megan turned to see Diego standing by the Otrolium tank. He was helping Steven stand, who had his arm draped over Diego's shoulder.

"I got this! Do it!"

Megan knew she was risking the lives of her entire team, but she also knew this might be their only shot. Mac had grown too strong, and in their already weakened state, a prolonged fight with him would only end badly. A small purple orb formed in her hand. It started to spin and glowed brighter with each passing second. She pushed herself to her feet and whipped her arm around her body.

The orb rocketed through the air toward Uranium. He reached out toward it as the ice started to crawl up his face. "NO!" he shouted one last time. The ice covered his face, freezing him in place.

Diego slammed his foot into the ground, causing a giant slab of rock to fire from the ground and shield the Otrolium tank.

The orb collided with Uranium's chest. There was a blinding light as the ice statue of Uranium shattered into millions of pieces. Fragments of the ice spun through the air and dissolved into steam in the heat of the explosion. Purple smoke billowed around the room, knocking Megan down and causing Dante to skid across the floor.

The floor cracked in all directions, and more pebbles and rocks fell from the ceiling above. Diego's rock wall buckled and cracked in the wake of the eruption. He fought with all his might to keep it steady.

Despite his efforts, a massive chunk of the ceiling split from its place and fell toward the tank. The twisted rock and metal were on a collision course of hundreds of gallons of Otrolium. Just before impact, the chunk disappeared out of thin air. The only thing remaining was a giant black portal, floating just above the tank.

Steven smirked and dropped his arm. The eruption finally came to a stop. Smoke floated in all directions as it dissipated into a fine mist.

Diego let his rock wall fall back into the ground. He immediately left his position and ran to Dante. He dropped to his knees next to him. Diego pressed his hands against the wounds on either side of Dante, trying to keep pressure on them.

"Dante!" he yelled, "hang on! We're going to get you out of here!"

"No," Dante argued between coughs. "We can't leave."

"You are going to die if we stay here!" Megan shouted at him. "We're leaving! That isn't up for discussion!"

"Nick is alone with Shotgun!" he screamed back. "I'm not leaving him!"

Megan sighed and turned her head away from Dante. She held a finger to her ear and activated her communicator.

"Nuclear, where are you?!" she demanded. "Blast is hurt... really bad. We need to get him out of here!" She waited for a few moments, but there was no response. "Nick! Can you hear me?! Dante is dying! We need to leave, now!"

After another silence, Steven pushed himself off the

wall he was using to hold himself up. He stumbled toward Megan and rolled out his shoulder.

"I'll go find Nuclear," he volunteered. "Get Blast back to the surface." Steven stepped forward, holding his chest to ease the pain from before. As he did, his boot had a hard time getting traction. He looked down at the floor in time to see a few drops of water roll across the ground. They traveled to a nearby drain and, one-by-one dripped in and out of sight. Steven slowly turned his head over his shoulder, meeting eyes with Megan.

"You don't really think..." she started, in awe.

Steven sighed and started walking again.

"Of course I do," he groaned.

CHAPTER 22: A FINAL FIGHT

The clashing of boots against a grated floor rung out down a hallway as Shotgun charged past. Nick was close behind in pursuit. Nick formed a fireball in his hand and took a shot at the Blade Leader. It sped through the air on a collision course with Shotgun's head.

At the last moment, Shotgun spun around and swiped it out of the air like a fly. The fireball flung to the side where it crashed into a wall and became nothing more than a puff of smoke and a burn mark. Shotgun continued spinning until he was facing away once again, all without losing an ounce of momentum. Shotgun reached the end of the hall and turned sharply to the right, disappearing into the next room.

Nick picked up the pace to try and make up some ground. He turned the corner and found himself in a dead end room.

It was a relatively small chamber but packed to the brim with equipment. Guns, ammunition, armor, and devices of all kinds. Nick held one hand out at the ready. Fire surrounded his hand, both providing light and setting up an attack in case of an ambush. Nick slowly stepped inside, being careful to check every one of his corners.

"Come out here, Shotgun!" he yelled into the darkest corners of the room.

Nick could see a glowing tank on the wall opposite him. The tank was blue in color and appeared to be full of liquid. As Nick approached, he could tell there was something more to it. Inside was a man, floating in the center of the fluid. His eyes were shut, tightly. A tube was wired through the top of the tank and attached to a mask which covered the man's mouth and nose, keeping him alive, and most likely, keeping him asleep. As Nick got closer, the features of the man's face became more distinct.

His head and shoulders sported deep gashes that were still in the process of healing. Blood was still leaking out in small quantities, floating off, and diluting into the water.

"Razor," Nick whispered to himself. "They're still using him. It's just like he told us. Strapped up to this thing like some sort of battery."

"A generator," Shotgun's voice echoed across the room, "in his own right."

Nick spun around and aimed another fireball. The echo made it impossible to discern the origin of Shotgun's voice.

Nick snapped back and forth, but never landed on a viable target. The light from his fireball illuminated every wall but never revealed Shotgun.

"Though, he is not the only key component to my operation. Not by a long shot."

Nick went to check another corner but stopped halfway there. His eyes fell on another machine in the room with him. It sat against a wall eagerly awaiting its next use. The device itself was small, but the glass tube attached to it was massive. Nick instantly recognized the machine. He could picture it spinning on Redman's screen. He could hear Redman's voice drilling the machine's importance into Nick's brain.

"The Matter Converter," he whispered. Surrounding it was a series of different things, including multiple potted plants, fruits, and even some cages containing small animals scurrying around. However, Nick noticed that some of the plants were shriveled up, decaying, and others were reduced to nothing but dust.

"Beautiful in its simplicity," Shotgun commented once again. This time, when Nick turned, there was no need for a search. Shotgun was behind him, slowly pacing. His eyelids were hanging lazily in front of his eyes like he was tired. In his hand was an apple, which he continuously tossed into the air and caught. His other arm was tucked behind his back in an attempt to make himself appear less threatening.

Nick still had his hand up, ready to attack, but was thrown by Shotgun's calm demeanor.

"The Converter is so powerful, and yet, a child possesses the mental capacity to operate it. Like giving an ape a button that fires a nuke. Something was bound to go wrong."

Shotgun's path changed slightly. He started to approach the Converter, never taking his eyes from it. He reached out and placed his hand on the machine, running it smoothly along the top, like he was admiring a work of art.

Nick was hesitant to attack Shotgun. Not only was the prospect of fighting Shotgun alone a terrifying one, but now Nick truly understood how similar he and his enemy really were.

He lifted his other hand and carefully examined the apple. Its brilliant red color seemed extra vibrant in few lights of the room. Shotgun held the apple to his face. He moved it forward and allowed it to roll out of his grasp. It dropped into the glass tube attached to the Converter and bounced to a stop in the center.

Shotgun traced his finger down the front of the Converter until it landed on a large lever. Shotgun pulled it down, activating the device. A plate slid across the front of the glass tube.

The apple was sealed inside as the Converter whirled to life. The apple began to twitch and shake around. Its bright red color started to fade. The crisp outer layer now looked soft and weak. The apple itself shriveled up until it could barely support its own weight. It eventually crumbled into nothing more than a pile of brown dust.

Shotgun reversed the switch and nodded. The whirling sound winded down and came to a stop. The plate slid out of the way, allowing Shotgun to stick his foot inside and kick the dust out of the tube and onto the floor. A panel on the front of the Converter happily displayed that it had absorbed all of the energy in the tube, and it was hungrily awaiting more.

"The energy it absorbs is what creates the Otrolium, but my goodness does it take a lot," Shotgun groaned.

"Who am I talking to right now?" Nick interrogated, still not comfortable enough to lower his hand. "Shotgun, or Scott Cells?"

Shotgun shook his head and once again began pacing.

"How different do you think the two really are at this point?" he asked, tilting his head up to meet Nick's eyes.

Nick slowly lowered his hand, but wasn't prepared to fully relax. He knew Shotgun was always dangerous, even when he didn't seem to be.

"You're a prisoner to Shotgun, Scott," Nick replied. "I like to think you'd stop him if you could."

"Why stop him? Especially when after years of work, we're so close to finishing this."

"And what exactly is '*this*?!'" Nick shouted. "You gave power to a psychopath with the intent of letting him loose on the streets. You want to send hundreds of innocent people to their deaths. Why the hell is this so important to you?!"

"Because Redman deserves to pay!" Shotgun yelled. He pointed his finger at Nick as his eyes started to glow. His veins in his wrist lit up. "Redman claims to be a man of the people, and yet all he does is feed us lies! He builds weapons that put thousands in danger and still, this city holds him over its head like a damned hero!"

"What do you blame him for?" Nick continued to question. The two were now pacing around each other in a wide circle, never allowing the other to close any distance.

Shotgun lowered his hand. His eyes were twitching with anger, but his words went back to that calm, collected tone.

"When Redman's street grid was introduced, protests were lining almost every road in the city," Shotgun explained. "I was one of the people involved. The R.A.N.T. they called us. Talked about us like we were some kind of street gang or band of thugs. The introduction of self-driving vehicles would mean me and hundreds of others were out of the job. Road workers, drivers, men in the gas industry, even entire car manufacturers were almost shut down. Redman didn't care. We were fighting for the people... and he was fighting for himself."

"So you lost your job," Nick surmised, "and to you, that's worth destroying an entire city?"

Shotgun almost looked disappointed in Nick. He

shifted his eyes away. Shotgun took a deep breath before speaking again.

"Do you remember when the grid was first activated, Nicholas?" Shotgun asked, avoiding Nick's question. "The immediate backlash?"

"Sure," Nick cautiously responded, "Redman told me about it." Shotgun returned his eyes to Nick. "He said there was a problem when they first came out. Caused the cars to lose tracking and drive off the road."

"A bug," Shotgun murmured. The lights in his eyes faded away. Soon the glow was completely gone. His eyelids dropped down and hung lazily over his eyes like he was tired. He finally turned his full body away from Nick. It was like he was staring at someone else in the room. Someone off in the shadows.

"That's what they called it," he reminisced. "'A bug.' I bet Redman avoided telling you what happened because of that bug."

"No, he didn't," Nick jumped in. "He told me everything. He told me one of them hit a boy."

Shotgun's eyes slowly closed. He sucked in a heavy breath of air and carefully exhaled it. After another second, his eyes opened again, this time looking directly back at Nick.

"He was six years old," Shotgun added.

The fire in Nick's palm started to fade. It disappeared back into his palm, drowning the room in darkness. The only light came from two small bulbs overhead, that were positioned just above Nick and Shotgun. Nick's hands unclenched as he listened to Shotgun speak.

"The vehicle had momentarily lost control."

Nick nodded.

"Redman told me," he said, quietly. "It was decided the manufacturer was to blame for all the issues with the software. Not Redman."

Shotgun looked away again. He didn't acknowledge Nick's words at all. He was in a different place.

"He was only a few feet away from me," Shotgun continued. "I could hear him talking to me." Shotgun returned his gaze to that same empty spot in the room. Shotgun chuckled to himself. "He was telling me about his day. The things he did at school. The things he couldn't wait to show me." Shotgun paused, like the next words out of his mouth were going to hurt.

Nick knew the feeling. The feeling of ripping open a scar that never fully healed. Some things, like what happened to Nick's family, what happened to Shotgun, never go away. It just gets easier to ignore their existence.

"And then... he just stopped," Shotgun said, in almost a whisper. "I went from hearing his voice, to hearing silence. I could see people screaming, covering their eyes, running toward us... but I just couldn't hear anything."

"Scott," Nick began, stepping forward. "You can't let that moment control your life. I understand..."

"You don't understand a thing!" Shotgun yelled. He snapped his head back to Nick. "I joined the Blades after Redman took everything from me. The RANT fought against the implementation of his grid, and when no one listened to us, I lost my son! I changed our mission. What was once a lowly gang became an army with the sole purpose of tearing Redman down. The explosion fused Otrolium into my blood and now…"

Shotgun lifted up his hands and gripped them into the sides of his head. He slammed his eyes shut and spoke through his teeth. Thin traces of water lined the bottom of his eyes.

"Now Shotgun will never let me forget what happened. He likes to remind me every single day of what Redman did to me. Now, all I care about is taking everything Redman has created and burning it right in front of him." Shotgun opened his eyes again. "He blames himself for the Faraday Center, he blames himself for what I became, and now, he's going to blame himself for the destruction of this entire city."

Shotgun stepped toward Nick. His hands were now down at his sides and balled into fists. Green light was cascaded out from the creases in his hand, circling up his arms, and waving into the air over his shoulders. His eyes were too bright to look at directly. "And then there's you. The straw that will finally break the camel's back."

"What are you talking about?" Nick demanded. Nick

knew Shotgun had plans for Redman, but it was now becoming disturbing clear how much those plans involved the Nitros.

"I warned you about the Otrolium poisoning in your blood. I want Redman to know what he did. I did it, so Redman will spend the next few years of his life watching as his greatest creation slowly dies in front of him, fully aware that it's all his fault. Uranium destroys Redman's city... and you destroy Redman's life." Shotgun held out his hands to the sides and tilted his head. "No matter what happens... I win."

Nick had heard enough. He charged from his position and leaped at Shotgun. His first swing cracked across Shotgun's helmet with a loud thud. The second and third impacted his chest. Each shot was harder than the last and made Shotgun stumble backward away from the assault.

"You'll never win, Shotgun!" Nick shouted. Fire surrounded his fist as he prepared for another devastating attack. "This is for my family!"

Nick's hand flew in like a comet. A trail of smoke and embers followed it toward its target. Just before impact, Shotgun's hand shot up and effortlessly caught it. Shotgun met Nick's eyes. Green light bled out from his hand and crawled its way around Nick's arm.

Shotgun pushed Nick's hand away and landed a massive punch on his chin. Nick stepped back, giving Shotgun enough room to hike his foot into the air and ram his boot into Nick's chest. Nick careened backward and hit the wall behind him. As soon as he pushed off, Shotgun was on top of him again. Two more punches collided. Nick managed to duck the third, leaving Shotgun's fist to bury into the metal wall.

"What's going to come of this, Shotgun?" Nick yelled while dodging attacks. "What would your son think of you now?"

Shotgun roared as he took another swing at Nick. Nick dodged again as Shotgun's fist ripped through the metal shelving in its way.

"You know what hurts more than wondering how my son would feel about me?" Shotgun asked. "The fact that he isn't around to tell me!"

Nick threw a fireball through the air. It slammed into Shotgun's head but bent around him like it was simply a puff of smoke.

"So, death and destruction... that's what you want? That's what will make you feel better?"

"Nothing will make me better!" Shotgun shouted back. "You really want to know what I want?! I want my son back!!!"

Shotgun slammed his hands together. A blast of green energy hit Nick in the stomach. The force was enough to lift him off the ground. He flew several feet away before falling onto his back.

Nick gripped his stomach. He was nervous going into

this fight that he couldn't stand against Shotgun alone. Now Shotgun was showing exactly why that was so frightening. Nick knew he had to win and yet he was terrified he couldn't.

Shotgun slowly approached Nick, like he was playing with his food. He stomped his foot down onto Nick's chest and pinned him to the floor. Nick bared his teeth and pushed both hands into the air. Two massive spouts of fire erupted from his palms. The fire engulfed Shotgun, wrapping around his body and climbing into his armor. Shotgun knelt down through the flames.

Nick could see his hand emerge from within the inferno. Shotgun continued to reach down until he could grip his hand onto Nick's head. Nick gasped at his touch as all of the oxygen in his lungs immediately escaped. The fire started to wilt and fade. Nick was finding it difficult to even keep his arms raised anymore. Eventually, the fire cooled, shrunk, and disappeared.

Shotgun's eyes turned red as he drained Nick of his energy. Nick's communicator began to activate and buzz to life. It was just static at first, but then a voice pierced through and began screaming. Shotgun was close enough that he could hear the frantic conversation on the other end.

"Nuclear, where are you?!" Megan shouted. "Blast is hurt… real bad. We need to get him out of here!"

Shotgun smiled under his helmet. "Looks like Uranium

is doing his job well," he remarked. Shotgun pressed his hand and foot down harder, making Nick cough and choke. "So how's it feel, Nicholas? Lying here, helpless, while your friends die without you?"

Nick continued to fight. He had to get to his friends. He had to save his cousin. He had to get through this.

Shotgun began laughing once again. It was like tormenting Nick was his single source of enjoyment. "Do you know what my favorite thing about this is?" Shotgun asked. A small trail of blood leaked out of Nick's mouth. He could feel his skin tightening around his muscles. His vision was turning black at the edges as he started to pass out.

"You hate me so much," Shotgun taunted. "You hate me because of what happened to your family." Shotgun released Nick's head but kept him pinned to the floor. "Well, I'm going to break you just like I'm going to break Redman." Shotgun leaned on his knee, so his head was lower and closer to Nick's. He was so close that Nick could feel the heat emanating from his eyes. "I didn't kill your family."

Nick's eyes shot open. He tried to speak, but his body was unable to make words. His lungs weren't responding, and his brain was questioning if it had even heard Shotgun correctly.

"You," Nick muttered through broken breaths, "you're lying."

"We're far beyond lying to each other at this point, don't you think?" Shotgun asked. "And the best part is, I know who killed your family, but… I think I'll hold onto that information." Shotgun laughed and nodded, pleased with himself. "I'll take it to my grave, Nicholas, and you… you will die without ever knowing the truth."

Shotgun stood up straight again and held out his hand. Fire surrounded his fingers and gathered in the center of his palm. The light from the fire illuminated his face in the darkness. His helmet covered his mouth, but Nick could tell he was smiling underneath. "See, I'm never going to kill you… but trust me… I'm going to make you wish I did."

The communicator clicked on once again. "Nick!" Megan called, desperately. "Nick where are you? Are you okay? Can you hear me? Dante is dying! We need to leave, now!"

Shotgun reached his hand down toward Nick's face. The heat of the fire instantly made Nick start sweating. Shotgun's hand was a few inches away when his sinister voice started up again.

"When you wake up," Shotgun croaked, "you'll be the only one left."

Nick ground his teeth together. Shotgun was right. Every one of Nick's friends were relying on him beating Shotgun right now. Nick couldn't give up here. He couldn't let Shotgun win. Nick fought his arms up and grabbed Shotgun's boot. He used all his might to shove it to the side, making Shotgun trip and fall forward. He caught himself on the ground but was now even closer to Nick. Nick pushed his hands together and forced them up into Shotgun's chest. Fire collected in his palms and blasted out like the nozzle on a rocket.

The sheer force was enough to launch Shotgun into the ceiling. He scraped off the metal and fell back toward Nick, who was already charging a second shot. Another eruption of fire hit Shotgun in his chest. It wasn't centered enough to bring Shotgun to the ceiling again, and instead caused him to twist in the air like his upper body was trying to pull away from his legs. Shotgun slammed down onto the floor only a few feet away.

Nick rolled to his side, trying to catch his breath and shake off Shotgun's attack. He looked around the room for anything he could use. His eyes scanned the area until they finally fell on the Converter.

He stared at the switch to activate it. His brain desperately tried to form a plan. Nick got to his feet and turned around. As soon as he did, Shotgun's hand wrapped around his throat.

Shotgun quickly stepped around Nick and wrapped his arm around his neck. He held Nick tightly in a sleeper hold. Both of Shotgun's hands were touching Nick's head and slowly draining the life out of him again. Nick's skin started to turn gray. His vision split into twos and fours. He could feel his life fading away. Nick knew he was in the end game.

Giving up at this point would be the last decision he would ever make for the Nitros.

"This is it!" Shotgun yelled. "Our fight ends here, but who knows? Maybe in a few years, once the Otrolium has had enough time to truly saturate your blood… you'll come crawling back to me. You and I will take Redman down together, and Nick Bruno won't be around to stop it. All I can say is… I can't wait to finally meet you in person… Nuclear."

Nick pointed his palms forward. Fire collected on his hands. Nick knew he had one shot left. Staying awake was becoming more and more difficult.

"Shotgun," Nick spoke, as loud as his lungs allowed. "Whether or not it was part of your game… you should have killed me when you had the chance."

The fire sprung forward, rocketing Nick and Shotgun in the opposite direction. The two launched perfectly into the glass tube attached to the Converter. The impact caused Shotgun to loosen his grip around Nick's neck. Nick fell forward and frantically reached toward the front panel. His hand landed on the lever, and as he fell, pulled it into the active position.

Shotgun shook off the attack. He went to step forward but was stopped when the plate slid into place over the glass tube, sealing him inside. Shotgun immediately realized what was happening. He slammed his fist into the wall, spider-webbing the glass around him.

"Nicholas!" he shouted. The Converter started up. The green light leaking out of Shotgun's eyes and hands suddenly changed direction. It wisped through the air and fed into the tube attached to the tank. The Converter began devouring Shotgun as he punched the glass a second time. The cracks in the glass multiplied, but the punch was noticeably weaker than the first. It looked like the light was being forcibly pulled from Shotgun's eyes.

Nick watched on as the machine worked against the Blade Leader. Nick was fighting against his urges to open the Converter and let Shotgun out. To end the pain he must have been feeling. However, after feeling Shotgun's power and hearing about everything he was capable of, Nick knew that simply wasn't an option.

"No!" Shotgun screamed. "Get me out of here!" Shotgun grabbed his own throat. He fell backward to support himself on the glass, coughing furiously. Unable to breathe, Shotgun reached both hands up and ripped his mask off his head. He dropped it to the ground and fell to one knee. He gasped for air but still, couldn't manage to inhale.

"Stop!" he yelled in a raspy, pleading voice. "Stop!" His eyes stopped glowing, and the light disappeared from his veins. His skin began to pull in around his muscles and bones like shrink-wrap. Shotgun's back arched and his hands came apart. He stared directly up at the top of the tank and let out a horrific scream. His entire body began to convulse. His chest puffed in and out, and his head snapped around in erratic and unpredictable motions. He lurched forward, coughing a splatter of deep red blood onto the glass in front of him.

Nick was barely conscious. His hearing was almost completely gone, and the edges of his vision were buried in black. He could see Shotgun's body fading away. This had gone far enough. Nick realized he was willing to do anything to stop Shotgun... anything but take a life. He refused to become exactly like Shotgun. With every last effort left in his body, Nick clawed his way forward. He reached for the panel on the Converter.

The outline of Shotgun's hand became visible in the blood splatter. It slowly scraped down, leaving a trail of clean glass behind.

Nick took hold of the lever and pushed it back up into its primary position. The whirling noise of the Converter started to slow, and eventually faded to silence. Nick fell away from the device and back onto the floor. The panel display change to say it now held enough energy to form a tank of Otrolium.

The glass tube slid open, allowing Shotgun to fall forward. He crashed onto the ground, chest-first. His helmet bounced out of the tube and rolled past Nick. Shotgun's body looked gray and cold. It was impossible to tell whether or not he was still breathing. At this point, Nick could barely make himself care. Nick dropped his head back to the floor. His vision blurred out once again, and everything faded to black.

CHAPTER 23: A RESOLUTION

Nick's eyes blinked open to a cold metal ceiling. His head was pounding, and it felt like someone was standing on his chest. He sat up and placed his hand on his forehead. He rubbed away some of the pain. Nick turned to the tank, only to find a puddle of blood, with nobody in sight. A splattered trail of blood led away from the puddle. It slinked across the room and led to Shotgun.

He was standing at a table, with his back to Nick. His hand was resting on the table and sifting through papers in front of him.

Nick slowly got to his feet. How was this possible? How could Shotgun possibly be standing again already? Was he even stronger than Nick already suspected? "Shotgun?" Nick asked. There was no response.

Shotgun continued to move tiny fragments of paper from one side of the table to the other.

"Shotgun?" Nick called out, louder this time. Still, he said nothing. Nick took a few more timid steps toward him. The more he thought about it, the more Nick realized why Shotgun wasn't responding. Maybe Shotgun wasn't there. He stopped about ten feet away and made one final attempt. "Scott?"

Scott's head turned to the side, and he looked back over his shoulder. His eyelids were hanging lazily over his eyes like he was tired. Nick now knew, he *was* tired.

Nick didn't see a man capable of the crimes Shotgun had committed. He didn't see a man desperate for revenge and violence. All Nick saw was a broken individual, tired from years of acting as a slave. A man worn out from atrocities he was never destined to commit. A man who's internal hatred was warped and twisted by Otrolium poisoning. A man who became a monster.

Scott closed his eyes and turned back to his table. "It's quiet," he said, softly.

Nick titled his head in confusion.

Scott lowered his chin. "This is the first time in years I haven't heard his voice." Scott lifted one of the scraps of paper into the light. Nick could make out the image of a boy on it. The boy was young, smiling, and happy. Scott stared at the photograph, unable to take his eyes away.

"Shotgun isn't here to remind me of what happened to my boy," Scott said. "He's not forcing me to remember him." Scott placed the picture down on the table once again. "And yet here I am." Scott sighed. "I just wanted a chance to look at him through Scott's eyes one more time. To see him as my son... and not a justification for everything I've done."

"Is Shotgun gone, Scott?" Nick asked, taking another step forward.

Scott lifted his hand off the table and looked at Nick again. "It seems like no matter how many times I explain this," he began, "you never understand." Scott lifted his other hand into the air, revealing a pistol aimed directly at Nick's forehead. Scott held the pistol firmly in his hand, with his finger gripped tightly on the trigger. "Shotgun will never be gone. I can already feel him, trying to crawl back out." Scott's bottom lip stiffened as he held back his frustration. "Why didn't you just let me die?"

"Scott," Nick tried. "Shotgun isn't in control of you, right now. No one has to die here. I could have let you die in that tube, and I didn't. I didn't because I'm a good person, just like you used to be. Put the gun down. You don't want to do this."

"I never wanted this," Scott whimpered. The gun shook in his hand. "Redman deserves this. Redman deserves to pay for what happened to my son."

"Revenge isn't going to solve anything," Nick cried out. "You want to know why I didn't let you die? Because that wouldn't fix anything. Good people can never feel happy about bad things. Your son's death was an accident. I'm sorry, I truly am, but this isn't the way to fix this."

Scott's finger was tightly against the trigger. "You deserve this. You deserve it."

Nick knew he was too weak to disarm Scott quickly enough. Scott was already back to his feet by the time Nick was awake. Not to mention Nick was struggling to simply stand, while Scott seemed almost completely recovered. He was at Scott's mercy, and it was clear he was breaking down.

"Sengre Malcolf," Scott whispered. His arm lowered, finally taking the pistol off of Nick.

"What?"

"Sengre Malcolf is the man you're looking for," Scott repeated. "He's the one responsible for the deaths of your family." Shotgun turned back to his table and shook his head. "Shotgun would never have told you. Sengre did business with the Blades before I became this. We sold him Otrolium. It's how we managed to build up our army. He was the one who was going to receive the shipment from the Faraday Center. When the explosion stopped that from happening, he blamed your father."

Nick's expression didn't change. He kept his stare locked on Scott. He finally had the name of the man who killed his family. He finally had a chance for closure. He finally had a chance to put this man away for good.

"Where is he?" he asked.

"I don't know. No one does. He was a mercenary who

came to the US for business reasons. Dealing with him was done in secrecy. That's all the information I have, but… you deserved to know as much as I did. Whether or not Redman was to blame for my son, at least I *had* someone to blame."

"We know how we can hold Shotgun back, now," Nick started. "Redman is already working on a way to cure us. All we have to do is keep Shotgun at bay until it's finished. We can be rid of our Otrolium poisoning for good. You can go back to being Scott Cells."

Scott laughed a little and placed his empty hand on the photograph once again.

"Redman might be a brilliant man," he said, "but so am I. I already have a cure for Otrolium poisoning. A way to keep Shotgun from ever coming back. However, with him controlling me, I was never able to cure myself until now."

"You have a cure?" Nick asked, astonished.

Scott nodded and faced Nick again. Their eyes met and locked on each other. Nick could see the sadness in Scott's eyes was also layered with a veil of relief. It was like he hardly knew how to be free anymore.

"Yes," he responded, "I have a cure, but for your sake…" Scott closed his eyes, "I hope Redman can find a better one."

In one swift motion, Scott raised the pistol and stuck the barrel underneath his chin. Nick's eyes opened wide.

"Scott, no!" Nick shouted, lunging forward.

The loud crack echoed through the entire complex. Nick's ears were filled with a high-pitched whine as he took in the scene in front of him. The photograph of Scott's son softly floated to the ground, covered with a fine mist of crimson.

Nick took some deep breaths. Nothing in the moment seemed real anymore. Despite seeing the Blades fall right before his eyes, Nick found himself wishing he could turn back the clock. A mission accomplished didn't feel like a mission well done.

He ran a hand through his hair in a rough, purposeful manner. When he lowered it, he could see red hairs speckled across his glove, now wet with fresh blood. Drops of Shotgun's blood leaked down Nick's face and dripped onto the floor underneath him. Despite knowing it was happening, Nick couldn't hear them landing. He had never heard anything so quiet. He had never before been in a room so empty.

The silence of the moment was broken by Steven charging in through the open door. "Nuclear!" he yelled upon seeing his teammate. "There you are! Jesus, we thought you were dead. Look… forget about Shotgun, we *have* to go, Blast is…"

Steven stopped in his tracks and few feet from Nick. His eyes fell on the body lying in front of him. He stared in disbelief as Nick slowly turned his back to it.

Nick walked past Steven but talked softly to him on his

way by.

"It's what you wanted, right?" Nick asked.

Steven didn't respond.

"In the end, all I can do is hope this helped you."

EPILOGUE

"The scene happened just last night in the field behind me, and over a mile underground," a reporter began. "That is where the Blades had set up their stronghold. It was found a mile underneath the quarantined area of Lattice Light, where the Faraday Center used to stand. The leader of the Blades, Scott Cells, found himself cornered within its walls, where he made the decision to take his own life."

"Scott's son, Damon, was killed in a car accident ten years ago, and police believe this was the event that caused him to turn to crime. Other notable members of the Blades such as Patrick, Matthew, and Miranda Zealo have been taken into custody and are currently housed in a maximum security facility outside of the city. The few remaining Blade gang members are still being rounded up, but without a leader, we can only assume that this is the end of their reign of terror."

"While the city is now much safer, authorities have stated that some high ranking Blades have managed to slip under the radar. These include Jason Powell, who has been known to call himself Razor, and Mac Sampson, about whom very little is known."

Images of the two appeared on the screen next to the reporter. "They are both to be considered armed and extremely dangerous. Any information on the two should immediately be reported to LLPD. The dissolution of the Blades is thanks to Dr. Phillip Redman, and of course, his team of biohumans known as the Nitros. For the first time in almost a decade, Lattice Light City can finally sleep easy, knowing they are watching over us. We'll have more on this story tonight at five."

The television flicked off. Redman set the remote down on the desk in front of him. The Nitros all sat together in the main chamber of the lab.

Diego and Megan sat at one table. Every now and again Megan would glance at the clock on the large screen and then look back down. Diego would close his eyes momentarily, whisper a prayer quietly under his breath, and then return to normal. After this continued for what seemed like hours, the door to the chamber slid open.

Dante strolled into the room, with bandages surrounding his chest. He was covered in bruises and cuts as well.

"I'll take it," he stated. "Chicks dig the 'injured hero'

thing."

Megan jumped from the table and threw her arms around Dante. Dante winced in pain but kept on a strong face as best he could. Diego was also standing up to greet his teammate.

"I'm so happy you made it," Megan spoke as she stepped away from him. "I'll be honest, since Project Nitro started I've kind of grown used to having you around. Didn't want that to end just yet."

Dante nodded and stretched a bit. "You're a pretty good time yourself. Hey, maybe I'll head down to those news stations and give them a little interview with the Dante," he reasoned. "Bet they want to hear from a real-life superhero."

"Do not go to the press," Redman announced from across the room. "There will be a time and place for the Nitros to formally address the public very soon, and it will not be in the form of Dante Bruno attempting to 'pick up chicks.'"

Dante folded his arms. "Ooh, I'm Redman," he pouted in a mocking tone. "No one have any fun. Don't hang those posters in your room. That music is playing too loud. I come up with dumb names for cars."

"Hey," Diego whispered to him, "what if we just went out tonight to grab some pizza? You know to celebrate? Redman doesn't have to know."

"Diego," Megan jumped in. "That's super irresponsible. It's completely against Redman's rules." She folded her arms and darted her eyes between the two. "So… are we thinking like ten o'clock or...?"

Nick was sitting next to Redman. His hands were together, and he was simply staring down at the table in front of him.

"Still nothing, huh?" Nick asked.

Redman shrugged and tapped his fingers on the table.

"No," he replied. "Still no word on this Sengre Malcolf, but we'll keep searching. Your family's killer won't escape for very long. We'll track him down eventually. In the meantime, work is being done to create a cure for Otrolium poisoning. We're already onto something, so there's no need for you to worry. Your time in the Blade base might have accelerated the process a bit, but we're still talking about years, even decades before there would be any effect. Shotgun was given an extremely high dose, while your case of Otrolium poisoning is much less severe."

Nick nodded. "And you're sure about that? Like… absolutely certain?"

"Well, it's difficult to be absolutely certain about anything," Redman replied. Nick frowned. Redman picked up on his rightful skepticism. "What I'm trying to say is, you're going to be fine. You're in good hands, Nicholas. I'd never let something like that happen to you."

Nick continued to have his doubts, but knew nothing would come from pushing the conversation further. At least not yet. Before Nick to move to another topic, Steven approached them. He sat down at the table and folded his arms.

"What's up, sunshine?" Nick asked, looking up at him.

Steven grunted. "I wanted to answer your question," he replied. Steven closed his eyes. His brain filled with images from the previous night. Shotgun lying on the ground. The conversations he had with Nick about Shotgun's past and what had happened to him. "You guys were right," he finally said. "I thought seeing Shotgun gone forever would finally fill the hole my brother left behind. It didn't."

Nick nodded and motioned toward Dante.

"Dante can be smart sometimes," he admitted. "He knows you're a good person, and good people can never feel happy about bad things. Seeing someone die will never erase the death of someone else. I think Scott Cells knew that, too. Shotgun managed to convince him otherwise."

Steven nodded. "I guess," he began. "I guess I just wish I knew, you know? I wish I knew why he left me. I wish I knew what he was thinking. I wish I could talk to him one last time. Could know what he was thinking the day he died."

Redman placed his hands down on the table in front of him and leaned forward. "Well," Redman interrupted, "maybe you can."

Steven turned to Redman. He didn't know what kind of trick the scientist was trying to pull. Steven honestly questioned whether he had even heard him correctly.

"What did you say?"

"You see, after Nicholas told me about Sengre, and the police's false report that Shotgun was to blame, I did a little more research into your brother."

Redman reached under his desk and sifted through a few files in his drawer. He pulled one out and flipped open the cover. "Your brother, Derek Reynolds, was discovered by police in Central Park."

"Yeah," Steven agreed. "They said he got caught up in something with the Blades. Saw something he shouldn't have."

"As far as we can tell, that's true," Redman continued, "but now that the Blades have been dealt with, more and more witnesses were willing to come forward about the events that day. Your brother was not killed in Central Park. That's where they left him, to make it appear that way."

Steven listened intensely. These were new details about his brother. Maybe he could finally know the truth of what happened.

"A man by the name of Andrew Hardings says your brother came into town to see him. Mr. Hardings is the head of Stel University."

"Oooh," Nick jumped in. "That's one of those fancy colleges. You know, the ones none of us could ever dream to get into. Not that we'd really want to... but I'm just saying."

"Well, clearly Derek thought differently," Redman
added. "He was there to tell your story. He wanted better
for you, Steven. He wanted to help you escape from the
life you were living. Derek wanted to give you a chance at
another life."

Steven looked down at the desk. He traced his finger
along the metal, trying to hide any emotions from sight. If
a tear tried to fight its way forward, he would quickly
scratch his eye, and hold it back.

"Derek ended up witnessing the Blades attacking a man
for protection money and tried to intervene," Redman
continued. "When that turned sour, he ran from the
situation, but the Blades chased him down."

Steven sighed and shook his head. "So, they caught
him," Steven quietly stated. "He was there because of me,
and he died alone, running... probably terrified." Steven
couldn't fight the tears anymore. They were flowing down
his cheek and dripping onto the desk. "That idiot." Steven
looked up at the ceiling. "Why couldn't he have just told
me? I could have been with him."

"He was alone," Redman said, "until..."

Steven looked back down at Redman.

"A friendly passerby noticed he was in distress. The
man was kind enough to invite Derek back to his home.
Keep him safe for the night."

Steven's eyes shot open.

Redman smiled and motioned his hand toward the others. "You may never know the last things your brother said," Redman began, "but at least, you know someone who does."

Steven turned around. His eyes fell on Diego, who was still laughing with Dante and Megan. Steven's brain painted a picture of Derek, scared and alone on a lonely road outside of the city. The Cortez family driving by and picking him up. They gave him shelter, and made him feel safe and at home. The images dove into loud, chaotic scenes as the Blades tracked him down and kicked in the door to Diego's home. Gunshots and screaming filled Steven's head. The last thing he could picture was Diego kneeling next to Derek. Diego was holding his hand. Despite everything that had happened, Diego was willing to be there so that Derek wouldn't die alone.

Steven didn't say another word. He stood up from the desk and slowly made his way to the table. The laughing immediately stopped as he approached.

Diego sighed and also got to his feet. "Look, Steve," he started. "I know earlier you were under a lot of stress. We all were."

Dante and Megan nodded, trying to keep the situation light.

"We say a lot of things we don't mean when we're angry," Diego added. "I just want to be friendly with each other, man. We don't need to be best friends if you don't want to. Hopefully, you're willing to put that behind us and…"

Before he could finish, Steven stepped forward and wrapped his arms around Diego. Steven pulled Diego in and embraced him. Unsure of what exactly was happening, Diego returned the sentiment.

Steven could see his brother. He could see Derek lying on the ground, looking up at Diego and for one moment, feeling like everything was going to be okay.

Steven closed his eyes.

"Thank you," he said quietly.

ACKNOWLEDGMENTS

Thanks to Nate Boyles, for his masterful cover art.

Kat Dooley, for taking the time to edit and help me finish this book (and for putting up with me).

Laura Silverman, and www.laurasilvermanwrites.com for editing this new edition.

Susan and Brian Dooley, for supporting me through all of this.

Rooster Teeth, for giving me so many opportunities to embrace my creativity.

The Rooster Teeth and DooleyNoted communities. Thank you for all your support!

Made in the USA
Monee, IL
29 November 2019